The UNEXPECTED CONSEQUENCE of BLEEDING on a Tuesday

The UNEXPECTED CONSEQUENCE of BLEEDING on a Tuesday

KELSEY B. TONEY

Random House New York

Random House Books for Young Readers
An imprint of Random House Children's Books
A division of Penguin Random House LLC
1745 Broadway, New York, NY 10019
penguinrandomhouse.com
GetUnderlined.com

Text copyright © 2025 by Kelsey B. Toney
Jacket photograph copyright © 2025 French Anderson Ltd/Stocksy.com
Interior drawing of uterus by hachi/stock.adobe.com

Penguin Random House values and supports copyright. Copyright fuels creativity, encourages diverse voices, promotes free speech, and creates a vibrant culture. Thank you for buying an authorized edition of this book and for complying with copyright laws by not reproducing, scanning, or distributing any part of it in any form without permission. You are supporting writers and allowing Penguin Random House to continue to publish books for every reader. Please note that no part of this book may be used or reproduced in any manner for the purpose of training artificial intelligence technologies or systems.

Random House and the colophon are registered trademarks of Penguin Random House LLC.

Editor: Kelly Delaney
Cover Designer: Angela Carlino
Interior Designer: Cathy Bobak
Production Editor: Clare Perret
Managing Editor: Rebecca Vitkus
Production Manager: CJ Han

Library of Congress Cataloging-in-Publication Data is available upon request.
ISBN 978-0-593-81151-1 (trade) — ISBN 978-0-593-81152-8 (lib. bdg.) —
ISBN 978-0-593-81153-5 (ebook)

The text of this book is set in 11.3-point Warnock Pro.

Manufactured in the United States of America
10 9 8 7 6 5 4 3 2 1

The authorized representative in the EU for product safety and compliance is Penguin Random House Ireland, Morrison Chambers, 32 Nassau Street, Dublin D02 YH68, Ireland, https://eu-contact.penguin.ie.

Random House Children's Books supports the First Amendment
and celebrates the right to read.

For anyone who's ever had
a really great day
ruined by
a really bad period,
this one's for you.

CHAPTER ONE

A WELL-BEHAVED UTERUS RARELY MAKES HISTORY

I've become surprisingly chill about waking up in a pool of my own blood.

Yes, whatever, I know menstrual fluid isn't technically blood, but come on. It's close enough.

Plus, if anyone else could see me, they'd definitely assume I'd been mauled by a velociraptor.

In the vagina.

"Not today. Not again. Please, not again."

I reached to turn on the light beside my bed and my belly clenched against the pain. Not that I had any doubts, but I aggressively flipped the covers back.

It was all-out carnage.

I winced. "No, no, no."

My pulse banged against the inside of my throat, in my

palms, my forehead. The clammy feeling on my cheeks spread across and under my nose.

To be clear, I was perfectly chill about the blood. It was the period that made me panic.

Lots of people dislike their period or think it's painful or annoying.

I don't dislike my period. I *loathe* it. Like, I seethe with all-consuming fury when I think about it.

I'm saying my period is the single literal worst part of my life, and if I could carve out my own guts with a melon baller and survive, I'd be in the car with my very last dollar on my way to Target right now.

I grabbed my phone—it was 3:24 a.m. on that fine Tuesday. I opened my period-tracker app to confirm . . . I wasn't supposed to start until Thursday.

I let my face fall into my hands and pressed my fingers against my closed eyelids, but tears leaked out anyway. I was supposed to have two more days—just a little more time. Maybe it was just really bad spotting. Maybe it wasn't the full-on period yet. But based on the fact that it looked like I'd been in an accident at the ketchup factory, I guessed it was.

Across from my bed, on the wall, my pinboard collected shadows along every clipped edge of every saved picture and printer-paper fortune: photos of women in scrubs and surgical caps, an ad for a line of stethoscopes "for women" (in soft pastels that I publicly hated but secretly loved), the promotional photo of the grounds of Gleeson University, and several handwritten mantras inspiring me to become the best gynecologist in the world.

I had to be the best, because I had to find an answer.

I had to figure out what was wrong with me.

I'd been chasing an actual diagnosis for years, but unfortunately for me, the medical community was all too willing to say my condition was just a girl being dramatic.

I rolled out of bed—instantly too woozy to stand.

I moaned through pursed lips. "This is not good," I whined to myself.

Nausea swirled in my stomach just as I raised my hand to twist the bathroom doorknob. I barely made it to the toilet before everything I'd ever eaten in my lifetime came screaming up my throat.

"Ah. How I love being roused by the sound of your vomiting in the wee hours of the morning," Regan said as she pulled open the door on her side of our shared bathroom.

"Sorry, baby sister," I whimpered into the bowl.

She squatted in the doorframe beside me and pulled my hair from my face. Her hands made quick work of a fat, messy braid with my dirty-blond hair. "I know, I know," she said. "Hang on."

Regan wet a washcloth as I flushed. I curled up in a ball on the floor just as she wrung it out and unceremoniously plopped it across my face before digging some over-the-counter meds from the cabinet.

"Thanks," I said, trying half-heartedly to sit up. "I'm sor—"

"Nope, nope, nope. Lie down and—I say this with love—shut up." She smiled down at me.

There were only a few extra seconds of silence. "But I *am* sorry—"

"Staahhhp," she said. Her eyes were stern now. I surrendered.

Since I first started my period, my life had been flooded with apologies for being a burden, for needing help, for missing out, for messing up plans.

I lay there on the bathroom floor with my head on Regan's lap, willing the pain to get better—not worse. She'd given me two ibuprofens that I washed down with a swig of anti-nausea medicine (that would probably keep me locked up for two days), but the nausea didn't fade. The lightheadedness didn't fade. And the pain? It grew by the minute.

I wanted to avoid a full-on panic attack, but when I couldn't figure out if I was actually panicking about school or about pain, that just freaked me out more. My breathing got quicker and I felt my cheeks get cold and my chin start to quiver. "I don't believe this," I said to myself, eyes stinging. "Why can't Elvira just keep a schedule?"

"She came early, huh? What is it? Two days? What the hell is her problem?"

"Trying to make a name for herself, I guess," I said.

I couldn't stand that Regan felt it was necessary to track my own period along with hers. It was embarrassing. I nodded.

"It's okay," she said. "You're going to be fine. Give the ibuprofen a few more minutes to kick in before you totally freak out."

"It's too late for that. The freakout is currently underway. And ibuprofen can suck it," I snapped. "It does nothing."

"Then why do you keep taking it?" she asked.

I pushed a moan through my lips as I rolled onto my back like roadkill. "Maybe this will be the time it works," I answered. My thinking started circling the drain again. "If I can't go to school today, I won't meet Dr. Steele."

Regan nodded in this way that implied she was waiting for me to keep going, but I didn't. "Sure . . . and you'll also get kicked out of the premed mentorship program altogether, and they'll give your spot to someone else, and they'll dock your grade because this forum is part of the advanced track, so your GPA will fall in the crapper."

"This is helpful?" I asked as my heart reacted to every new word she said. "I know. Yes. I know that all the rest of it is tangled up in today too. I know. But Steele." Desperation made my chest heave as my lungs struggled to take in air. "If I could just meet him, talk to him. I know in my gut that he would believe me. I know he could help me figure out what's wrong with me." The lack of oxygen had made my lips start tingling.

"You have to breathe," Regan said, pinching my lips together with her fingers, which brought sensation slowly back to the rest of my face.

I tried to pull my lips apart, but she gripped tighter.

"Oww cad I breev if yur odinng by libs togeddr?"

"Through your nose."

I rolled my eyes and sniffed a little whiff of air.

"You're stubborn as hell," Regan said, letting go of my mouth. "Come on."

She began inhaling the way I should have been. She guided me to follow along, in and out. Slow and steady. It took a few minutes for the sparks in my vision to recede to the outer edges until they faded from my periphery entirely.

Believe it or not, this early pain was nothing—a 7 or 7.5. The real pain was coming, and the accompanying dread made every part of my body and mind seem to freeze. Every time I felt the first hint of calm, that fear whispered to me, *You're not strong enough to handle this pain.*

Regan helped me get up and sit on the toilet. She fished a super-mega pad from under the sink and handed it over.

"Thank you. You're such a good sister," I said softly.

"Are you kidding me? I'm the best sister alive," she said, winking. "I'm gonna go pull your dirty sheets and put on your shark sheets. I'll be back."

She turned on the water in the shower to let it get warm and then stepped into the dark of my bedroom while I sat on the toilet, slumped over so that my shoulder rested on the countertop. A few seconds later, a fresh set of underwear smacked me in the face.

Sometime after four, I was settled back in bed, desperately hoping my heating pad would work a miracle.

I squeezed my lips together and breathed heavily through my nose. I stayed like that for over a minute, thinking about how it felt like my life had been racing toward this junction for years.

My period was heavy right from the start, and my cramps were tough (but survivable) from day one. Literally day one, which was Valentine's Day, when I got my first period and bled through my light pink shorts during the sixth-grade sweetheart party. (I'll never forgive myself for opting out of my red pants that day.) But over time, things got worse and worse, and as slowly as freezing water, my ability to handle that pain seemed to weaken. Or at least that's what I believed was happening. I'd go to school and hide in the bathroom, biting my fist to keep from making sounds while my body raged. I became less and less able to deal with the pain. Eventually, Regan made the surprising suggestion that I wasn't getting weaker, but my period was getting stronger.

That made way more sense.

Mom and I asked Dr. Pauly (my first OBGYN, and the same doctor who'd delivered me and Regan) about it, and when we left that appointment, Mom and I had both been convinced that Regan was wrong: Periods hurt, and I just wasn't used to that. It takes time to build up an understanding of how much pain is normal. I mean, I was in middle school. What could I possibly know that a doctor didn't?

It was a few months later that Mom found me at the bottom of the stairs with a broken wrist. I'd passed out and fallen from about halfway up. My period pain had shut my body down.

When I told her that my broken wrist didn't hurt *half* as bad as my uterus, we were finally convinced.

This wasn't normal.

Something had to be really and truly wrong with my body, right?

Dr. Pauly had seemed willing to listen, but in the end he chose to stick to his guns rather than believe me. We asked for a second opinion, so he gave me a referral to another doctor in the practice. Dr. Li gave me the respect of a meeting before repeating exactly what his colleague had said. Almost word for word. My doctor when I was in eighth grade, Dr. Zimmern, made me think we were onto something, but she insisted on a whole year of "watching for change" before I realized I was in another dead end. It was early in freshman year of high school when Dr. Dimitri broke me. She told me I'd get over it . . . with time and maturity. She told me it would get easier once I stopped being scared of it.

I snapped. I knew she was wrong. I knew everyone who'd doubted me was wrong. And I found some faith in myself, in knowing that I was right. I'd figure out what was happening to me with or without them. I went into study mode, found my focus. I locked in for those first few months of ninth grade at Stockwood, my fancy college-preparatory high school that gives students very little time to be undecided about the future before the guilt trips and pressure to define your life trajectory officially begin. So, after first term, I was ready to leave the general program and join the premed track. If my doctor wouldn't figure out what was wrong with me, then I'd figure it out myself. I'd go all the way to med school to do it. I spent ninth and tenth grade looking for answers, while my annual appointments with Dr. Reyes and Dr. Thomas (my fifth and sixth doctors) made it very clear that there were dozens of things that could cause pain like mine—and the process of elimination would take years. And none of them actually wanted to spend those years investigating, which trapped me in a cycle of doctors waiting and watching before starting at their personal "square one," which was almost always birth control. Nobody seemed dedicated to solving the problem. They only seemed interested in telling me to learn to live with it.

When one name kept popping up in my research about pelvic and period pain, I fell face-first into idolatry: Dr. Jacob Steele. Dr. Steele was one of the world's most acclaimed experts on pain like mine, and in a stroke of great luck, he worked out of Dallas, only a few minutes' drive from Stockwood. More than anything, I wanted him to be my doctor. But getting in to see him proved impossible. He traveled a ton, had a surgical calendar that was filled up a year in advance, and didn't take new patients except during brief, unannounced windows of time, as he'd started to move more into teaching and lecturing around the world.

I couldn't get so much as an email to him until the last semester of my senior year, when my school announced that our premed program mentors had been selected based on our areas of study, and miraculously, he'd agreed to match with me.

I was going to meet him. Talk to him. He'd be able to teach me. He'd tell me about conditions, and maybe one of them would be mine. He'd get me into top programs and help me make the right connections. He wouldn't be my doctor, but he'd help me become one. And maybe then I'd finally find an answer.

But not if I was dropped from the program for missing the ceremony today.

Not if I couldn't get my butt out of this bed and over to school.

Today and only today.

"Maybe you can rally? Maybe it will pass? Maybe they won't drop you?" Regan whispered, putting a hand on my shoulder.

"Dean D'Agostino was crystal clear. There are too many alternates, too many other kids who'd take my place. There was no loophole: If I miss today, I'm dropped from the mentorship program. No exceptions—"

Another jolt, and I pressed my pillow to my face to stifle my sobs. When the pressure released, I fell quiet, and Regan reached up and pulled the pillow down.

Regan's voice was sharp. "God, I'm sick of this. I can't just sit back and watch this anymore. I can't." Her own eyes were full of tears, which made my heart snap right in two. She got up to leave—totally understandable, in my book. I'd want to leave if I were her. Loving me had to be exhausting.

I said, "I understand. I'm so sor—"

"Delia. No, you don't." She rolled her eyes. "I'm not *abandoning* you. God, you really are so freaking annoying sometimes. I'll be right back." She had a weird, wild look in her eyes, and she mumbled, "Maybe you'll say no, maybe it won't work, maybe you'll rat me out, but I don't care. We have to try."

"Rat you out? For what?"

"My secret weapon."

CHAPTER TWO

AN ACT OF DESPERATION

When Regan returned, she helped me sit up. The light from my lamp made a pink glow, and everything in my room looked soft and red. A couple of years ago, Mom had found a set of kid's sheets that were soft blue with great white sharks all over them. Knowing I'd find them hilarious, she bought them so I wouldn't have to feel bad if I bled through and stained them. The bloodstains would just look like the sharks had chomped somebody's arm off or something. Regan pulled the corner over and smoothed the shark sheet out flat with one hand. Her other hand was tucked behind her back.

Regan swallowed hard. My ever-cool kid sister was visibly nervous.

What she pulled out and set down on the bed was not at all what I'd expected. I don't know what it was that I did expect, but it certainly was not this.

A little glass bottle with a black rubber dropper tip sparkled in the soft light of my room. I picked it up and looked it over. The entire surface of the bottle was crusted with black glitter.

And (if I could trust the cartoon versions plastered all over the novelty items in the lone edgy gift shop at the mall) there was a pot leaf—an actual crispy, dried pot leaf—glued down and painted over with clear craft sealant. She'd put tiny black gemstones at the tip of each tiny point.

"Are. You. Serious?" I said, shaking my head from side to side. My face was almost instantly boiling hot. A stream of rejection flowed from my pinched lips, but I kept my volume low so Mom wouldn't hear. "You think I'm going to do some . . . what is that? Liquid *pot*? I didn't even know that was a thing. The thing about pot and minors is that, generally, grown-ups aren't that chill about them together. Oh, and hi, I'm Delia. Have you met me? I am not a drug user, okay? I'm what's called risk averse, Regan, good god. And who even sold this to you? Was it Travis Hewitt? People talk, you know that? Travis is totally a drug dealer, isn't he?"

She was trying not to laugh. "You're freaking out."

"Isn't this when I'm *supposed* to freak out? When you are committing crimes in our house? In my *bedroom*?"

"It's one tiny little baby crime. And we go to a private school, Delia. Of the fifteen people you know who currently deal, Travis Hewitt's not one." She shook her head as if this should have been obvious. She added, as an aside, "In his defense, his face just looks like that." I felt my eyes get big as I started trying to think of who else made up the seedy underbelly of Stockwood Prep. "And I didn't buy this," she continued, holding up the bottle. "I made it!" She broke into a smile, far bigger than seemed reasonable given that she was revealing her bedazzled homemade weed drops and not a handprint turkey in a picture frame made of bottle caps.

I blinked a few times as the rest of my face stayed frozen. "I think that might be worse, babe." I unscrewed the lid and sniffed the liquid. "Oh. Super. Fantastic. Smells like alcohol. Excellent."

She shrugged—"It's vanilla flavored"—and dropped her head in a sort of pout.

I snapped my fingers in front of her face. "Focus. What do you mean you *made* this? What are we dealing with here?"

"I mean, I . . . well. I got seeds from the internet and grew a small, very pitiful, very ugly plant with like four leaves, which I then harvested, baked, macerated, and infused into a small amount of vanilla vodka and water. It's a tincture!" Her smile was back, and she was nodding enthusiastically.

"A tincture. A weed tincture," I clarified.

"A vanilla-flavored weed tincture. Yes." She nodded some more. "Oh, and then I mixed glitter with white glue and—"

"This is not a glittery pot bottle tutorial!"

Regan's grin melted away and she held her hands up in surrender.

"You're sixteen!"

"And you're seventeen! So what? I'll be seventeen too in, like, two months."

"That's not the point. Even in the best-case scenario where

pot is magically legal all over Texas, it certainly won't be legal for you, a minor, to grow pot in our house, steal Mom's vodka, and make your own Super Syrup and think putting glitter on it will make it okay!"

"But . . . the glitter."

I held my hands up to calm myself down. "Why? Why this? Why weed? Why is this your 'secret weapon'?"

"Because I read about how the THC in weed can—for some people, in small doses—provide game-changing pain relief. I was trying to help. It's called pain management. Look it up."

"I'm not looking it up, Regan. I appreciate the gesture. Kinda. Maybe. But you know that Mom let me try some of those CBD gummies from the store down the street, and I didn't notice any real difference. At least that was legal."

"Don't be a snob just because you don't smoke—plenty of respectable people use medical marijuana, and plenty of doctors prescribe it. Don't pretend you don't know that just because you want to be right about this or mad at me or whatever. You know damn well that CBD and THC aren't the same thing." She paused, and when I didn't reply or say anything at all, she shook her head with a disgusted look on her face. "Fine. Whatever. I can't believe you're being such a jerk about this. I really was just trying to help, okay? But what is this garbage about not believing the testimonials of thousands of people's medical experiences, huh? I thought you didn't like it when people did that to you—"

She fell silent again just as a flood of excruciating pressure crawled up my back and forced me to bend over. As if on cue, my guts seized, and every bit of blood drained from my face. A deep moan of pain followed as I let Regan guide my head back to the pillow.

She reached over then, grabbed my phone, and shoved it into my hands.

"God, Deels, you'd better just get started then," she said smugly.

I stayed silent for several more seconds before I could get words out of my mouth. "Started with what?"

"Email Dean D'Agostino and tell him you're sick and can't come to the mentorship-matching ceremony. Give him some time to take your name off the list and start processing the paperwork documenting the complete and total failure of your life and your removal from the program. And tell him to tell Dr. Steele you'll be back on the waiting list for a consult in spot number three thousand seven hundred twenty-one."

I stared at my phone but said nothing.

We both knew that I couldn't survive that happening.

Another squeeze. Black edged my vision, and my eyes bulged as I held my breath.

"You've tried every over-the-counter pain pill, patch, and cream." She spoke calmly as she counted off on her fingers. "You've tried multiple different birth control pills. Heat therapy. Cold therapy. You've waited months and months to get in to see a new doctor only to be told to try some nonsense Epsom-salt bath for sixty days before they'll try something else. I hate seeing you like this. And maybe this idea was completely ridiculous, and maybe it doesn't even work, but according to my research, a little of this could not only sap your anxiety, but it could dim your pain enough to get you to school. To get you through a conversation with the doctor-of-your-dreams who already chose you to take under his wing." She paused, and her eyes got sadder. "You're tired, man. You're so tired. Even if it just lets you get some rest, it would be worth it, right? You *deserve sleep,* Deels."

I looked at her and back at the phone in my hand.

"How can it just keep getting worse?" I asked softly.

Maybe I was a fool for being so focused on meeting Dr. Steele. But I just knew he could figure this out. He was the guy. He'd have answers. Of course he would.

Illegal drugs, though? That was not my vibe. It felt reckless, desperate.

But desperate was exactly how I felt. I could do nothing and definitely lose this chance, or I could do this one single unbelievably reckless thing and maybe, possibly . . . not.

"Fine. I'll do it." I bit my lip and gave my sister a tight nod.

She didn't wait for me to change my mind. Ray picked up the bottle, unscrewed the lid, and brought the dropper over my mouth as I closed my eyes.

"Lift your tongue. I'm just giving you two. It may sting, but leave it under there for as long as you can."

CHAPTER THREE

VERY DISHONORABLE DISCHARGE

Now, I'm not saying Regan's drops were literally magical, but what do I know? Maybe she'd conned a fairy out of some dust. I am just saying that I can't remember the last time before then that I was able to sleep through the first hours of my period. My alarm went off three times before I actually got out of bed to get ready for school a few hours later. The weird part was that I really didn't feel impaired. I expected to feel like every stoner character from mom's Y2K teen movies—wanting to have Flamin' Hot Cheetos for breakfast and practice skateboarding in a beanie. Instead I hobbled to the bathroom, gingerly, and took another shower. I wasn't pain-free. But I was able to stand, and that felt like a victory.

When I got out, my uniform was hanging on the back of the bathroom door. A plastic cup on the counter, full of a pinkish-purple smoothie, dripped condensation down its side.

"Mom?" I yelled, opening the bathroom door to my bedroom. I hung my towel on the hook and started getting dressed. Shouting through the sliver of open doorway, I added, "Thanks for the breakfast!"

"ShhhhhhhI'mgonnapunchyourfacewithmyface," Regan moaned. The little black sheep is clearly not a morning person. She was dressed, but had opted out of a shower. Her feet were dangling off the edge of my bed like she'd been sitting there waiting for me, but the top of her body was lying back so she could try for a few more moments of sleep.

Mom was busting out a Mariah Carey song from her tween years—my favorite Mom era. (Regan prefers the alt bands of Mom's emo teenage years.) Regan pulled a pillow over her face and screamed.

"Girls, don'tcha know you can't escape mayyyy. Ooooh, darlins, 'cause you'll always be my babayyyyys," Mom wailed from the doorway. Her phone made dozens of clicking sounds as she took photos of me holding my bookbag and the blended breakfast.

"Mom, you know Mariah wasn't actually singing about her children in that song?" I asked, grinning.

"Shut up and look like a doctor," she said, gesturing for me to spin.

I stood near the foot of my bed and spun around nice and slow. I watched my vintage posters of nineties heartthrobs whir past my vision, followed by my bed, desk, and bathroom door.

Mom then circled toward the other side of the bed, and panic snatched my eyelids back as I noticed, still nestled in the folds, the glittery bottle with its pot leaf emblazoned and bejeweled on the front. She was still focused on her phone screen when I kicked Regan's foot, and somehow that kick transmitted all the necessary information, because Sleeping Beauty jolted up, swept her hand as she rose, and pulled the bottle against her hip and then under a pillow.

"Come on, Ray. Button your shirt and stand by your sister," Mom said.

"Oh my god, Mom, our faces are the same as the last time you saw us," Regan whined. She did up the last couple of buttons to hide her My Chemical Romance T-shirt and straightened her tie, even though it was still loose. Then she put her arm through mine.

Mom wears pink pajamas with tiny sheep on them. Most of them are white, but there is one tiny black sheep right over her left boob. We always joke that the black one is Regan—her edgy, acerbic spawn—and I'm the light pink sheep at her hip, which looks slightly like it has a stick up its butt. Mom's hair was a soft halo of frizz, and even though she looked tired, she's always pretty. Mom's skin is tan with olive undertones and her hair is mostly dark brown. She passed her coloring along to Regan, who frequently tries to minimize how much they look alike by dying her hair black and blue.

"I hate taking photos in my uniform," Regan said.

"Let me see," I said after Mom's thousandth photo. I stepped forward and snatched the phone, and my mom grabbed my smoothie out of my other hand in retaliation.

"Hey!" I said. "That's mine!"

"Let that be a lesson to you. Mother can smoothie giveth. Mother can smoothie taketh away."

In the picture, Regan and I stood side by side. Regan is taller and darker and always looks cool. Her oversized uniform would have looked disheveled on me, but Regan just looked effortlessly aloof. Me, on the other hand . . . well, I stood in my perfectly tailored uniform with the same posture I'd used my whole life (except when I was doubled over in pain). I kept my back straight, feet locked together, my dirty-blond hair pulled into a side braid running down over my shoulder. I pulled my fingers apart to zoom in on my face. My blue eyes were squished because my smile was so big. I was sickeningly pale. Like actually sick-looking.

"Here, take another one," I said, handing the phone back to Mom. "I'm standing too straight."

"You always stand straight," Regan said.

"Yeah, well, you don't, and you always look cooler than me. I always look like the manager of a store that only sells corrective orthopedic inserts for granny shoes."

"I'm not cool." Regan scoffed, missing the point that her thinking she wasn't cool always made her even cooler.

"You're both cool." Mom said, smiling at her phone screen.

"Hear that, Ray? Mommy thinks we're cool!" A playful thumbs-up before I raised my arm and set my elbow on Regan's shoulder. I let my posture relax, one hip cocked out to the side. She snapped another photo and then pulled it back up for review.

Mom gave an impressed look and said, "Okay, wow. Delia, you actually should stand like that more often 'cause it really does make you look like a badass." She melted with gooey mom pride. "Awwww. It's like I made my very own best friends with my very own vagina." She dabbed an imaginary tear.

Regan took the smoothie cup from Mom's hand and said, "I have asked you a million times if you would please not discuss the *one single time* I exited your vagina?" She took a glug of smoothie, then took a step and nudged the laundry basket out of her way.

"Are those the shark sheets?" Mom gestured to the bed and then to the basket of dirty sheets from last night, and gasped, her face turning white. "Oh my god."

Regan confirmed, nodding. "Demon uterus."

"Honey love. Why didn't you tell me? Are you okay? No wonder your color is all wrong."

"Yeah. Started last night," I said, grabbing my backpack and swinging it over one shoulder.

"And . . . you're okay?" she asked, coming over and taking my hand in her own. "I thought you weren't starting for a couple more days."

I felt my gaze lower for a moment. That same, unreasonable shame at her knowing my body's schedule. It was the same feeling that drove me to push Mom out of my doctors' appointments since the start of senior year. No matter how willing she was to go with me, I pressured myself to handle some of this—any of this—without leaning on everybody else. "Yeah, I'm okay. So far," I said, glancing at Regan over Mom's shoulder. My sister pulled her lips back tight so her teeth showed in an awkward smile.

Mom gave me a squinty sort of look and said, "Seriously? You're just . . . fine?"

"Well, I, uh . . ." I could only imagine how guilty I looked. "Not fine. Just having a lucky start, I guess? I mean, I can't miss today anyway—you know that. And I have my fingers crossed that the worst of it won't hit for several hours."

"Delia, the drive into the city alone is almost an *hour*. If it really hits you, you might be behind the wheel; you might pass out. Hell, you might barf all over your doctor crush, and then what would we do? I'm sure they would excuse you. It's an emergency."

"I'm sure they won't. They wouldn't care if a tornado took our house to Oz this morning. I have to be there."

"I'm calling the school," Mom said.

"Absolutely not," I snapped back, reaching for her phone. "Don't you dare."

"Don't tell me what to do, little girl. I'm the boss around here."

"Oh please. Tell me right now that you're not wearing underwear with smiley faces on them. Go on. Tell me."

"Ha-ha! Joke's on you!" Mom reached down, turned, and flashed her bare bum at Regan and me.

"Damn it, Mom!" Regan barked. "What is wrong with you?"

Mom laughed at herself a little more and then turned to look at me seriously. "I have to call the school. I have to try."

"What are you possibly going to say, Mom? I mean, honestly."

"I was thinking of the truth," she said, lifting her chin defiantly.

"Hard pass," I said, holding my hand up. "I have survived, clawed, and scraped myself through the years at Stockwood without the entire front office knowing that the reason I'm always absent or taking makeup hours is because of my *period*. They may think I have kid cancer, or maybe that I'm trying to be a teen-movie star and I have a ton of auditions. Whatever they're filling the gaps in with, they don't care. *I* don't care. So I'm certainly *not* telling them why now. I can't. It's too embarrassing. I wore my period on my sleeve in middle school, and we all know how that turned out."

"That sounds gross."

"Oh, shut up, Regan. You know what I mean."

One of the unusual perks of going to Stockwood is that there are a whole bunch of things the administration just doesn't seem to care about. It's been the school for five famous child actors, one pop star, two super-genius ten-year-olds, a professional skier, and an Olympian from the US swim team. Oh, and the kids of two governors. These are kids who miss school. The reasons don't matter as long as you make up the credits. There is only one exception: program-based mandatory days. Everyone has a few times each term that absences won't be excused. Today was one of mine.

"Listen to me," Mom said. "I know you don't want anyone to know about your period problems, but you are like a *month* away from graduation and then you'll probably never see any of these people again. A month. Who *cares* what they think? If I can get him to excuse you and let you still keep your mentorship, shouldn't we try? You've literally never asked for an exception. You've managed to miss school and make up every single hour and credit for four years. Maybe this will be something they are compassionate about. Maybe they will understand. We don't know if we don't try. I mean, what do you have to lose? Have you even considered what this means for Gleeson?"

My mind pinballed its thoughts back and forth. In the chaos of the last few hours, I'd been more focused on meeting Dr. Steele than on my college track. Gleeson University in Boston, the school of my dreams since my first A+ on a test that everyone else failed, partners with Stockwood and had issued early acceptance letters last fall to all the seniors who were approved to be matched with mentors for this program. I had made it into a college anyone would do anything to attend. If the mentorship fell through, would my college acceptance be in jeopardy? I'd already taken illegal drugs—maybe I was actually losing my mind. What was one more brush with insanity?

I nodded, just half a nod, and Mom stepped away, dialing. I reached across her and tapped the speaker phone button. The call went through and we stayed silent, listening for an answer. Regan sat on the bed and lay down again.

"Dean D'Agostino, please . . . I know he's got a big morning, but it's sort of an emergency."

The secretary made an irritated sound, got Mom's name, and put us on hold.

Anxiety spiked in me while we waited.

"This is Dean D'Agostino." His voice sounded dark and low. He was in full effect—he probably already had some of the guests arriving now.

"Hi, yes, this is Miranda Bridges, Delia and Regan's mom?"

"Good morning!" His voice brightened slightly. "I hope Cordelia is ready for her big day. What can I do for you?"

Mom continued, "Well, she is *so* excited, of course—it's just that, well, she's having sort of a medical emergency, and I need to know if there is any way for her to be excused from this super-cool, premed match-o-rama today—"

He cut her off by clearing his throat. "Medical emergency? That sounds serious. Is she in the hospital?"

"Well, no. No, she's not in the hospital."

"Oh. Well, do you have formal diagnosis paperwork from a medical provider that states she is on medically required bed rest?"

"No, we don't. I—"

He audibly sighed into the phone. "Emergency medical-care paperwork would specify if she's contagious. Is she contagious?"

"Wow, do you use a teleprompter or what?" Mom chuckled awkwardly and was met with equally awkward silence. "So, um, no. She doesn't have an official diagnosis, but she's very close to one. We've been working on it. Getting diagnoses takes time, as I'm sure you know. And it's so complicated to find the right doctor." She coughed and continued, "I don't mean to be vague about the details of her medical situation, but it's somewhat sensitive in nature."

Mom paused once more, looked at me, and asked with her eyes if I would allow her to tell him the truth about what I was going through. With few other options, I gestured for her to go ahead.

"Delia has really intense . . . like, whew, really intense, um . . . pain sometimes—well, monthly, I guess—and I was hoping you could make an exception for this one day's attendance requirement."

Every cricket in the world could have chirped in the space that silence left us. "Ms. Bridges, surely you understand that we cannot make exceptions at an institution like Stockwood— especially without formal documentation of a serious, specific medical diagnosis or hospitalization. You can only imagine how many times we've had students attempt to dodge due dates, deadlines, and expectations for all sorts of reasons we can't abide."

I moved to the bed and sat beside Regan, who had already pulled back up to sitting. I covered my head with my hands. Here it was. The embarrassment bomb was ready to drop. Mom paced and her jaw was clenched until she opened it to speak again. "My daughter isn't avoiding anything. My daughter has medically significant period pain. It's excruciating pain—"

The dean cleared his throat, and I could almost hear his shudder and cringe through the phone as he said, "I am sorry to be blunt, but I really am short on time. Stockwood has been very accommodating with Delia's schedule. She has made up credits and worked extra hours to keep up with her missed schoolwork. We've even approved an absence for her this week on Thursday." (I often put in a pre-scheduled absence for the first day of my period, since knew I'd feel so horrible.) "But each term there are nonnegotiable attendance days for special milestones, and this is one that she can't miss. There is simply far too much competition for this program in our school, and on the national scale, to allow her to miss it. Especially for something as commonplace as . . . cramps"—he cleared his throat again—"which are a part of Cordelia's development that she will have to learn to navigate without asking for special treatment. There are academic expectations linked to this mentor-matching day: grade points, assignments, lectures, written assignments based on the session today. Without one of the very specific medical excuses that we can accept, if she can't be here, she will have to be replaced. That's it."

Mom turned and tried once more with her back to Regan and me. "Sir, I understand, but if you would let me explain. These are not just 'cramps.' These are like the Godzilla of—"

"I'm sorry. I do hope to see Cordelia here in just a bit. I have to go. Goodbye."

The phone clicked and Regan and I watched Mom's shoulders rise and fall. My palms were sweating, and I wiped them on my skirt.

Mom didn't turn around. "You're sure you don't want to be a plumber?" she asked me.

"I'm afraid not. I'm surprisingly bad at righty tighty, lefty loosey."

She nodded, still facing the other way.

"I have to be there, Mom. I have to go."

"If you have to go, I can at least put my foot down about having you behind the wheel. Regan: you've been promoted to primary driver of the Woolly Mammoth." She spun around, pointed to my sister, and then let her face fall with worry.

Regan couldn't help but let her excitement out in a little bounce. "Of course!" Even though we both had provisional licenses until eighteen, I had a year more experience, so Regan was rarely the one entrusted to drive all the way to Dallas—especially without an actual old person riding shotgun. Our household had two cars: the pleasant little sedan that Mom drove around Blythe, and the brownish, twenty-year-old minivan (with both the world's strongest air-conditioning and the world's highest safety rating) that we called the Woolly Mammoth. She added, "And, Mom, I'm going to the mentorship-matching ceremony thing too. We, the plebes of Stockwood Prep who still haven't selected our career track, are supposed to attend, so I'll be there. And I promise I'll take a bunch of pictures."

Regan smiled, but Mom's worry-face was still on. "You shouldn't be forced to be at Delia's thing," Mom argued. "Your history test is this afternoon. You should be studying during your free hour this morning."

"They want us to go so we'll be shamed into choosing our entire life's future *instead* of doing something as pedestrian as *studying*. Whatever, Mom, it's fine. I reviewed some last night. People did stuff a long time ago. Blah-blah. I'm good."

One glance at Regan and I realized it was true. She *had* been up late before finding me in the bathroom. She *did* have a huge test today, and she'd barely gotten any sleep. She had once again put her needs aside and placed me in the center of her focus.

Mom paused to consider before adding half-heartedly, "Maybe I'll just cancel the rest of inventory at the store today. I can go. I'm glad you're miraculously fine right now, but that may not be the case in an hour."

I shook my head. "No, Mom, I'll be fine. You can't leave the whole back of the store half done, or you'll need to start over," I said. Mom was the store's manager, so Regan and I were small-town grocery store nepo-babies. Sometimes, we'd come up and work for an allowance and hang out in the stockroom. I patted her hand and tried to sound reassuring. We both knew that my period would most likely be in full effect, violent and shocking, in the next few hours. We both knew that sometimes things seemed fine, and other times I thought my body was going to literally explode on the spot. The fuzzy softness in my brain drew my attention back to the tincture that had given me rest and made the pressure in my guts a deep, steady throb rather than searing knives. Sometimes the worst of it would rise so fast and fade even faster. If the tincture had worked for the past few hours, maybe it would work for the next few too. "I'll be fine. Really. Now go remind Regan which one of the little pedals on the floor of the car is the one that goes *zoom-zoom* and which one makes the brakes go *screech*, and I'll be right down," I said with a grin.

They left, and I spared ten more seconds for questioning my fate before sticking my hand under the pillow.

The glittery bottle with its sparkly pot leaf felt heavy in my hand. I had no way to know when the stuff would wear off, but I knew for sure that there was no chance I would survive without it. Even its modest relief was more than I'd experienced in as long as I could remember. I shoved the bottle deep into the pocket of my plaid pleated skirt.

Just in case.

CHAPTER FOUR

~~NO~~ SOME REGRETS

The auditorium doors were still closed when Regan and I arrived at the hallowed halls of glimmering, glittering Stockwood Prep. The dark wood walls and light stone floors of Stockwood give it distinctly historic feels, but the truth is, the campus was designed and built to look old in 1967.

Mom makes a reasonable middle-class income, but her dad was in and out of big money starting in his twenties. Over his lifetime, Grandpa gained and lost enough money that it would have been a fortune if it had all been tallied on the positive side of the line. But it wasn't, and at the end of his life his balance was pretty close to net zero. With one exception: somehow, in a moment of clarity, once Mom got pregnant with Regan (just before our dad took off, ne'er to be seen again), Grandpa set aside legally restricted educational trusts for Regan and me.

Since the money couldn't be used for anything but school, it was assumed that Regan and I would use it for college someday. But the summer before freshman year of high school, everything in my social life got shredded to confetti, and I was dead serious when I told Mom I was going to drop out and run away if I couldn't go to some other school for ninth grade. Thanks to Grandpa, we had the money to pay for not just any school, but the best school. Stockwood is worth every penny to the families who want their kid on the fast track to an elite future. It's part of a network of prep schools that partner with top colleges through career trajectory programs that are badly named and nationally renowned. MedSci, my program, is for everyone who wants to be a doctor or work in bio science. But there's also BusFin (business and finance), PoLegal (political science and law), CompTec (computational science and technology), and a few others.

At Stockwood, knowing what you want out of life is a mandatory part of the high school experience. After the struggles my period had brought to our lives, it became clear to me that the fastest track to an answer for my medical mysteries might just be turning into my own medical expert, so I joined MedSci after first term of ninth grade. I was only briefly one of the poor lost souls (like Regan) on the general-studies track, a.k.a. Genny. Most Gennies desperately want to get out and into one of the other programs as fast as they possibly can. Regan totally doesn't care (at least that's what she wants us to think), and is a Stockwood anomaly as an eleventh-grade Genny.

As Regan and I approached the crowd, she turned to me,

said she'd see me inside, gave my arm a little squeeze, and peeled off to find her girlfriend.

I took the opportunity to slip into the bathroom.

In the time it had taken to get ready, leave our house, and get to Stockwood, I could tell I'd absolutely maxed out my tampon and my backup pad, and of course in my haste I had forgotten to put on some backup booty shorts under my skirt, so I couldn't just let it ride for a while.

I closed the stall door and sat, bending over to dig around in my backpack for another tampon/pad combo, when I felt a pain like someone had put a hook on the base of my spine and was trying to pull it down into the toilet. Wincing, I slammed my hands out sideways against the walls of the stall, dropped my mouth open, and squeezed my eyes shut. My heart started racing and spots danced in my vision. Fear flooded my whole body.

Fear not just because the pain was particularly bad in that moment. Fear at the realization that the relief I'd been feeling was temporary. At any second, pain could still crash into me and knock me to the floor. I couldn't take another wave like this morning's. I lowered my arms and felt the bump in my skirt pocket. The tincture. It had been over five hours since Regan put that stuff in my mouth. Time flies when you're fighting the urge to lose consciousness.

My underwear had been mostly protected, but since I'd been seated in the car for the better part of an hour, the purple and white stripes had two large red spots near the back where I'd bled through.

"Your panty-saving skills are bullcrap," I mumbled to the

eye-scorchingly pink-wrapped pad as I changed out the old and stuck the new into place.

In my other pocket, my phone pinged. It was a text from Priya Balakrishnan, one of my two best friends (other than Mom and Regan). Priya, Keisha Perkins, and I had been a full set since I'd arrived at Stockwood freshman year. I'd been relieved to find friends so quickly, since I'd practically fled regular public school. Eighth grade had ended in a spectacular dumpster fire of embarrassment and heartbreak when my childhood best friend, Ruby-June Walker, and I abruptly ended our friendship at her birthday party in front of everyone we knew. *The Bloodbath*, I call it. But middle school nonsense faded deep into the background as I started focusing on my future instead of my past, and my new friendship trio was unshakable: Key, Pri, and D. Rock, paper, scissors. Snap, Crackle, Pop.

PRIYA: Where are you?

PRIYA: I saw regan, and she told me you started today

KEISHA: Your uterus is traaaaaash

PRIYA: Elvira is the worst. I'm so sorry, friend. Are you okay?

DELIA: I'm fine. I freaking bled through my underwear though. Again ugh

KEISHA: D, I swear to god, why didn't you order those period panties yet? I told you they would change your life

> DELIA: I know I forgot. I keep meaning to, but it's hard to remember things when your cramps are trying to MURDER YOU

KEISHA: LOL

PRIYA: Will you get out here and stop texting in the bathroom! you've definitely got poop particles on your screen now!

> DELIA: GROSS. Okay okay. I'll be right out.

A dull ache filled my abdomen, like a hum in my ear. I put my phone into my pocket and pulled out the glittery glass bottle.

The forum was starting in thirty minutes. My choices were to take more of the tincture, or risk screaming in the middle of the auditorium or passing out and ruining everything.

Oh my god, stop overthinking and just do it.

I twisted off the top and filled up the dropper. Regan said she'd put two under my tongue, but I was nervous about taking too much, so I just squirted one dropperful into my mouth, cringing against the bitterness for as long as possible before swallowing it down.

It was done.

No takesies backsies.

I put the bottle into the side pocket of my purse, finished my business, and went to find my friends.

"Today's the big day! I am *so* excited for my baby doctors." Keisha blinked away tears from her big brown eyes as she hugged us. "And I promise to represent you in every medical malpractice suit you ever face." She was in the prelaw track and the judge she was matched with last week for the PoLegal mentorship already had her gearing up for her eventual appointment to the Supreme Court.

"Awwww. That's so sweet," Priya laughed. "How are you feeling, D? I can't believe Elvira came early and gave your plans the ole middle finger, today of all days." Priya flipped her middle finger out for about one quarter of one second before hiding it back in her skirt pocket.

"Shhh! Hey"—I scolded her and looked over my shoulder— "don't talk about it. I'm fine. Don't worry. It's fine. I'm fine."

The relationship between me, Priya, and Keisha is solid gold. The relationship between me, Priya, Keisha, and my period . . . that's more complicated.

Even once I trusted them, my middle school emotional baggage made it hard for me to completely let my guard down about my period. The self-doubt was so brutal, and it made me feel childish and separate, and insecure. The girls had seen firsthand how much pain I was in, but when everyone around you just takes a little Tylenol and goes about their business, the worry sets in. They were my best friends, but I still wanted them to think I was strong enough to handle what everyone else faced without flinching.

For two to three weeks each month, I felt like one of them, one hundred percent. But the other times, the bad days, I just wanted to do anything I could to keep them from looking at me with pity (at best) or doubt (at worst) in their eyes.

Keisha gave me a little squint. "You don't look fine."

"Gee, thanks," I said.

"No, I just mean, I never get used to how white you get when you start. I swear."

"*Shhhh.*" I held a finger up to both of their lips.

"Okay, whatever. Love you guys," Keisha said, giving our shoulders a squeeze. "Knock 'em dead."

After she walked off, Priya said, "I *do* want to punch Elvira right in the cervix."

"Priya!"

"I used the code word!"

I hissed, "Priya, it doesn't matter if you remember to say *Elvira* if you also say *cervix!*"

"Okay, okay. So, subject change. Are you excited? The doctor of your dreams is behind those doors!"

"To say I am excited would be a huge understatement." I nodded, which made my head felt a little bit like a water balloon. "How many questions did you prep?" I asked.

"Ten. But I have another ten backup questions in my bag."

Priya smiled and tucked the front bit of her hair behind her ear. Her soft, round face glowed beautifully thanks to some expertly placed highlighter, and her eyes were lined with a soft blue color, flicked out in a tiny little wing that perfectly coordinated with the voluminous blowout she'd given her glossy black hair.

We started to walk toward the open auditorium doors, slowly making our way through the crowd of our classmates. Everyone in the auditorium was from MedSci, but only twenty of us had been chosen for the mentorship program. Priya and I were among the elite.

As we entered the auditorium, I saw the mentors communing down in the place of honor—the ring of tall stools where the participating doctors would spend the next few hours in conversation with us. The doctors were easy to spot: each of them was wearing a white lab coat over their fancy clothes. Dr. Steele was there. Right there. I was starstruck. His gray-and-golden hair was cropped short and sort of swept over to one side. He wore sneakers with the gray trousers that showed below the bottom of his lab coat. He was talking to another doctor, a younger Black woman with green-framed glasses who had thick braids draped over one shoulder. Even from a few rows up, I could see that they had the same logo on their long white coats. I wasn't sure, but I thought she might be the protégé who had started making a splash in the online pain forums.

I was heading down the steps, Priya's shiny hair bouncing in front of me, when I felt a surge of dizziness. I stumbled a little and almost tripped, when Regan appeared out of thin air and grabbed my arm.

"Easy there, sister. You okay?" she asked.

"Sure, sure, suuuuuure. You came out of nowhere. Where did you come from?" I said to Regan's face, particularly to her eyeballs.

"You don't look okay. Here, let me help you down to your seat."

"Did you know you have two very nice eyeballs?" I said, genuinely concerned that she might not know.

Regan picked up the pace, pulling me down to the front two rows where the other mentees had reserved seats. Priya had already stepped into the row and started moving to the middle, but Regan waved her back to the seats on the end, right beside the steps.

"Hey, Ray," Priya said to my sister and her eyeballs.

"She should sit on the end," Regan said. She guided me so I was sitting in the first seat in the row, and Priya sat beside me in the second seat. Regan took the seat directly behind me, just outside the reserved section.

"Why, what's going on? Are you feeling okay, D?" Priya asked.

"Of course. Stop being weird," I said, positioning my book bag and my purse at my feet. "Did you guys notice that they're wearing the same costume?" My eyes wide, I lifted a hand and pointed at Dr. Steele and his companion, then turned to face Priya and gasped. I was smiling so hard, my cheeks started to ache. "Oh my god, do you think they're gonna sing a little bit?"

"Sing? Before or after these highly respected leaders in their field sit for hours answering questions?" She laughed.

"After, hopefully. I really love a well-timed musical number," I said. The noise in the room was growing fast, which was the only reason nobody other than Priya and Regan heard me start singing: "LADIES AND GENTS, THIS IS THE MOMENT YOU WAITED FOR. OHHHHH OHH—"

Priya pushed my hands down, stopping me before I could finish the melody.

"Oh my god," Regan said behind me. I turned and watched the mouth right under her eyeballs mutter, "Oh my god. Oh my god. Oh my god."

"Whoa, weird." I looked at her quizzically. "Did your words get stuck or something?"

"If one of you doesn't tell me what is going on, I'm going to lose it," Priya said, but Regan was already bending over so her head was at my shoulder.

"What did you do, sis? Tell me? Is this some sort of delayed reaction? Or did you take more?" she asked, nodding.

I thought for a second or two before my nodding joined her nodding and then we were both nodding. "I was worried it would get bad again, and then it *was* starting to get bad again, you know? But I didn't want to take too much, so I took one. Just one." I held up my pointer finger right in front of her best eyeball so she could count it herself.

She smacked my hand away. "One drop shouldn't make you act like a weirdo, singing *Greatest Showman* in front of Dr. Steele!"

"A drop? A drop of *what*?" Priya's face was all spread out. Like her eyelids were pulled back, and her eyebrows, too.

"No no no. One *dropper*," I emphasized. "One dropper. Drop. Per. Drop . . . per."

CHAPTER FIVE

STOP, DROP, DROP, STOP, ROLL, AND ROLL

"Oh, Delia, you didn't." Regan started shaking her head side to side while she looked at me, and at first I shook my head along with her. But then my shake turned back into a nod. Affirmative. I definitely did.

"Regan!" Priya snapped a whisper, and a teeny-tiny little ball of spit flew from her mouth and landed on the armrest between us. "Information, now, or I'm calling your mom."

Regan started to answer her, blissfully unaware of the little spit bubble, when someone began to edge between them to take the seat behind Pri and me, beside my sister.

"This seat's taken," Regan barked.

"By who?" the guy asked. "I don't see anybody sitting there, Ray-gun."

"By the ghost of the last guy who wanted to sit beside me

in a room full of empty seat options that don't require us to share an armrest. Bye, Stephen!"

My face did that same shocked, stretchy thing that Priya's had, and then I started to giggle.

"That. Was. So. Awesome. And rude, but mostly awesome," I said, but the giggling didn't stop. I started laughing louder until I remembered Priya's spit beside me, and then I stopped.

Priya was still staring at Regan, unblinking.

Regan leaned toward us again and whispered. "She took some of a tincture. A lot of it, actually."

"A tincture? What is this, a medieval apothecary? A tincture of what?"

Regan paused, and then dropped her head.

I whispered, "The devil's lettuce." I reached down and pulled open the side pocket of my purse and, without removing it, let Priya take in the glory of the beautiful glittery bottle of weed juice.

Priya eyed me and then Regan and then me and then she started to say something that would have been loud and then Regan started talking first.

"Marijuana. That I grew. In my closet. And then prepared. Secretly. Over a few months of sneaky middle-of-the-night work. For her—for her pain." She raised her head then, her voice earnest. "Priya, even when she tries to hide it, you know how bad it is. She can't function . . . for days sometimes! And it's getting worse. It used to last, like, six days, but her last three periods have lasted twelve days. Twelve!"

"I know," Priya said. I saw pity in her eyes, but it only lasted a second. "But what were you thinking?" she said, eyes closed, shaking her head.

"I was trying to help—"

"Not you." Priya's eyes snapped open, and she glared at me. "Delia. What the hell were you thinking?"

I tried to pull the corners of my smile down, but they just kept going the other direction. Damn my uncontrollable smile corners.

"It's going to be fine," Regan said, "She just needs to get through the first part of this, and then we can get her out of here and she can fake the rest of the day that isn't quite so . . . in the spotlight?"

"I'm staying to the end," I said. "I have to meet Dr. Steele. And can you believe that's his real name? I bet he's an evil comic-book character in real life. The Evil Robot Doctor Steele. DOC-TOR STEELE!" I brought my hand to my mouth to cover my laugh. "Actually, it's also kinda . . ." I whispered this part: "It's kinda like a cheesy stripper name, right? Like, 'Up next on the main stage, it's Professor Cashmere, but first, get your dollars out for Doctorrrrrrrr Steele!'" I waggled my eyebrows. Neither of them thought it was funny. At all. Then I stopped suddenly, fear in my voice. "Wait. Do either of you have any cash?"

"Esteemed students and guests," Dean D'Agostino said into his microphone. "Can I have your attention please?"

The three of us—well, four if you count the spit bubble— and everyone else went silent.

And then, full-voiced, I declared with a smile, "Yes, you sure can!"

Many, many eyeballs pointed in my direction, including the dean's. He did his signature throat-clearing sound and then said, "Thank you. We are so glad to have you with us this morning as we honor the twenty seniors who have been selected for the prestigious Medical Science Mentorship Program. Stockwood Preparatory School is pleased to announce that we have the highest number of chosen candidates of any participating private preparatory school in the country."

The room, full of my classmates as well as younger students from the MedSci and Genny programs, burst into applause.

Dean D'Ag continued. "The twenty physicians seated before you have selected the twenty students we honor today for an incredible opportunity. Not only have our MedSci students been earning college credit for all dual-enrollment courses here at Stockwood, but they're also being given the chance to work alongside these fine doctors during their first, formative four years of college at one of four partnering institutions of higher learning: Gleeson, Perrince, Brickbriar, and Milton Universities. While taking their first years of premed undergraduate courses, they'll have the incredible opportunity to sit in on lectures, discuss career goals, and seek guidance several years before ever applying to med school. These relationships have the power to change the course of your careers," he said, now speaking directly to those of us in the front two rows. "It is a distinct honor. I am so proud of the fine people you've become, and I can't wait to see you change the world of medicine in the years ahead."

The room filled with applause again.

The dean began inviting the doctors up to introduce themselves and then calling us up one by one to shake their hand, pose for a photo, and return to our seats.

When Priya's mentor (a dermatologist) was called, Priya rose, slipped past me, and crossed the open space with smooth steps. It looked like she was flying.

Regan stuck her phone out over my shoulder and I could see her screen while she took a photo of their handshake. Then she leaned over to my ear. "Just like that, Delia. When he calls your name, you just have to walk over, shake the good doctor's hand, and come back. Nice and slow. Okay? Now just wait right here. Don't move."

Dr. Steele stepped toward the microphone and made his boring, non-musical-number introduction while I pretended to be a statue in my seat. "My name is Dr. Jacob Steele, and I started the Center for Pelvic Pain Care. I am sorry to say that this is my last year taking on a new mentee in this little rodeo. But fear not, underclassmen. This is Dr. Erika Dubois." He gestured with a flourish to the doctor beside him, who waved but stayed in her seat. "Dr. Dubois is another expert at CPPC, and I'm trying to convince her to take my place next year. We'll see if she thinks it looks like fun after watching me work with this promising student here." He gestured to my statue-self.

I whispered to Regan. "Got it. I'll fly just like Priya did."

"What?" Regan asked just as the dean called my name.

I stood, stepped deftly over my purse, and floated and down to the row of doctors.

Nice and slow. Nice and slow.

He extended his non-robotic hand in my direction with a grin.

"Nice to meet you, Dr. Steele," I said.

"Same to you, Ms. Bridges," he said.

"Delia," I whispered. "You can call me Delia. Short for Cordelia. Ms. Bridges isn't short for anything. It's long for something. So it's not as fun to say." A little bruisy feeling bloomed in my low belly and I felt my eyelids cover my eyeballs for longer than normal.

He grinned a little, nodding and lifting one eyebrow as he stood, and we positioned and posed for the formal school photo. A strong shock of pain made me flinch, so naturally I checked with the photographer. I whispered as softly as I could (which might not have actually been that softly), "Can you be sure it doesn't look like I just got a cooter punch in that photo real quick?"

The photographer's eyes went wide, and he gave me a little nod to look down at his preview.

"Nice. We're looking goooooood, Dr. Steele. If that is your *real* name," I said, giving myself the giggles again.

"Are you all right?" Steele cocked his head in curiosity, and Dean D'Agostino shot me a confused sort of look.

"Well, now that you ask . . ."

"Please take your seat, Ms. Bridges," the dean barked.

I'm pretty scared of dogs, so I turned and shuffled back to my seat.

I sat and Regan patted me on the back. Priya took my hand and gave it a squeeze.

Regan hadn't been able to hear much of what had been said away from the mic, so she asked what we'd been muttering about up there, but I couldn't really remember, so I just ignored her. Plus, I was basking in pride. I'd done it. Even though I felt weird, like my head wasn't attached to my body. The hardest part was over.

I started to giggle again, thinking about my head being a balloon connected by string to my shoulders.

This time, though, I couldn't stop laughing. Priya squeezed my hand. Regan leaned over and tried to shush me. I wasn't making much noise, but I could feel my shoulders bouncing. I covered my mouth with my hands.

When Dean D'Agostino opened the forum and asked for questions, my hand shot straight up.

Priya and Regan both tried to stop me, but the dean saw me first, and before I knew it, the room was looking to me to ask the first question of the forum.

I stood, my balloon head floating up, pulling me out of my seat.

"My question is for you, DOC-TOR Steele." I sputtered a spray of spit through my lips, trying to keep it subtle, and then I dramatically extended my arm and pointed to where he sat. He smiled and dressed his face in a slightly amused, very confused expression.

"I can't decide if I think your name sounds more like it belongs to a dark robot mastermind from a comic book about space doctors or . . . to a stripper. Which do you think?"

"Oh my god," Regan said, and her hands were on my shoulders.

Dean D'Agostino's face was doing the shocked, pulled thing. There were gasps and giggles spreading throughout the auditorium.

I tried to keep my mouth closed, but I buzzed out a second spitty laugh through tight lips.

"Dean, Doctors, I'm so sorry. My sister's not feeling well today. She should have stayed home. Dr. Steele, she's been wanting to meet you for years; she's your biggest fan. She respects you deeply. Really. I'm so sorry, but I should take her home."

"I think it's a valid question!" I said, jerking my shoulders away and trying to regain my footing.

The dean's face wasn't stretched anymore. Every part of it was squishing down in anger.

Regan started pulling me out of my row.

"Stop, Ray," I said. Then my shoe caught on my purse, and before I could blink, before I could breathe, my purse and my body went flying.

I hit the hard tile at the bottom of the aisle and felt my body stretch over the floor. It might have hurt, but I didn't care because I was laughing so hard. Until I pushed up a little and Regan appeared behind me, trying to pull my skirt back down. I glanced over my shoulder and for half a second saw purple and white stripes. My skirt had flown up around my waist, and my bloodstained underwear was aimed right at the stadium seating.

And then, in slow motion, I watched the glittery glass tincture bottle roll out of the side pocket of my purse across the open space until it bumped into the leg of one of the stools. Of course it was Dr. Steele's.

He bent to pick it up, then extended his hand to me and pulled me to standing. Then, in the tiny circle made by the doctors, the dean, my sister, and me, he asked, "What do we have here?" He gave it a look, running his thumb over the pot leaf, before handing it to Dean D'Agostino.

"That'd be m' weed," I answered.

Regan and Priya, along with Dr. Erika Dubois, helped me get situated and brush dust and dirt off of my sleeves. Dr. Dubois tried to catch my eyes, but they were securely in my skull. "Are you okay? What's in that bottle? Can I feel your pulse real quick?"

She tried to reach for my wrist, but I was distracted. "Dr. Dubois, Dr. Dubois," I said, placing my hands on her forearms. I dropped my voice to a whisper: "Do you think it's too late to pretend that I've taken some other medication instead of, you know . . ." And then I brought my pinched fingers to my lips to mimic the traditional pot-smoking gesture.

My sister resumed trying to drag me away in the next second, while the rest of the room gasped and giggled. Dean D'Ag had already started scowling and gesturing for another teacher to come be my escort.

"Ms. Bridges, report to the front office immediately and wait for me there." White splotches rose to the surface of the dean's skin, and the top of his bald head started to turn red.

I glanced sideways to see the row of doctors frowning—including Dr. Steele. I turned my head the other way to see the entirety of the MedSci program: most of them had their mouths covered. When I looked back at the dean, I reached out to take the glittery bottle from his hand. "I'll just take—"

He snatched it out of reach and put the bottle in his pocket. "Now."

"Okay, jeez," I said.

I started walking up the stairs, Regan at my elbow. But I only got a few steps away before I turned and faced Dr. Steele again. I pointed, and a sly smile broke out on my face.

Regan pushed my hand down and tried to interrupt, but the room was too quiet, and I had had a revelation.

I bonked my head with my palm, as if this answer were suddenly obvious. "Duh. Doc, it's gotta be more of a stripper name. You spend way more time around naked ladies than you do in comic books."

CHAPTER SIX

GIVE ME A TIME MACHINE OR GIVE ME DEATH

At some point they loaded me up in the car and took me home. I don't remember how Mom and Regan got me upstairs and into bed, but I remember my dreams.

Vibrant, colorful, beautiful dreams.

About bald angels and spacemen and vaginas of steel.

My eyelids felt like sandpaper when I opened them at 8:22 that night.

I got up slowly, sure that I'd feel hungover, but I didn't.

I'd been a little hungover one time after a big party sophomore year. I got home smelling like beer, and Mom in classic fashion offered to let me try a shot of anything from her liquor cabinet. I thought she was so cool. That is until I was throwing up at two in the morning. She still swears her method was a stroke of old-school parenting genius. It's hard to argue, because of course I haven't so much as sipped a beer since.

Well, unless you count the vanilla vodka in the tincture.

Mostly I felt stiff because I'd slept too hard to move around much. I waddled to the bathroom to check my undies, and sure enough, another pair bites the dust. I took a quick shower, grateful to not have much pain.

I padded downstairs and found Regan and Mom sitting on opposite ends of the couch in silence. Both looked like they'd been crying recently but had since stopped.

"Hey," I said.

"Hey," they answered, shifting and gesturing for me to sit between them.

I pulled my feet up and sat cross-legged on the cushion. All three of us stared at the TV that wasn't on.

"So," I started. "How bad was it?"

"You don't remember? Really?" Regan asked.

Mom pulled her feet up underneath her and reached behind the couch cushion for a secret stash of candied almonds. She offered me some, which I declined with a *what is wrong with you?* face at her inability to determine appropriate snack timing, while Regan recounted the whole thing.

Regan had texted Mom to say she needed to leave work and come to school immediately. It was going to take almost an hour at the best of times, but thanks to mom magic, Mom was already halfway to Dallas from Blythe. She'd asked James to handle the rest of inventory and set off toward school on sheer mom instinct, hoping she'd catch part of the ceremony and check on my early period arrival at the same time.

When we got to the front office, things got extra bad.

Apparently, we were sitting in the waiting area when the dean walked through for only a moment between fifty other tasks he was juggling with all the students and special guests transitioning to the library. That's when I asked him how much money he'd saved over his lifetime.

On shampoo.

Because he's bald.

It was at this point he called the nurse, who I believed was a literal angel, and she insisted on calling an ambulance because my blood pressure was so low, and I kept blacking out over and over each time a surge of pain would rise up inside me.

This was when Regan realized that both things were happening at once: I was very, very stoned, and I was also still experiencing pain, off and on, while everything was falling apart.

They let me lie down, but seeing the nurse leaning over my bedside made me suddenly very sure I was dying, and that was when the panic set in.

I began to cry uncontrollably, telling my sister all the reasons I loved her (one of them being her very nice eyeballs), and then began eulogizing myself in third person.

Apparently, it went something like this: "Here lies me. Cordelia Erin Bridges. May she be remembered as more than her bloody underwear." And then, apparently, I pulled up my skirt—to reverently reveal the aforementioned bloody underwear—and crossed myself like a Catholic (I'm not Catholic) before raising one hand to my forehead to salute myself and laying my hands across my chest to look like a dead body. When the astronauts (paramedics) came to carry off my corpse, obviously, I started singing a funeral dirge.

Loudly.

Then I decided I didn't want the astronauts to take my body to space, and I begged the angel to let me live. Nurse Phelps tried to calm me, but I got up and tried to hide under her cabinets.

Regan started cussing about how they should give me space and how I might have a panic attack if they didn't give me some room.

Mom arrived right as the paramedics were trying to restrain me.

Regan ran from the corner, where she'd flattened herself against the wall with guilt, and set off crying and explaining bits and pieces that no one could understand.

Mom didn't react well to the sight of the spacemen trying to put me on the table so they could fly me to heaven.

"What the hell are you doing? Get your hands off my daughter!" she screamed. "I mean it. Step back!"

She pushed herself in between them and me, grabbed my face, and told me to breathe.

"Y-Y-You missed m-my funeraaaaal!" I cried.

"You're not dead, baby. You're not dead. In and out. Come on."

She sat on the floor and pulled me onto her lap.

Regan said the room got quiet then. The paramedics and the nurse looked at each other from the doorway.

Mom rocked and shushed me until I was calm, and then she looked up at their faces and demanded information. She demanded to know why I was reacting outrageously to my pain.

For a few moments Regan couldn't speak. Then she decided she couldn't be silent, either.

"She took a very big dose of a tincture. A marijuana tincture."

Mom and the nurse screamed, "How much?" in almost perfect unison.

Regan did some calculations in her mind and then sputtered, "It's hard to say. Maybe fifteen milligrams? Twenty?"

Nurse Phelps immediately began consulting her phone and talking with the paramedics.

Within a half hour the paramedics were gone, Mom and the other adults were talking behind closed doors, and Regan was sitting at my side on the stiff, plastic-covered nurse's bed.

When she finished recounting the whole story, I looked around the living room, noticing the tiniest things I could find. A stitch in the cushion. A bump in the paint on the wall.

All I could say was "Wow."

For a few minutes the silence was all mine.

I asked, "So did you talk to Dean D'Agostino? What did he say?"

"Well, for today," Mom said, "the primary goal was getting

you home safe and letting you sleep it off. We have to meet with him tomorrow morning. But I'm telling you, kid. It's not good."

"Oh man. Mom. I don't know what to say." My throat clenched. "Maybe I'll get lucky and that whole 'being a good kid' thing will pay off?"

They both looked doubtful.

"One possible card we can play tomorrow," Mom said, "is plea deal–style negotiation. Are you willing to rat out which kid sold you the stuff?" She crunched a few more almonds.

I wasn't sure how much they'd hashed out, but somehow Regan had kept her nose clean. I looked over at her to use our secret sister powers of communication. Regan's eyes were still streaked with tears, but when I glanced at her, ever so slightly, she shook her head and then, unmistakably, dropped her gaze in crystal-clear shame.

"I . . . I don't know."

"You don't know?" Mom scoffed. "Who on this *whole* planet could be worth lying for right now, Delia? I swear." She rolled her eyes at me and then turned to Regan. "Do you know? You obviously knew she took it because you knew how much she'd had."

Regan swallowed. "I don't know."

Mom turned her head back and forth between us and then shook her head. She looked me right in the eyes. "Whatever. I don't know what to tell you two other than I wish either of you had paused for one second to just *think. Especially* you, Delia. I can't believe you put that stuff in your mouth. *That's* why you were willing to scamper off to school today while you knew your pain would be coming on? This was the big plan? What were you thinking?"

"Mom, come on."

"No, okay?" she said. "I deserve to be Mad Mom for just a while! You took drugs *to* school and *at* school, called the doctor you've been dying to meet a stripper, and had a paranoid breakdown, and you may get kicked out of your college program entirely, Delia. You were so worried that missing it would get you disqualified, but you didn't consider that your own bad decisions might do the very same thing?"

She stopped. Her eyes were starting to water, and she had the most pained expression on her face.

My skin was hot immediately. I was embarrassed, sad, ashamed, angry. I felt every negative feeling I'd ever had in my life all at one time.

"Mom, I'm so sorry. I really am." I sniffed, but my nose couldn't keep up. I reached for a tissue, which made me somehow start crying more. "I'm so sorry. And I know you think this was just some immature, shortsighted teenage decision, and maybe it was." My voice cracked and got warbly. "But you have no idea how *desperate* I felt, Mom. How totally trapped. How helpless. How alone. Stockwood, and getting into a good med school, and becoming a doctor, it was a path. It was a way to get me from where I am to an *answer*. But then Dr. Steele entered my life's equation and he was a shortcut. That long, long path to a diagnosis had a teleport from *now* to *then*—how could I not try to take that shortcut? I had to go because I had to meet him because I can't . . ." I felt my voice catch in my throat, so I stood up as if that might make me sound strong. "I can't keep going like this, Mom. You want to understand, but you can't. You have no idea what I'd give for an answer . . . or what I'd give up. I would never have been able to forgive myself or move on if I had just not showed up. I don't know. At least I can say I made a memorable first impression?"

I sputtered a pained laugh, quick and loud. Standing, face toward the ceiling, my good humor rang out a few notes, and then, just as fast, the giggles melted into sobs, and I brought my hands to my face, hiding my tears and my shame.

"So you accidentally destroyed the road you were driving on. So what?" Regan said softly. "You'll build a new road. A bridge? A tunnel? Insert the right metaphor, okay?"

Mom leaned over and pulled me back onto the couch along with Regan, squishing us all together in a pile. "Your impression will be *lasting.*"

"At least the part in front of my classmates wasn't that bad, right?" I asked my sister.

"Well, that depends. How bad is it when all of MedSci sees your bloody period panties?" Regan asked, cringing.

"No!" I growled, deep and slow. "No! I thought that part was just my nightmare!"

I was powerless to resist the flood of memories from four years ago. Ruby's party. Everyone laughing. Everything changing. It was the Bloodbath all over again. I stood up while Mom and Ray covered their mouths waiting to see if I'd need them to follow me down the path of coping with laughter or tears. This time, I felt something in between. I dropped dramatically to the floor and covered my head with my arms. "Oh my god! I can never show my face at that school again!" My laughter was weak, but it was my brain's only option as my past echoed in my ears.

Regan picked up on my shift and tried to keep the jokes rolling. "Didn't you already say that once before, when you were in eighth grade?" Regan's punch line pulled a cautious smirk from Mom. Our fragile smiles faded one by one. "Anyway," she continued, "I'm glad I was there. It was *way* more interesting than a test, I'll tell you that much."

"Oh no! Your test!" Regan waved me off, but I kept going. "Regan, you're at the end of the semester. The last thing this family needs is for you to mess up in school too. You can't tank your stuff trying to take care of me. I can't stand it."

"It's nothing," she said. "I'm gonna ace the makeup exam. No sweat."

I had a whole new batch of guilt cramming itself into the clown car of my brain.

"You have a doctor's appointment super early before school, like seven a.m., and then we're supposed to go meet with the dean at nine. But, honestly, I think maybe we should cancel the doctor's visit, hon. I'm sure they'd let you back at the top of the patient wait list." Mom said.

"Oh god. I totally forgot about the new doctor."

I sat for a second—we all did. Staring. Quiet.

I knew that the doctor's appointment tomorrow might end up being a waste of time. But the thing at the core of all of this was answering the question of what was wrong with me. Solving the mystery of my angry uterus. I'd started down this premed road because I was willing to do anything for an answer. And then I'd put all my eggs into the basket of Dr. Steele, sure that he would be able to look at me and tell me what was wrong in an instant. But if that option was gone, was that really the end of all hope?

Somewhere, somehow, there were doctors who figured this out for their patients. It happened all the time. People got lucky and found out what was wrong. The right person, the right doctor, the right symptoms, the right medication, the right tests, and *bam* . . . their questions had answers.

I'd been led around by my guts on a leash for long enough.

Maybe the answer to not giving up is sometimes to just stop giving up.

"I'm going," I said to the quiet room. "I'm going to that appointment. You know how long I've been waiting to get in to see the next doc on the list. I can't get bumped to the back of the line again . . . not now."

"Are you sure, honey? This is all so much . . . and if it doesn't go well—"

"Well, then I'll go to the next one. And the next one. And the next one." I stood up and paced around in a few tiny circles. "I'm done with not knowing. I'm not going to keep living without knowing what's wrong. I need answers, and I'm going to keep looking until I find them."

Regan gave a sort of sarcastic slow clap and said, "All right, tiger, I like that rage!"

I smirked, but then I doubled down. "I'm serious, though.

I'm not going off into my adulthood in chaos. I'm not going off to college and just bumbling around in painful bodily anarchy."

"Yeah!" Regan egged me on. "You stay in those stirrups until you get answers!"

"Tomorrow I'll meet my seventh gynecologist. Seven doctors in six years, and I don't know anything more than I did when I was twelve years old."

"I get it, baby, but what else can you do about it? You're already doing everything you can. Maybe you should let me come with you." Mom's eyebrows were scrunched together with sadness.

"No, it's fine. I can go on my own. But I'm not waiting a year between doctors anymore. I'm going to keep going to new doctors until I find someone who'll listen. If I have to see a new doctor each week, then I will."

Mom didn't want to tear down my plans, but I could see the skepticism on her face. She said, "Well, in the meantime, we should probably get some more medicine in your system, 'cause underneath all this you are still on your period."

"Oh my god. My period. When we made the appointment, we thought I wouldn't have started yet. I can't have a pap smear on my period, can I?"

"You can." Mom gave a reassuring expression and reached for my hand. "You need to tell them in advance and let the nurse know, and it's not ideal, but sometimes it happens. You'll be fine. I promise."

I pouted and rolled my eyes. "Oh god, they're all gonna hate me. This whole appointment is going to be hell."

Regan tossed an almond up and caught it in her mouth. "Of course it's going to be hell. You're getting a pap smear while you're on your period. It doesn't get any worse than that."

Just then, Elvira sent a crush of a cramp coursing through my legs as if to say *challenge accepted.*

CHAPTER SEVEN

STAR-SPANGLED PAP SMEAR

Few things are as awkward as sitting your bare butt on a paper tablecloth, with another paper tablecloth draped across your junk, and a paper vest gaping open over your chest, while you wait for the gynecologist.

You never see the doctor beforehand, when you're still dressed and look like a reasonably put-together person. No. You get to meet the nurse. *They* get to see your cute shoes and compliment your sweater, but then they set out the paper goods, and you're forced to strip down to nothing. And then you do the ritualistic hiding of the underwear, where you stuff your undies under your folded pants or whatever so that the doctor can't possibly know that you even dared to bring underwear into the exam room. And then you have to navigate that paper ensemble, so when the doctor comes in and reaches out to shake your hand (something the old ones always seem to want to do), you have to decide if it's worth the risk of your crotch cover sliding onto the floor or your boobs making their own introduction first.

When I told the nurse I had started my period but didn't want to miss the appointment, she was very understanding and told me to get prepped for the exam anyway. She graciously put a special sort of pad on the end of the exam table for me to sit on, just in case. The doctor would have to decide, ultimately, if the pap smear would go forward or not. I was sitting there, trying desperately to focus on what I wanted to say, when I heard a whisper-soft knock on the door.

Dr. Leavy appeared to be, approximately, 897 years old. His website was woefully overdue for an update. The photo with his bio depicted hair and teeth, both of which had, unfortunately, since disappeared. His skin was pinkish white, his eyes deep green. Age spots peppered his face and hands up to his forearms. I could see under the cuffs of his shirt that beyond his wrists his skin hadn't seen much sun in a very long time. His smile was kind, though, truly, and his eyes were gentle. My worry continued to fade when he spoke with a strong and steady voice. The exact voice of an old white dude who has all the answers. Hey, I'd take it. Let him have all the answers for me.

At this point, I was willing to take answers from just about anybody. If a stranger on the street tried to tell me they knew what was wrong with me, I'd probably have listened.

My first two gynecologists, in sixth and seventh grade,

respectively, were men: Dr. Pauly and Dr. Li. After those two doctors made it clear they weren't willing to do very much of anything other than make me feel like I was a child with a wild imagination, my friends and family convinced me, at thirteen, that maybe I'd have better luck with a doctor who had had a period before.

Dr. Zimmern and Dr. Dimitri were the third and the fourth. Both women, and both gave me such hope at the start of the process. Both spent several minutes commiserating with me about the "annoyance" of periods, and in the case of Dr. Zimmern I invested almost a whole year in her care before we all realized it was a dead end. She'd told me that birth control pills might be all I needed to manage things. I couldn't help but get my hopes up. Regan was taking birth control pills by then . . . They made her periods way more bearable. The doctor explained that for a lot of patients, just having their periods be extremely predictable and consistent made all the difference. I tried to tell her that I tracked my period religiously—predictability wasn't the problem. She told me to "just try it for a few months." During that trial, I experienced mood swings with rage and paranoia, and she still urged me to hang on, since it takes bodies a long time to adapt to new hormones. When I stole Mom's car and drove it without a license on the straight-shot highway all the way to Oklahoma one night, out of a chaotic urge to outrun my pain, we all realized that even though it was a lifesaver for some people, that pill wasn't working for me—it had to stop. When grand theft auto didn't keep Dr. Zimmern from urging me to continue taking it anyway, my family and I knew she wasn't listening.

The next one, Dr. Dimitri, really hurt. She was the first doctor I saw after leaving Blythe Middle School and Ruby behind, and I was especially sensitive about people seeing me as making it up or being dramatic. She was a little older, well-respected, and had been on the receiving end of some of the fanciest births in North Dallas since the eighties. She was a superstar doctor, and I held out hope that she'd be supportive, but when I told her that my period pain was the worst thing I'd ever felt, she told me and Mom flat-out that I would get used to it. She told us that it was normal for newly menstruating kids to freak out at the "discomfort." She told me that all girls since the dawn of time had survived their periods and that I would too. I think maybe the worst part was that for some reason I believed her. I believed her for months. I believed that I was weak and broken. I believed that my former best friend had been right. I believed that I was less than every other woman on the face of the planet for all of human history. When she told me that my complaints were unrealistic and unlike those of the other young patients she had, I believed that that meant the problem was mine. I believed that I was the only person who'd ever suffered this way.

Dr. Reyes, the next one, was a man, followed by my one nonbinary doctor, Dr. Thomas, last year. Placement on the gender spectrum didn't make a lick of difference. Each one of them let me leave without an answer in exchange for little more than a lollipop.

Again, sitting on my paper-draped exam table, I was at the mercy of optimism. I took a breath and an extra-long blink. Maybe I'd get lucky this time, and this doctor would be different.

"Good morning," he said, reaching out a hand to greet me. "I'm Dr. Leavy."

I, an expert, have perfected the belly-button paper-clench technique. I hold the paper that's draped across my lap and cinch it together with my little paper vest in my left hand's tight fist, right at my belly button. Nothing falls open. An expert move. I confidently took his hand and gave it a shake.

"So, we're going to do a little exam, but the nurse says you started your period?"

"That's right," I answered without flinching.

"Well, it's not ideal, and sometimes it can impact the results, but if you're here and willing, I'm happy to do it, and we'll revisit if your test results come back abnormal, okay?"

"Okay."

A promising start.

The nurse entered as he asked if I'd lie back on his examination table, which was unlike any other I'd ever seen. It was huge—way bigger than any exam table I'd ever been on, but I followed instructions and put my head back on the paper-draped pillow. Above my face there was a poster of a cloudy blue sky with small text in the top corner that said simply THE LIMIT.

I managed—successfully—to not gag or make a sarcastic comment, which felt like a win.

"This exam table makes it easier for me to see what I need

to see," he said. "It might feel like you're gonna slip off the back, but I promise you're not."

This was meant to be reassuring; however, it was not. "Wait. What?" My eyes bulged.

The nurse came up beside my head and provided what I assume was emotional support as I heard the doctor bring his foot down hard on a pedal I hadn't noticed at the base of the table. A jerk and a clank and then motorized motion. *Oh dear god, I'm moving? Why am I moving?* My legs went up and my head went down. The whole table inverted to what felt like at *least* forty-five degrees. As promised, I was almost certain I was about to slide, headfirst, backward into the floor.

Every muscle in my body instantly tensed as I saw my life flash before my eyes.

"You're okay. You won't fall, I promise." He chuckled as if this was his literal favorite comedy bit of all time.

Right about the time he should have been telling me that I needed to scoot to the end of the table—because you're never close enough to the end—I was preparing myself for some sort of junk-in-the-air crab walk that would defy gravity and allow me to climb back up the table and get my butt to the edge. Then he clicked another button and a big latch disconnected.

The entire last quarter of the table, the part directly under my tush, released and collapsed, folding under itself, creating a whole new table edge perfectly poised at my tailbone without my scooching. My eyes grew wide, and the nurse grinned at me with this blank stare, as if that was comforting.

The contraption of ergonomics, clearly designed to allow

this ancient creature to do exams without pain or discomfort, had me angled, head toward the floor, feet in the air in stirrups, butt hanging off the end of a no-longer-existent portion of the table.

At least one of us would be comfortable during the exam.

Then he had the nerve to say, "There we go. Perfect."

The nurse leaned just a few inches closer to ask, "Everything okay, hon?"

You mean aside from the fact that I feel like I'm about to get launched backward out of the world's most horrible waterslide without the promise of a snow cone after?

"I'm okay. Thanks."

"Gonna be a little cold while I insert the speculum. Are you doing okay?"

"Uh-huh." I said. Possibly telling the truth. I was too disconnected from my brain to be sure.

There was a slippy sort of feeling as he inserted the instrument, and then a bit of vague pressure until I actually managed to relax a little, and then I heard the clicking of the speculum locking into its open position.

With my medical history, I'd done more than my fair share of basic research about the instruments, what they looked like, and what they did. So I could picture the business end of my exam, which made the whole thing easier to handle.

Once the device was locked open, and all my various muscles had had a few seconds without change, I really did get a little calmer—until he started humming.

It was such a shock, the sound of music wafting up from

where his head was positioned in the open space between my knees, that it took me an extra moment to recognize the familiar tune.

Is that . . . the national anthem?

He got through "the dawn's early light" and then paused. "Okay, I'm going to use my hand now to check on a few specific areas."

The nurse, who had a clear view, was dutifully observing his work. He pressed one hand on the outside of my belly while the other hand made a few careful prodding motions along the inside of my vaginal wall. This man was honoring his country while giving a pelvic exam.

"You okay?" he asked, standing tall now so his head was visible from behind the paper sheet.

"I . . . I am, yes. How are you?"

Every muscle in my body tensed as embarrassment took over my brain. *How are you?*

Dr. Leavy ignored me completely, humming his patriotism with increasing gusto, this time getting all the way to "the perilous fight" before saying, "Okay, now you'll feel a little pinch."

Lying there, mostly upside down, fighting the urge to bring my right hand over my heart, I squeezed my eyes shut. This part was the actual pap smear, where the doctor uses a little tool to sort of brush or scrape cells to test and screen for cervical problems. That's the "pinch," and it is not very fun. It *almost* really hurts, but doesn't quite. And it doesn't last very long, except when the doctor tells you that the pinch is coming and then you're anticipating it for seconds that feel like minutes.

His humming approached its crescendo.

And just as those bombs started bursting in air, he made contact.

There. Ouch. Ow, ow, owww.

Done.

He removed his instruments quickly, and a tiny knot of ache settled deep into my guts, fading quickly but not completely gone.

A few minutes later I was dressed, back up on the paper-draped exam table—which had thankfully been returned to its fully horizontal position—and Dr. Leavy had left and re-entered the room so we could talk about my issues.

Everybody else with a period gets to navigate it privately—but my period is always run by committee. At the start of twelfth grade, I decided it was time to practice handling my doctors on my own. I had a desperate desire to be independent in this one tiny way. And even through the acrobatics I'd just endured, I was confident about not needing Mom to be at the appointment with me no matter how willing she was to be there. But once he crossed the room and sat on his little stool, I wished I hadn't been so stubborn. I just wanted my mom.

He asked all the usual questions about how often it hurt and how long the pain lasted. He asked me to rate my pain most of the time (a 7 or 7.5, maybe?) and compare that with the worst it had ever been (a strong 9).

Regan had asked me that question so many times. How

bad was bad? How painful was the very worst of it? I couldn't ever bring myself to declare my pain a 10. I didn't want to lock myself into a scenario where I pushed their belief. And I didn't want to tell myself or anyone else that it couldn't get worse, because somehow, every time, there was always room for it to get worse.

"So, I think that based on what you've described, you're probably experiencing pain from an ovarian cyst." Dr. Leavy was reaching behind him to the place on the counter where a dozen glossy pamphlets said things like SO, YOU HAVE SYPHILIS and HOW TO TALK TO YOUR DOCTOR ABOUT BIRTH CONTROL.

"A cyst?" I asked. "But I've been having this pain for years . . . and it's been getting worse."

"Well, it's possible that you've had one very small cyst that's been growing, but it's also possible that you've had a few different cysts over the years. You had an ultrasound several months ago for another doctor, and I was able to review those images. There is a spot that might have been a small, fluid-filled cyst. That could be the culprit."

I found my voice, suddenly, and said, "But I have some other symptoms that seem worse than they should be. Pain, but also migraines, back pain, so much fatigue—"

He interrupted. "What about achy muscles? Diarrhea? Constipation?"

I nodded, a tiny spark of hope lit inside me. I wondered if this was the beginning of a line of questions that would finally bring me into the light.

"All the symptoms you're describing are pretty typical for

a lot of periods. That doesn't mean we have anything out of the ordinary here. Unless I'm right about that cyst. What I'd like to try is a birth control pill while we wait it out."

This part of the appointment always feels like it's going at supersonic speed. Like, I wanted to interrupt to say that I needed him to try something else, but before I could form a word, he'd already pushed ten sentences past me, and I was struggling to catch up. I was overwhelmed, but I tried to keep listening and processing everything he said. He rattled off information about the pill he wanted me to try and why it should prevent new cysts from growing.

"Do you have any questions for me?" he asked.

I felt dizzy. "I . . . well . . ."

Dr. Leavy was getting a lot of things wrong, but he was also kind enough to give my brain a few seconds to catch up and ask the question that was stuck.

"So, are you sure? Is this it? Is this a diagnosis? No other doctor has thought it was a cyst . . . but if it is, what do we do? And if it isn't, what do we do then?"

He continued, "You're right. It may not be a cyst at all, and that's why waiting it out is always our first course of treatment. So, with that in mind, birth control is a great place to start, and this pill is the one I recommend to all my teen patients because of its low dose of hormones. It makes menstruation lighter and more predictable. It solves the problem for a lot of girls who struggle to handle their periods."

Struggle to handle.

Struggle to handle.

"I'll get this prescription sent over for you," he said, tapping the notepad and standing. My mouth really, really wanted to speak. I swear it did. I wanted to tell him that I'd tried birth control before and it hadn't gone very well. I wanted to tell him that waiting through months of pain to find out if we were even moving in the right direction wasn't right. I wanted to tell him that I wasn't going to take that pill, and we'd have to keep looking. But I didn't. I couldn't.

My jaw was locked from a very specific fear that I desperately wanted to shake, but I absolutely couldn't.

There was always a chance that he was right. It was possible—it had to be—that I really was just that one feeble girl who couldn't figure out how to handle this thing that was an unavoidable part of life for half the world's population.

So, even though I wanted to speak, I couldn't. Not a peep.

Then he gave me a smile, brought the edge of his hand to his forehead, and gave a little salute of goodbye before he walked out of the room.

CHAPTER EIGHT

GUILTY UNTIL PROVEN GUILTY

The car ride conversation with Mom shifted from my initial disappointment into hysterical laughter and a full-volume duet of "Yankee Doodle Dandy." The endorphins were very much appreciated because then, Mom asked me what I wanted to do next.

"All I know is that I'm not going back to that exam table from hell. I'm not going to wait him out. I just can't. The receptionist said it would be almost four weeks before his favorite ultrasound tech could get me in—"

"He's making you wait for his favorite ultrasound tech? Does this person add a snazzy baseline to his uterine serenades or something?"

"Dr. Leavy has a tech on staff that is his personal favorite. She is the only one he likes to use for cyst checks. She does these sort of drawings of what she finds and I don't know, dude, it's just what he said. But I don't have a month to wait and then two months to wait again, before we do a follow-up to see if his guess is right." Mom nodded along while she looked out the windshield. "I told you yesterday, and I'm not kidding. I'm going to see which doctor is next on my list. I'm going to college in just a few months. I don't have time for this."

Mom got too quiet too fast, and I knew it was because my mention of college had her doubt all riled up again.

Mom and I arrived at Stockwood for our meeting with the dean. Regan originally wanted to blow off school and come with us to my doctor appointment, but it would have meant getting to school late. Mom told her she had to take the Woolly Mammoth to school without us (and get there on time). While Mom and I waited for the dean, I texted Priya and Keisha, who came up and saw me for a second between classes but they just kept doing things like patting my hands and hugging me. I imagine they would have treated someone on their deathbed exactly the same. I shooed them off after the fifth time they took turns asking if I was okay.

After that, it felt like we sat in the waiting area for an hour before anything happened. During that time, I called Dr. Steele's office twice. Once, I left a voicemail, and the second time, I left a message with the receptionist for him to please call me back.

The dean's office was painted a deep, navy blue. There

were several large leather chairs in front of the solid oak desk in the center of the room. Dean D'Ag sat behind it with his hands in his lap. At the sight of the pink skin of his bald head, I felt my heart start beating faster.

"Have a seat," said the dean. I watched his shoulders rise and fall with a deep breath.

"Let me just say, my daughter's medical condition complicates this already complica—"

"Ms. Bridges, pardon me, but it will save us a great deal of time if you'll allow me to explain the situation." The dean took another inhale and exhaled silently through lips parted in a tiny O.

My mother's confidence was shaken. It was crystal clear to me that she'd expected to set the ball rolling and talk first. Her posture stayed strong, but I noticed her spinning the rose-quartz ring she wore on her thumb. She spun it around and around, pausing every few spins to run her other thumb along the band. I wished I had a ring to spin. Everything I wanted filled the open space of the room. It was like I was breathing in my own hopes instead of oxygen. Logically, I understood that I had made a huge mistake. One of the tenets of Stockwood is taking responsibility and learning from our mistakes, so the administration would expect me to make amends, and I would. I'd do it—anything—to put this behind me so I could get back to my plan. Even if Dr. Steele never spoke to me again, the diploma from Stockwood was still a golden ticket to almost *anywhere*—I would still get into med school and eventually figure out what was wrong with me.

"Delia?" Mom asked, apparently for the second time, since I'd zoned out.

"Sorry. Yes?" I pulled on the sleeves of my cardigan until they were over my thumbs, then straightened the Stockwood logo as I closed my sweater across my chest.

"Did you hear what I said?" Dean D'Agostino asked.

"I'm sorry. Could you repeat it?"

"I said that we all know you're an incredibly smart student. You make excellent grades. You're involved in chorus and volleyball. You have a virtually blemish-free school record."

The corners of my mouth tugged up just a little, an involuntary smile at his compliments. He was right. I was a good kid. A great kid, maybe, by some standards. A wash of relief splashed against my face like cold water.

Mom nodded her head silently beside me.

The dean hesitated and looked over at the bookshelf for a moment. Then he slowly nodded. "Unfortunately, your glowing record and your standing until now have no bearing on the action we have to take."

The tiny smile vanished. This wasn't the time to have a half-sincere grin on my face. Of course they'd have to punish me. I interrupted: "I completely understand. It was irresponsible and shortsighted of me both to take the tincture and to bring the bottle to school. I have no excuse for my behavior. I made a bad decision, I disrespected Dr. Steele, my classmates, Stockwood, and you. I completely accept that there will be punishment. I know you can't just let it slide. But I promise you I won't let my work slip in the meantime. I'll keep up with everything, and after that time is served—detentions, suspensions, whichever and for however long you decide that should be—I promise I will be the same Cordelia Bridges you've always known to be a responsible and dutiful student. I promise."

He couldn't ask for more than that. It was a perfect apology. And as cheesy as it might have sounded, it was a sincere one.

The dean bowed his head for a moment before saying, "Delia . . ." It was strange hearing him use my nickname rather than Cordelia. My heartbeat picked up speed again. "Not detention . . . or suspension. Expulsion." My heart stopped in my chest. "Unfortunately, you won't be returning to Stockwood . . . at all. As of today. Permanently. I truly am sorry."

A sound like rushing water filled my ears, until it was the only thing I could hear. It roared for a moment, then got softer again. My heart restarted and took off running.

"What?" Mom and I said in unison.

Dean D'Ag took another deep breath. "The Safety Resolution of 1996 requires the expulsion or alternative placement of a student who brings illegal drugs to any school campus. As Stockwood is a private school, not a large public school, we don't have alternative placement options, and beyond that, our school's bylaws are absolute and not subject to exceptions. Any Stockwood student found with drugs, alcohol, tobacco, weapons of any kind . . . they're expelled. It's in the morality clause you signed at the start of freshman year. You knew this would be the consequence of the choice to bring that bottle to school. You agreed to it. Right here."

A crisp white piece of paper bearing my name lay on the desk in front of me. It was there. In black and white.

My heart wasn't beating fast anymore.

All the blood in my body fell still all at once, lurching forward and back as it rocked to a stop.

"Wait. Delia and I were both prepared for the chance that she'd be kicked out of the mentorship, or even the pre-med program itself, but kicked out of the school? There are only a handful of days left until graduation. I'm sure we can work something out, right?" Mom asked. She didn't give him time to respond before her frustration streamed out. "*And I thought zero-tolerance policies were over.*" She was finding her voice again. "I thought the educational system on the whole had figured out that one punishment with no consideration for context was problematic, racist, ableist, patriarchal bullshit!"

He didn't even flinch at her words. He must have been ready for a blowup.

"Ms. Bridges—"

"Would you please just call me Miranda while you take this whole thing way too far and demolish my kid's hopes and dreams?"

"Miranda." The dean locked his chin in place. "Zero-tolerance policies are definitely questionable at the best of times, but the short answer, in this case, is that your child brought an illegal drug to school and was also under the influence of that illegal drug at school, and that's simply *always* going to be against the rules. Furthermore, because of that legislation, we have no choice but to remove her from her regular educational setting. Public schools often do have more options like alternative placements. But Stockwood has no other programming. There isn't a homebound version of our special programs, and there isn't an alternative campus. She has to be removed from the school where the incident occurred, and it will be marked on her transcript under the disclosure-mandate portion of that legislation, which means that wherever she goes to school next will know about the reason for her expulsion."

I startled myself so much when I stood. I took a step closer to his desk. "I . . . apologized. I took responsibility. How . . . how can I fix this?" The rushing sound was back in my ears, and I raised my voice to be heard over it.

"Delia, you might not believe me, but I hope someday you will understand . . . You can't fix this. And neither can I. I can't change the law, and I can't break the law. Our school must remain compliant."

The room was quiet and still until I asked, "Could the mentorship with Dr. Steele continue outside of Stockwood?"

The dean blinked four times before speaking. "He left the forum yesterday before we could speak about this situation specifically, but honestly . . ." The dean paused to restrain his overwhelming disbelief at my last scrap of hope. "You know the mentorships are part of a collegiate program intended just for select students of participating prep schools." He turned to Mom. "She won't be eligible once she enrolls back in a public school. I sent word to the principal at Blythe High School that you'll enroll on Friday—according to our records, you had a prescheduled absence tomorrow—Thursday, right? It was already approved. At least it buys you a day to process. It's not much, but it's all I can do."

"Wait. I have to go back to *Blythe*? No way. Mom, you know I—aahhhhhssshhhhhhh." Pain gripped me, shocked me out of nowhere. I closed my eyes and tried to breathe as I started rocking forward and back, holding the ache in my guts.

"Let's go. We need to get you home," Mom said, supporting me under my arm.

The dean called to me before we walked out the door. "Cordelia, I really am sorry."

"Me too," I said.

Mom and I hobbled down the stairs and outside to the car. She helped me get in, and I pulled the lever until my seat was laid back all the way flat.

I pulled out my phone and texted my friends their patiently awaited update:

DELIA: Welp, my period just ruined my life.

CHAPTER NINE

READ BETWEEN THE LINES

Mom and I didn't really talk much on the drive home, and when we got there around lunchtime, I went straight upstairs and crawled into bed, and she went to work.

From my bed, my line of sight pointed straight at my vision board. So many little scraps of paper meant to inspire me to keep my goals in mind. So many little scraps of paper meant to keep me on track and moving in the right direction. I flipped over and looked the other way.

I couldn't even imagine it was possible that I'd go back to Blythe High. Back to Ruby.

Ruby had hurt me so badly on the last day of our friendship and she really, truly, never even tried to fix it. At various times over the years I'd thought of her, sure, but I'd never expected to see her face again for the rest of my life. It's just so hard to come back from something like that.

Ruby hadn't started her period yet when things fell apart. Even though she'd helped me so much during the first couple of years, by the summer after eighth grade she just absolutely could not manage to get her head around what it was like for me. She became irritated at my absence and my unwillingness to hang out while I was in pain. On that last day, she let fly the truth she'd carried for a long time: She simply didn't believe me. She thought that even if it wasn't on purpose, I was making it all bigger than it was. Nothing could have ever hurt me more than that. My worst fear come true.

A notification pinged, so I skimmed the preview, but this was obviously the sort of news that needed to be read on a much larger screen. I leaned over and pulled my laptop out of my bag, bracing myself for the worst.

In a few taps I read the most recent email from the admissions department at Gleeson University. There it was, in big type at the top of my screen.

My early acceptance to Gleeson University had always been conditional—it was directly tied to my mentorship. I had been accepted to my dream college. I was supposed to be there in just a few months, when fall would be hitting New England and painting the streets with fiery leaves that Texas never seems to get. But without the mentorship, my acceptance had vaporized. Gleeson had dropped me.

Adrenaline surged in my body as I opened a new email and started to compose.

Damage control.
Okay.

Good evening, Dr. Steele,

My name is Cordelia Bridges, and we met briefly at Stockwood Prep yesterday during the mentorship-matching ceremony.

Not that I actually remember it.

I know that morning was

the day my entire future got launched like a rocket right up the devil's fiery b-hole

complicated and likely confusing to have witnessed. I apologize for any frustration or offense I undoubtedly caused. I'm sure that Stockwood has provided some basic information regarding the situation and their required response to

my getting higher than Rudolph and going to school, where I proceeded to flash my bloodstained panties to not only almost every kid I know, but to you and about a dozen other adults whom I respect

the complicated events of that morning, but I want you to know that this event is not reflective of my preparation or dedication regarding my medical future. The truth is, and I hope you can empathize with this personal detail,

Okay, keep your head on straight, Delia. Mentorship or not, you have to try to turn this catastrophe into a consult.

I have been suffering from debilitating period pain for several years now, without any hope of a diagnosis. I am seventeen years old, and I will soon visit my eighth gynecologist.

Don't ask what happened with the seventh.

Each has their own theory, and none of them have had any solutions. I have to admit that I am an admirer of your work not only as a future doctor, but also hopefully as a future patient.

Niiiiice.

I would love nothing more than for this mentorship to somehow survive my horrible mistake, but if it can't, I would appreciate your consideration in regards to meeting with me to discuss my case.

My pride has already been destroyed, so why not toss my professionalism in the blender too?

Unfortunately, my conditional acceptance to Gleeson has been

screwed up, ruined, set on fire

revoked, but I am no less determined to find a way forward toward my goal of being a doctor who, if I'm lucky, will have a reputation much like yours for listening to patients.

So now, to prevent my imminent explosion from waiting,

I would appreciate a quick email or phone call at the number below so that we might touch base and connect sometime in the future. I'm truly devastated at how our meeting played out, and I really can't apologize enough for what I said about your name. I'd love to have the chance to talk to you sometime about how my attempt to self-medicate my pain went so badly wrong.

Cordially,

With shame,

Cordelia Bridges

Send.

I closed my laptop and shoved it to the edge of my bed and then tossed my phone on the floor for good measure.

I leaned back and stared at the ceiling and curled my knees closer to my chest. Then I turned again, back toward my corkboard. I tucked into the fetal position, kicked off my boots, and pulled the blanket over my legs. A tear ran out of the corner of my eye, and then it soaked down into the fabric of the pillow. The cold wetness spread, and it bloomed against my cheek.

I stared so hard, willing that cold, wet spot under my cheek to warm up so I wouldn't feel it anymore, but another tear welled up, and the wet spot grew bigger.

It was silent in the house, and that soundlessness pressed down on me, and my cheek kept getting colder and colder.

Like lying on a cold, wet swimsuit.

My life: more uncomfortable than it had ever been. My future: broken.

I took a deep breath and screamed.

My sobs came, furious and shaking.

Then I screamed again.

Loud and piercing, slapping down the silence until it was irreparably broken too.

Hours later, I woke and found Mom and Regan whispering in the kitchen. "Why are you guys being so quiet?" I asked before grabbing Regan's arm and taking a bite of her pizza while it was still in her hand.

"Obviously we were talking about you," Regan said.

I laughed. "Obviously." The round-robin of two of us talking about the other one was perpetual in our household. We had all learned to live with the understanding that we would *definitely* be discussed behind our back. "How was your makeup test?" I asked.

"It was pretty hard, actually. But it's fine."

"How hard?" Mom asked, turning to face her.

"I'm so sorry, Ray. I am so sorry. I'll make it up to you. I can help you study for your final?"

"It's a deal," Regan said. "But stop trying to change the subject."

Mom started in, "Yeah, Ray and I were talking about what this means, and what we need to do next to get you into a good school."

"I know. I can't *believe* I don't go to Stockwood anymore. And I really, really can't go back to Blythe. Obviously."

"Not high school," Mom corrected. "College. Hon, you're going to Blythe High. While you were napping this afternoon, I went up there and got the enrollment all done. You're a Blythe Badger. Congratulations." She pointed to the table, where a packet of registration papers was topped with a brand-new shiny class schedule for me to follow on Friday. Her eyes were full of judgement and even though she managed to keep from saying it out loud, I could hear the *I told you so* in her mind. She had tried—she really had—to convince me to do the reasonable thing and apply for a few backup schools. But this thing with Gleeson was a certainty in my head. I knew I was at the right school with the right grades and the right background. I knew I'd get matched with someone. I didn't have any reason to doubt it. And I was right, of course, I did get matched and get in. But nothing could have convinced me my period would cause me to lose that acceptance. Nothing.

"And, honey, you're not going to Gleeson. Ship. Anchor up. Sailing away. Deck swabbing. Stockwood is done. Gleeson is done. And we need to make absolutely sure we have a few good second-choice college options if you don't get full acceptance to Gleeson *without* the mentorship program. That is, assuming you want to reapply as a regular, basic-ass person." Mom stared at me.

"Mom, in what universe am I basic-ass?"

"In what universe are you *not*?" Regan asked instantly.

"Okay, so, whatever. Worst-case scenario I get a diploma from BHS, but I'm still a competitive candidate for Gleeson—with or without Dr. Steele. Right?"

"Of course you are," Regan said. "But . . . without him and that mentorship and Stockwood, you're just a basic-ass senior from a basic-ass school, and without all the special courses and your extracurriculars and stuff, your transcript is literally basic-ass. A perfect GPA isn't enough. It never is. So you have to have a backup plan. Because you're what? Basic. Ass."

My posture slumped. I was so tired. Emotionally and physically. I felt it in every muscle in my body. I didn't know a brain could have so many thoughts and feelings in such a short amount of time. The dean, Mom, and Regan. Stockwood, Blythe, and Gleeson. Dr. Leavy, Dr. Steele, and . . . Dr. Me? Really? Without Gleeson, was med school too far out of reach? My palms became itchy and my lips felt like they were being stung by bees. Ruby hadn't believed me. Doctors didn't believe me. I'd probably lost my shot for a magical diagnosis from Dr. Steele, and I was at least a decade away from being able to diagnose myself.

Everything had crumbled, not to rubble, but to dust.

I'd felt sure I was weak, but now I really knew it.

My mouth parted a little, so eager to refute what she was saying, but there weren't any words that would do the trick. Mom saw the crisis flush my skin and reached for my face. She held it in her hands as my eyes filled with tears, which eventually fell in wet streaks down my cheeks, over my mom's thumbs. Eventually, I whispered the word, "Maybe . . ."

"I know you're sad, and I know this is disappointing, but your plans—your original plans—aren't going to happen the way we wanted them to. And I'm sorry. And I know it isn't fair. You know I know it isn't fair, right? But that doesn't have to mean your future is over."

My head was still immobilized, but I looked down with my eyes anyway.

"No, look at me. Deels, you're going to have a beautiful, beautiful life, my love, and it's going to be okay. You are still going to graduate. And you'll get into a phenomenal college. You're still going to help people and make a difference in the world. You'll be on the other side of this, eventually. It's not going to be Stockwood, and it's not going to be Gleeson." She noticed the argument threatening to spark behind my eyes. "But it's going to be *something*. It's going to be something unexpectedly beautiful and right. And I know you're sad, but I need you to focus on what we're going to do *now*. We're going to start by applying to some backup schools— amazing ones—and plan for getting you into med school just like everybody else who didn't go to Stockwood Prep. Maybe some will have some late admissions process, but maybe not.

Maybe we have to wait through the fall. Maybe we have to try again next year."

Regan chimed in as she gnawed on her pizza crust like it was a dog bone. "Don't worry, *Cordelia* comes before *Regan* in the alphabet. You'd still cross the stage before me."

Her joke hit me in the heart. Mom could tell, and she reached over and smacked her in the knee.

"Too sharp. Too soon. Sorry, sis."

I listened to her words, but it felt like my brain was stuck in a fog.

"And Friday . . . you're going to Blythe High School for the last few days of school. You're going to go, and you're going to be fine, and it will be over before you know it. And I know you're worried about the thing with Ruby, but I'm sure everyone has long forgotten about it. You don't owe her your forgiveness or your friendship."

"Right." I nodded, and she let go of my face. She pulled me against her chest and held me.

It should have been this poignant, healing moment of connection, but somehow I just felt numb . . . and entirely, completely alone.

CHAPTER TEN

THE BLOODBATH

I spent the whole day on Thursday in mourning. I cried here and there, watched an unreasonable number of shows, and ignored every ping on my phone. I felt sick—physically and mentally. Two days in, my period had settled into its cycle of pain. Waves of crushing pressure, skin tight over my belly, head pounding relentlessly, and shocks of terrible searing suffering peppered on top. That night, the night before my first day at Blythe, Priya, Keisha, and I swarmed the pizza box and then settled on the patio's worn wicker furniture while I told my two friends everything about the meeting with the dean from the day before.

"I can't believe it," Priya said, wiping her mouth with her napkin. She'd pulled her hair back into a clip to give her maximum pizza-chomping ease.

"Believe it, Pri. Believe it."

Keisha pulled her feet up into the chair and sat cross-legged. She propped one elbow up on her knee and rested her chin on the back of her hand. Keisha was taking a break between protective styles, and for now she wore her hair natural and short. "What you're gonna do is you're going to walk into BHS and just . . . get through it." Keisha used her hand like a blade in the air.

I hung my head. "Don't even get me started on BHS. That's possibly the worst part of this whole thing."

"Seriously?" Priya asked leaning forward, putting her hands on her knees. "Worse than losing the mentorship?"

I shrugged. "Maybe? I started this whole becoming-a-doctor thing in part because I wanted to prove to the Ruby who'd been living in my head rent-free that there was something *actually* wrong. There was a reason, a disease, cancer, *something*. Then I started chasing Dr. Steele because I believed he could diagnose me. So, yeah, facing real-life Ruby again and still not having proof that she was wrong about me? Proof that this is real? It's the worst thing I can imagine."

"Okay, *enough*." Keisha crossed her arms over her chest and rolled her eyes.

"*What?*" I recoiled.

"It has been four years of you teasing this story and *refusing* to tell us what actually happened with that girl. You've got to get this out in the open if you want Pri and me to be able to tell you everything is going to be fine . . . or maybe tell you that you actually do just need to move away and assume a new identity. But this is getting annoying. We deserve this—we've been patient enough. What exactly happened?"

I blinked a couple of times.

Priya nodded and said, "Definitely. You tell us you lived through a social failure that you call 'the Bloodbath,' but you won't tell us what happened? It's just not reasonable."

I had no way to argue with them. It was true. If I was going to be facing Ruby, I'd have to be able to talk with my best friends about everything without leaving big gaps. Maybe retelling the story would make it seem not so bad. It had been four years. Maybe time had healed these wounds after all.

"Okay, fine. Fine."

Ruby-June Walker and I first met in fourth grade. We were desk buddies in Mrs. Branch's class, and once we realized we had the same purple-and-teal backpack, we were inseparable. Ruby and I did everything together.

She had the reddest hair I'd ever seen in real life, lovely and orange and heavy. Her eyes were dark brown, and she had wildly crooked teeth that her parents tried to wrangle with braces just as soon as they'd all come in. Her Texan accent was heavier than almost anyone else's in our class for reasons I couldn't quite understand. Her mom and dad weren't overly drawly, but I think she took after her grandma more than her parents anyway. She had collected dozens of very silly-sounding sayings that she recited in her granny's tone, and it made her sound like a cowboy cartoon character half the time.

She was louder than I was, more wild, more outgoing. She was effortlessly popular, but not in an obnoxious way. She was popular because she was really and truly liked and likable. She had her first crush on a girl in sixth grade and her first kiss with a boy in seventh grade. But it was in eighth grade that she found herself immersed in little love bursts with every person she daydreamed about. *My* eighth grade had a different focus—by then I'd been navigating my period for two years.

During the sixth-grade Valentine's Day party, I'd been sitting, reading notes from my little mailbox, when I felt my shorts were wet. I stood up, and sure enough a little splotch of red was sponged onto the plastic orange seat, and even though I couldn't turn around backward, I knew it must be visible on my butt. A boy in our class, like a robot with a sensor, tracked onto the spot within seconds. Of course, he brought it to everyone else's attention, and as I prepared to disintegrate, Ruby took my arm and loudly proclaimed that, yeah, I'd started my period, but so what? That made me older and cooler than any of them, and somehow her Ruby magic worked, because nobody made fun after that. They all thought I was in fact older and cooler, and I felt like I was too.

As the months rolled on, though, my period got more and more complicated and harder and harder to live with. A year or so in, I passed out at school for the first time in the middle of the library. Ruby and I had been working on a project, and suddenly I was just out cold on the floor. She had to finish it on her own. Maybe that was the first time my period annoyed her.

Of course, I had no way to gauge what periods were usually like. I had no way to know if my period was worse than anyone else's. I would cry in pain sometimes, and the other girls picked up a fair bit of anxiety about their own looming changes. But somehow Ruby's tone surrounding my period had helped shape the culture of our middle school group. Thanks to Ruby in those early months, I wasn't overly quiet or ashamed about my period. I could pull a maxi pad from my backpack, carry it boldly to the front of the class, and ask the teacher to go to the bathroom without flinching or stuffing it up my sleeve. If I turned green and clammy or felt like throwing up, I was willing to say why. She made me brave about my period. She told me that I could do it . . . I could handle it . . . I could get up and keep going . . .

At first it felt like support, but over time it shifted toward exasperation.

Ruby's magic couldn't last. The other kids became less and less forgiving of my taking up space with my period. Loud admissions that I'd thrown up and quiet crying in the back of the classroom got old. Eventually, I was seen as a drama queen—just trying to keep the attention of being one of the only girls to have started. Because as other girls did start, most had normal periods, and the culture shifted back. *They* didn't have to go to the nurse every month. *They* didn't pass out on the floor of the cafeteria. *They* didn't scream and cry and need their moms to come pick them up early. They handled their business in between classes—they didn't need to be excused every other hour to keep from staining their clothes.

They just had their periods. They wore dark jeans once a month. They asked each other for ultrathin pads when it caught them by surprise, and they giggled at me when I pulled out one of my supersized ones.

As bold as I'd started, I ended up just as quiet and embarrassed as anyone else was about their period. And eventually I was just another girl with a pad stuffed up my sleeve and a sweatshirt tied around my waist.

Ruby wanted to be like every other middle schooler. For a while I nervously accepted her invitations to hang out, go shopping, or see movies, but slowly my yes became maybe and then my maybe turned into no. I couldn't bring myself to go to places where I felt sure I would get sick and not be able to sit down. Even days that weren't period days were questionable. Headaches popped up. I would get nauseated for no real reason. And I didn't want to be at Six Flags on the day I expected to start for the month. I didn't want to be shopping and worried about barfing all over the perfectly folded T-shirts. I disappointed Ruby. Over and over and over. As it happens, she still hadn't started her period even though our birthdays were only a couple of weeks apart. Not in sixth grade, or seventh, or eighth.

Our small fights started piling up. She would ask something of me or I'd tell her I needed something and, slowly, we soured. She wanted me to suck it up, and I needed her to understand that I couldn't.

Ruby's birthday was always the week or two before school started, and the birthday party she'd planned in the summer before going off to high school was going to be epic: an into-the-evening, twinkle-lights-in-the-bushes, music-and-dancing-and-kiss-sneaking pool party. The kid she liked was going to be at that party, and she was convinced that if her party was perfect, she and Nate would become *more than friends.*

A few days before, I knew I was doomed. I'd definitely be on my period the day of her party.

There was no way in hell that I was going to be in a swimsuit, let alone in a pool, on my period. I mentioned it to Ruby, but she just kept saying, "It'll be fine. It'll be fine." And when I gave in and told her I would come, but I probably wouldn't swim, she waved me away and said that I should use tampons and figure it out. Easy for her to say . . . she still hadn't had her first period, and tampons can be kind of intimidating when you've never used one before. The next afternoon I really tried to learn how to use them. Mom and I went through a whole box, but they all ended up in the trash. The experiment concluded with me tearfully opening the bathroom door and asking if there was such a thing as a micro vagina because tampons just wouldn't fit in there.

A few hours before the party I told Ruby that I'd started my period and there was just no way I could swim. I told her I felt dizzy already, and nauseated, and I was worried about being sick while I was there.

She just said over and over that I would be fine. I would be fine. I just needed to show up and I'd have so much fun, I wouldn't even think about my period.

I so wanted that to be true. I put on shorts and a tank top and went.

When I got there, Ruby was glad to see me, but she was also obviously irritated that I hadn't worn a bathing suit. Ruby knew on some basic level that if one or two kids didn't want to swim (and god forbid *Nate* not want to), other kids might not want to either. We were all totally obsessed with being sure that everyone thought we were doing the cool thing. Throw in a mix of budding hormones and newly acquired body insecurity, and the delicate social dance of a boy-girl pool party was seriously in jeopardy.

"You're fine." She swore it. "You're gonna be fine."

She begged me to put on a suit. She went and got one of her mom's wraparound cover-ups. We had only a few minutes until the rest of the kids were supposed to show up, and somehow guilt (and a deep fear of disappointing her) convinced me. She thanked me a dozen times and left to go answer the front door. I grabbed an extra swimsuit from her drawer. A one-piece that felt like the safest, least flashy bet. My guts weren't too sore yet. They'd barely begun to ache. So I changed my pad and stuck a new one into the bottom of the swimsuit and wrapped the sarong around my waist. I checked myself in the mirror and couldn't see anything, other than the fact that I looked physically uncomfortable. The plasticky wad of the pad was invisible as long as I kept my legs tight together. My "swelly belly," as I called the intense and painful bloat that often accompanied my period, was pushing out my stomach several inches, and it felt absolutely awful.

But I wanted to be a good friend, and to just be normal. I really did.

I went downstairs, and the party was getting going. Kids all stood by the side of the pool, hands awkwardly on their hips or crossed over their chests. Ruby and Nate were talking by the big stack of towels, gesturing to the water and asking each other if they should get in or wait for more people.

Nate grabbed her wrist, and they took a few steps before jumping into the pool hand in hand. The other kids followed them immediately, the boys making violent waves while the girls were up to their necks at the edge, obscuring their bodies from the eyes of the boys. I managed to not feel like a weirdo sitting perched on the side of the pool with my feet in the cool water. It was all going to be fine. I caught Ruby's gaze, and she smiled and mouthed *thank you*.

My choice was invisible to everyone else until the hot tub pile-in started. The whole group decided it would be hilarious to get every last one of us into the hot tub. Like, fifteen kids.

"Get in, Delia!" All the boys were squawking at me to help them complete this completely asinine mission.

By this time, everyone was in. Everyone. Except for me.

Ruby was listening to all our other friends urging me to get in, and she knew why I didn't want to. I looked down at her, her brown eyes big and pleading.

I tried to play it off cool, saying things like "I really can't. I don't want to get wet. I'm just not feeling up for it."

I was seconds from trying to figure out how I could turn around, get up and out, and leave without anyone seeing me when hands started to grab at my legs. Many hands, of so many kids.

And then Ruby, too. She grabbed my wrist and yanked.

I splashed down into the water, my limbs going in all directions, and the warm water all but obliterated the measly adhesive on the back of that pad. Impossibly, inevitably, it came out and rose to the surface. The beginnings of my period, ruddy and brown, face up in the waterlogged pad, which quickly rose and fell, tumbling in the bubbles from the jets.

Everyone had been laughing at my graceless splash into the pool, but those laughs quickly turned to shouts of shock and disgust.

One boy shouted, "We're swimming in her period!" And another answered, instantly, "It's a literal bloodbath!"

That comment drew laughter from almost everyone, followed by a chorus of "ewwwww" and "gross," and soon everyone was out of the hot tub *except* me.

I started trembling from shock; my heartbeat was so loud in my ears. My eyes were instantly stinging with tears as I started to pull myself out of the water.

And then, because my life is clearly the universe's favorite laugh track, my cramps chose exactly that moment to kick me right in the junk.

I doubled over, holding myself, and gasped. I couldn't make myself breathe, and once I did, I moaned a deep sob.

At that, everyone got quiet. No laughs, no pointing, just nothing. Pale, red wetness found its way down a drip's path, making soft pink swirls in the water.

I looked up, and each party guest was making a different facial expression: disgust, pity, secondhand embarrassment. Every single person was looking at me . . . except Ruby.

She stood there, silently, staring at the ground. She refused to raise her head, to look at me with scorn or comfort or anything. She wouldn't look at me at all.

And then I did what any thirteen-year-old would do when faced with a public shaming: I turned and ran out of her yard and out the side gate. It slammed behind me, and I stood there with my back against the rough wood, panting and listening.

My skin prickled and my guts raged, but I kept waiting for Ruby to appear behind me to check on me or ask me to come back.

She just . . . didn't.

The music turned on, squeals of laughter rang out, and then the dull boing of the diving board came again and again with loud splashes as the kids all jumped in to the (un-period-contaminated) deep end of the pool.

Ruby wasn't coming to check on me because Ruby didn't care.

And she didn't care the next day, or the next day, or the next.

Our friendship didn't go out with fire and fighting.

It evaporated in a moment made of water and silence.

Keisha and Priya had twin mouths gaping open.

Priya finally said, "Dude, middle school was so horrible. Couldn't pay me a million dollars to go back to that."

"Hard same." Keisha took a chomp of her dry, chewy pizza crust. "I bet you figured out tampons real quick after that one, huh?"

Funny, but I couldn't bring myself to laugh. "I sure did. The next day, actually."

Priya grinned, "Seriously? What about your micro vagina?"

"Ha-ha," I droned. "Turns out stress creates tension in the body."

"Who knew?" Keisha said. "So you just . . . literally never spoke to her again?"

"Yeah." I shook my head a little. "I didn't talk and she didn't talk and then it was just gone."

"That's rough," Keisha said. "And tomorrow you're just supposed to see her? After all this time? That's going to be so awkward."

"Key!" Priya scolded. "Don't make it worse."

"What? I'm just saying!"

I laughed. "It's funny 'cause it's true."

"I think you're gonna talk it out," Priya said, twisting a strand of her hair around her finger. "You're smart, Ruby was obviously dealing with her own stuff, and I'm sure she's realized by now how trivial it all was."

I shrugged. "I mean, maybe? But even if she realized she was being a bad friend, it doesn't mean she believes me about any of the rest of it. She made it crystal clear that she thought I was full of crap."

CHAPTER ELEVEN

QUEEN OF FIRST IMPRESSIONS

My eyes felt all scratchy because I'd stayed up so late looking at the profiles of all the people I used to know—the people I used to call friends—who would now be smack-dab in the middle of my dance space.

I spent most of my time snooping on Ruby.

We hadn't blocked each other. It was this undiscussed window that I guess neither of us wanted to fully close. I used to look at Ruby's profile fairly often, but as months became years, and as I got more and more distracted by my life and school, the time between creepings increased.

Of course, she posted less too—we all did. The photo dumps slowed down as we all got older.

I fully expected Mom to insist on driving me to school for my first day, but I was still on my seventeenth possible outfit by the time Mom absolutely needed to leave to get to work on time, so I told her to go on without me. Regan was making her second solo drive all the way to Dallas, and so she had taken off early too.

I would have to walk.

I locked the front door behind me and hoisted my backpack higher on my shoulders. I looked down to make sure my skirt was straight and my black tights didn't have a snag. In late April, Texas is plenty hot—my upper lip started to sweat before I got to the edge of our block—but I was still on my period, and you'd better believe I had double protection, plus totally opaque tights, for this important day. No more underwear flashing for this girl. When I got dressed this morning, I realized I hadn't dressed how I wanted for school in, like, four years. The freedom was hard to handle. I tried on nearly everything in my closet before essentially deciding to cosplay as my sister. A miniskirt and a concert tee from Paramore's first stadium tour (a gem from Mom's band T-shirt collection—a glorious treasure trove which she had bestowed upon us as her most precious family heirlooms). My Docs clip-clopped on the concrete, and I settled in to their rhythm and tried to keep calm as the tension in my belly got worse and worse. I'd been fine all morning. Absolutely fine. But here I was, just around the corner from the school, and the sweat in my body suddenly felt cold. There was a drainage ditch on the side of the street, past the sidewalk, and I made a beeline over to it, arriving just in time.

I bent over, one hand holding most of my hair behind my

head while the other instinctively wrapped around my waist. The quiet of the street on this spring morning was violated by the sound of my retching again and again.

"Whoa, whoa!" A guy's voice sounded worried beside me, but I couldn't make myself stand up. I could only see his shoes, and then a moment later his backpack on the ground.

At any other time, I would have freaked out at having a strange dude that close to me, but my mind was on the pain in my body, and it was a reasonable guess that the backpack and shoes belonged to another person from school, so I couldn't bring myself to care.

Just as I thought it was over, another round came roiling through me, and I heaved again into the grass.

"Here, oh god. Are you okay? What should I do?" The voice was calm even though the words were panicked. Then I felt hands reach up, gently sweep the rest of my hair back away from my face, and hold it out of the way.

A classmate was holding my hair while I puked in the street on my first day.

Awesome.

The cramps vanished, instantly, and I lifted my torso halfway up. Tears and snot streaked my face, and I didn't even want to think about my mouth. I was just going to have to die bent over. There was no way for me to stand up and look at this guy. A plaid flannel shirt appeared under my view, between my head and the ground. He held it out and said, "Here. Use this. Are you okay? Damn."

"Thanks," I said, using my own hands to reach for my hair

and giving him the chance to let go. "But I really don't think you want me to use your shirt for this."

He chuckled a warm sort of laugh and said, "There's this thing called a washing machine. Get this: it takes dirty stuff . . . and washes it."

I gave a sad laugh, still hunched over, looking at the ground, and then reluctantly took his shirt.

I used it to wipe my face, still unsure if I'd ever actually have the guts to walk upright again. The shirt smelled fresh, in a good way that made me sure he was one of those teenagers who understood the power of deodorant and baths.

Impressive.

Slowly, I brought myself up, and said, "Thanks. That's really cool of you. I'll wash it and—" And then I saw him.

Of course.

He had beautiful deep brown skin and a soft pile of bleached blond curls on top of his head. His eyes were dark and warm, and his smile (because of course he was smiling) was absolutely electric. He looked old enough to be an upperclassman, and he was wearing a gray hoodie with bold flowers up one side. It looked like it was hand-painted.

"I'm Caleb. You okay?" he asked. "That did not look fun."

"Oh, yeah, sure. I'm fine. Please don't be late to school on my account."

"Doesn't seem fine to me . . . maybe you need to turn around and go back home. I mean, nobody wants your stomach bug over there, I assure you." He gestured over his shoulder to Blythe High around the corner.

"It's not a stomach bug."

He smiled again. "You sound pretty confident. So, why are you sick on the side of the road, then? You've got me curious."

He reached in his pocket and pulled out a container of gum, snapped open the lid, and offered it with a nod.

I let the moment cover my silence and stepped a little closer. I held out my open palm, and he reached toward it, slowly, gently, cupping it with his own. His skin was soft and warm, and it almost felt like he gently traced one finger on the back of my hand as he shook a couple of pieces out for me.

"So?" he asked again, smirking this time, as if he was already halfway to laughing about my response.

One thing I knew: I did not want to be Period Girl. My years at Stockwood had served me just fine. My period was private, and I was certainly not telling random other kids about my business. No way. Ruby was going to be in there somewhere, and other kids who knew more about my period than they should, but I wasn't doing it again. I wouldn't be called a drama queen again. I panicked, desperate to come up with any reason people threw up in the morning that wasn't related periods or pregnancy. I started chewing the gum, letting the gesture infuse a little confidence into my tone, and said, "I guess I must be hungover."

What? Delia, you are completely freaking bonkers.

He let out another longer laugh that time. "Hungover, huh? On a Friday morning? You're a special kind of mess, aren't you? Should I be worried? I mean, more than I already am, of course."

I could tell he didn't believe me, but he didn't ask again.

"Why are you so curious about me? Don't you have any more interesting things to think about this morning?"

"More interesting than the new girl barfing into a ditch?" he said, letting one corner of his mouth curl up just a little.

He was flirting. I was almost definitely sure.

"Who said I was new?" I asked, hoping he'd think I was flirting back.

"I've been at BHS for four years, and I've never seen you."

"Yeah, I'm new. Ish. Well, mostly."

"I guess all your answers to my questions are gonna be messy, right?"

With the exception of my body being a hot mess, I was clearly a very put-together girl. Great grades, great friends, hardworking. My room didn't smell like Cheetos like Regan's did. I smiled. "No, actually, I'm usually pretty poised. I'm not usually throwing up in the street."

"I just got lucky, I guess?" he said.

I turned, picked up my bag, and then, with every hope of looking cool and aloof, I took a few steps backward and said, "Thanks again for the shirt, Caleb. I'll get it back to you. I promise."

Another step, and I turned again, away from him.

He called over, "Wait! What's your name?"

I didn't turn around, but I kept walking, and just as I was about to answer him, the toe of my boot caught on a slightly raised patch of concrete, and I tripped.

I stumbled forward, catching myself with my other leg

and taking a couple of quick steps to stop myself from hitting the ground.

Just kill me. Honestly.

Caleb was by my side again within seconds.

"You're sure you're supposed to be out of bed today? 'Cause if I had one more of those, you'd catch me getting back under the covers."

I smiled, but I didn't feel fun or flirty anymore. I felt awkward. Uncool and ridiculous and awkward.

Over our heads, the sound of the zero-hour school bell rang out. Obviously, I'd read the entire BHS student handbook from cover to cover before falling asleep, so I knew that bell was indicating we were about twenty minutes from the start of first period. We were still a street away, but the tone carried up on the wind and through the young leaves on all the trees.

"Shit. I am meeting a friend to study for finals. I've gotta run. But I'll see you around, Trip!"

CHAPTER TWELVE

MY REPUTATION PRECEDES ME

The buildings are old, but in good shape. The brick is deep red, and there are large gray stripes of some other kind of rock running all around the top and bottom of the first and second floors. Unlike Stockwood, BHS is actually old. It's what most would consider a historic building—it would be perfectly suited for any number of movies set in the forties or fifties.

I made my way past a bunch of other students, up the front steps, and through the double doors.

As I walked, I rested my hand on my lower belly, right over the sorest part, and rubbed it just a little. It didn't help, but it still made me feel a little better. I took a breath and started checking the markers on the wall until I found my locker. It was way at the end of a row that was new and shiny and had been added to the right of a long section of ancient, rusty dented ones.

I tried my combo about four times before I realized something was wrong with the lock.

I glanced at the clock and realized the late bell was going to ring in less than five minutes. I started speed walking to the office again to find help.

When I got there, the room was full of buzzing students, teachers grabbing mail from their boxes, and a thousand different conversations. Everyone was moving, but something even faster and more frantic raced through the side of my vision.

"Get your tails outta my way!" I heard the voice chirp. The mostly orange blur shoved through two more people and to the last door on the corner of the hall, nearest the nurse's office—a single-seat bathroom with a locking door. I heard it click closed and the latch turn.

"When you gotta go, you gotta go, huh?" I said quietly to myself, or at least to no one in particular.

The late bell chimed while I was still second in line for the chance to talk to the woman at the front desk. I'd be late for my first class for sure. Perfect. When it was my turn, she helped me quickly (I'd transposed a 12 for a 21 in my locker combo), and I set out to drop off my stuff and get to my first class.

I got to the big double glass doors of the office and put my hands on the cross bar at just the same time as the blur from before. When I looked up, I couldn't help but chuckle, because it felt so obvious—it was, of course, Ruby.

"Well, holy hellfire," Ruby whispered. She looked like a perfect fifty-fifty split of exactly-how-she-used-to and totally-and-completely-brand-new. She still had orange-red hair, but now it was chopped bluntly into a shoulder-length bob. Her eyes were still brown, as were the uncountable number of freckles from her chin to her cheeks. She still had a broad smile, but her braces were gone, leaving impeccably straight teeth.

I was stunned to the point of being unable to speak.

She was mirroring my look of disbelief.

Her—the girl who had embarrassed me, accused me, and discarded me.

Me—the girl who had declined too many invitations and left without turning back.

We both opened our mouths twice to say something, but neither of us could think of a single reasonable thing to say.

Then, suddenly, Ruby's eyes got big, she turned, and she *ran* back toward the bathroom by the nurse's office.

Part of me wanted to wait for her to reemerge, but I was already late, and I didn't have any reason to expect that I'd figure out what to say to her that would be anything other than salt in the same old wounds I had worked so hard to heal from.

So, as fast as she'd run to the back, I ran out the front and made my way to my English class. I entered the class-room without drawing much attention to myself because the end-of-the-year vibes were in full effect. Students were talking to the teacher at his desk, and the volume of chatter in the seats totally drowned out the clunk of the heavy door shutting behind me. I flashed the teacher my new-student schedule and he gestured to an open seat and mouthed that he'd introduce himself in a few minutes. In my chair, I pulled a new spiral out of my bag, uncapped a pen, adopted my standard perfect-student posture, and only then took a second to look around. There were some vaguely familiar faces, a couple of waves, a few double takes as people tried to remember why I looked familiar, and then the class just resumed as usual. Most of the faces in the room were only barely recognizable.

Under my desk, I rubbed my belly again. It was aching dully, and I would have to take more ibuprofen soon. It barely worked. But barely was better than nothing.

This record-breakingly bad first day continued when the teacher called the class to attention and set into his instructions for their work. He said the class was continuing a group project and they would be doing independent work with their groupmates for these last couple of weeks. I wouldn't be able to sit and disappear into a lecture. I'd have to be in the middle of an already established team. Perfect. After everyone else got up and moved to their spots, the teacher came over and said hello. After a quick explanation of the assignment, he gestured me toward one of the clusters of kids that had gathered in a clump on the floor in the hall.

I lowered myself onto the cold tile and took note of the faces in the circle. None of them seemed all that familiar except . . .

"Wait, are you Nate?" I asked the boy on my right.

The boy smiled at me and his eyes got wide. "Oh my god, Delia! No way! It's actually Iggy now."

I smiled back at him. "Wait, how did you get from Nate to Iggy?"

"Ignatius," he said. "Remember?"

Some dusty corner of my brain had that little grain of sand in storage, and I nodded. "Sure, Ignatius, yeah. Nate. Iggy. Cool." Iggy's family was from Mexico City, but he'd been here since fifth grade. He'd been Ruby's eighth-grade crush. Iggy had rosy brown skin, shiny black hair that he'd clipped very short, and eyes that were almost black. His nose was slim, and that matched his whole body. He'd always been skinny, but these days he was skinny and tall. I could tell—even sitting down—that he was at least a foot taller than me now.

"What are you doing here?" he asked. "I thought you moved to Australia."

"Australia?" I chuckled and screwed up my face in a twist of confusion. "I did not move to Australia. Where did you hear that?"

"I dunno. It's just what I heard." Iggy was texting in between sentences, glancing up and down from his phone.

"Heard?" I smiled. "Heard from who? That's so weird."

"Well, it would have been Ruby, I guess."

My heart pounded a little when he said her name.

He continued, "When you weren't here . . . when we started school freshman year, Ruby said you'd moved to Australia. Before that, basically everyone assumed you'd just gone into hiding or whatever after Ruby's birthday party." My eyes popped open and I almost choked on my gum. "Oh. Sorry, dude. I shouldn't have brought that up."

My mouth was so dry, my gum stuck to my teeth when I started chewing again.

A girl in the group chimed in. "Oh, I feel like I vaguely remember something about a girl who kinda made a whole big thing about starting her period in the pool. That was you?"

"I—no—I didn't make a—"

"Shut up, Sarah. Nobody needs a recap." Iggy's phone pinged again, and he sent another text back.

Sarah gave me a *yikes* sort of face. I was embarrassed but also completely overwhelmed. Way too overwhelmed to actually try to respond to her impression that I'd made anything up that day years in our past. The other kids were only mildly interested or altogether not listening. Nobody except Iggy was from our original friend group, so I guess they didn't care very much. It was a relief, anyway, that the mention of it (including Sarah's jab at me) hadn't pulled their attention very hard.

I changed the subject to the only topic that I could pull into my head. "Are you and Ruby . . . uhhh . . ." I made a vague sort of hand gesture that waved from side to side.

The girl, Sarah, fake coughed and said under her breath, "Not today. But ask again tomorrow."

Iggy laughed, smiled, and gave her the finger. Then he said, "Nah. No, me and Ruby are just friends."

I raised one eyebrow and glanced back to the girl, who was clearly dying to gossip.

"What! Sarah! You know we're friends." He looked around the group with a sly smile on his face and added, "Sometimes we're just really, really *good* friends." He smirked at her, raised his eyebrows a few times, and then turned back to face me before reaching over and pulling my schedule out of the top of my notebook, running his eyes over the words. "You only have this one class with me, and none with Ruby. Anyway, she really is dying to see you."

"How do you . . ."

He held up his phone and waggled it in his hand. "She told me."

He'd texted her as soon as he saw me.

I let the rest of the group carry on with the project and spent the rest of the day chatting with old acquaintances in the hallways. I ate a salad in the courtyard on my own and wasn't mad about it. And nobody else even mentioned the Bloodbath. In fact, most people seemed not to remember me at all.

That would work. I would take it.

That afternoon, home after a wild first day, I was putting my key in the front-door lock when Ruby's greeting made me jump out of my skin.

"Hey," she said from the porch swing.

"Oh my god!" I squealed. "Oh man, Ruby! You scared me. What are you doing here?"

Without talking, she got up and moved to just a few steps from me, and I couldn't help but soften my posture. She had been my safest place, my closest confidant. My first soulmate and my first heartbreak.

Running through the memories made my body tense up again. I had every reason and every right to be angry at Ruby for what she'd done.

I was just about to raise my finger up to her face when . . . she pounced.

CHAPTER THIRTEEN

JUST LIKE THE GOOD OLD DAYS, EXCEPT WAY WORSE

I gasped, but didn't know why, and then my brain processed that she was hugging me. Tight. The muscles in my back loosened their squeeze.

And then I was hugging her, too.

Her hair still smelled like strawberry shampoo. But something had changed. Her features were softer. Rounder. The shape of her had filled in all the empty angles.

"I'm sorry. I'm sorry. I'm sorry." She just repeated it over and over and over into my shoulder. She was crying. I noticed it once I felt her shoulders start to shake.

I felt the words *it's okay* get stuck on my tongue. Part of me wanted to say them to help her feel better, but it wasn't okay, not really, and I didn't want to say that it was.

I loosened my grip from around her and tried to scrunch

my brow back into a frown. I used all my mental strength to prop my emotional walls back into their usual positions.

As if she could sense my defenses, she started talking again, in her soft, steady drawl, and this time she didn't stop.

"Deels, you have no idea how sorry I am. I don't want to just blame all the times I was a jerk on the fact that I hadn't started my period and didn't know what you were dealing with, but I really didn't understand. And I was awful about it—my empathy was just plain underbaked and I was being a selfish shit-ass. But then I got my first period, and the next year I started pooping *a lot,* and I really, really found out what it felt like to be hot-glued to a toilet seat, and it was embarrassing in new and horrible ways every day. And I know I should have reached out or called or something, but I was ashamed, I think, and I mean, I couldn't see how it would matter if I apologized or how it would even be useful to you with your new friends and your new life. You would still be gone either way."

My head was spinning a little. I was out of practice on Ruby's speed of speech and her drippy long vowels.

"Okay, hold on. Hold on." I paused for a second and Ruby basically panted waiting for me to speak. "You started *pooping*? What in the world are you talking about?"

Ruby's eyes got wider and she grabbed my shoulders while she said, "Oh girl, I started *really, really* pooping. Whew." She made a funny little wave with her arm. "Do you know what IBS is? Irritable bowel syndrome?"

I chuckled a little. "Well, I mean, I've heard of it, I guess. But I don't know much about it."

She rolled her eyes back and whistled a long, swirling note. "It's a damn doozy is what it is. Sometimes it feels like a meaningless umbrella term since it's not exactly diagnosable, but that's all I've got. My gastrointestinal system is absolutely hosed. Top to bottom. I mean, just take me out to pasture. Some days it's unbelievable how much of my time is spent pooping . . . or trying to poop . . . or trying to stop pooping."

My little smirk faded with sadness.

"Let me put it into terms you can understand. Imagine if every single poop of your life was a period poop."

A look of horror hit my face like a brick. "Oh dear god." Tummy troubles were a super-common symptom of my period. If anyone was going to understand living through bathroom nightmares, it was me.

"*Exactly.*" She laughed but turned sad again in an instant. "Deels, I'm really, really sorry I didn't follow you." Her focus softened, looking past my shoulder. "I can still remember the sound of that splash, me pulling you into that pool, and how—"

"Stop. Please."

Ruby quit talking abruptly and held up her palms in acceptance.

"Subject change," she said. "What are you doing here? Why are you back at school?"

"Well, *that* is a really unbelievable story, actually . . ." I waved my hand casually. "It involves my period, marijuana, and referring to my future med-school mentor as a stripper in front of most of my school and its administration."

She nodded her head, impressed, letting her lips draw

down to a deep frown before saying, "Not bad, Bridges. Way to keep it simple."

"You know me . . . I'm stacking up scenes for my eventual memoir of public humiliation."

She gave a small, sad laugh. I'd gotten just close enough to the story of our demise to bring it back to the foreground. "I am truly sorry, Deels. I've spent a whole lot of time thinking, especially when I'm alone, sitting on the toilet, especially if I forget to bring my phone in there? I mean, I might as well be in a black hole if I get going and don't have anything to pass the time. But anyway, I sit there a lot, thinking about all kinds of things. I know now just how bad *bad* can be, and I'll probably never forgive myself for not believing you."

The sounds of little birds chirping filled the space where her talking had suddenly stopped. We let the quiet stand alone for a beat or two.

I took a deep breath. "Thank you. And honestly, I'm sorry too. I'm sorry I wasn't there for you so many of the times that you wanted or needed me to be. Maybe there were times that the fear kept me home more than the pain."

Ruby looked over my shoulder at the front door of my house. I asked her, "Do you . . . um, want to come in?"

She stepped up and passed me, pushed open the door, and walked into my house, moving surprisingly fast. She spoke to me over her shoulder as she went: "Well, it's that or crap my pants, so, I'm gonna say yes."

She disappeared down the front hall to the bathroom she'd used plenty of times before. I heard her shout back to me in the living room, "I'll be back in either four or forty-five minutes!"

CHAPTER FOURTEEN

HONORARY WEIRDO

"I'm just saying, who *does* that?" I said, spinning the pricing gun on my finger like a cowboy spins a pistol. "What kind of doctor hums the national anthem while he's elbow deep in your vagina?"

Ruby tried with mild enthusiasm to defend the indefensible. "What was he supposed to do? The man had a song in his heart!"

"And his hand in her vagina!" Regan said, sending Ruby and me rolling with laughter all over again. Then she started humming and slowly covering her heart with her right hand while her left flailed wildly, conducting in the air in front of her. She abruptly paused. "You have to start recording these appointments."

"Oh, come on," I said.

"I'm serious! Nobody would believe you if they heard some

of the things these doctors have said to you. Turn on your phone; record the conversation. Just imagine the experience of telling this story with an actual soundtrack!" She pulled out her phone and started frantically typing something while resuming her patriotic serenade.

Ruby had settled into an absolutely unhinged goose honk of a laugh while Regan put on her little display. By the time Ruby was finished in the bathroom (it had taken her an hour), Regan had arrived home from Stockwood to change clothes before heading to Mom's store, Gunderson's, to earn a few hours' pay. I'd wanted to join her and had convinced Ruby to ride along with us, sure that Mom would be excited to see her after such a long time. On the drive, Ruby had filled Regan in on her bathroom woes, and I'd filled in a few more gaps in my story about my exodus from Stockwood (still leaving the tincture maker's identity a secret). In the stockroom at the store, it was just like old times. The three of us had spent hours here during younger years when we'd wanted a little cash (which Mom paid us, though we definitely hadn't earned it) and had been bored enough to find a grocery store entertaining.

I tried not to laugh at Regan's patriotic refrain. "I *know* it sounds funny, but you weren't there!"

Regan interrupted herself. "You had better just count yourself lucky that he was humming the national anthem instead of 'Deep in the Heart of Texas,' or you would have been in a world of hurt!" She started humming our state's unofficial song, and Ruby executed the iconic *clap-clap-clap-clap!*

"You Bridges girls are not normal. Not a one of you," Ruby said.

What could I say? Ruby was right. My evenings were often spent discussing my reproductive system with my smart-mouthed sister while sitting on huge crates of canned goods in the stockroom of Gunderson's Grocers waiting for Mom to finish one of her clandestine tarot card readings in her office.

Not normal.

"Aha! Right here. Got it." Regan shouted, jumping down off the large stack of boxes and running over to show me her phone. "Texas is a 'one-party consent' state—most states are, actually—so if one party of a conversation, in person or on the phone, wants to secretly record the conversation, they can! It's your appointment, so you can record it."

I rolled my eyes at her and shoved her playfully away.

"Hey, girls." Phil, the night manager, walked through the big swinging doors and found the cart he'd piled high with dog food. Mom had been busy all evening and hadn't seen Ruby yet. She'd had two phone meetings, three interviews for new checkers, and now a client for her secret fortune-telling side hustle.

The big lights with their wire covers swung back and forth when Mom opened the door lettered LENNART GUNDERSON in flaking gold.

"Remember," Mom said in her most mystical voice, hugging her client close, "every new beginning comes from some other beginning's end. Think about it, okay?"

The lady just nodded and looked at my mom with large,

wet green eyes. She sniffled and wiped her runny nose with the sleeve of her shirt. "Thanks, again, Miranda. See you soon."

"Yes, you will." Mom winked at her and waved with one hand while holding open the big metal side door of the stockroom. Once she was gone, Mom let the door slam against the budding summer's dim light.

I looked over at Regan, still standing between the crates. She glanced up at me, grinning; then we rolled our eyes in unison. Don't get me wrong. I like tarot. I have crystals and wish I were a thousand percent more mystical. But tarot-card readings were mom's fourth DIY backroom business in the past few years. First came leggings, then homemade bracelets made of found objects, and then "intentional consulting," which Mom could never effectively define.

"Now, am I imaging things, or did you just pass off the lyrics to that song about closing the bar as advice to that sad lady?" Ruby's voice was iconic, and Mom spun lightning quick with a grin on her face as soon as she heard it.

"Oh my GOD!" Mom screamed, and ran forward. Ruby was already in motion.

While Mom and Ruby were hugging, Mom caught my eye over Ruby's shoulder. She mouthed *Are you okay?* And gestured with one finger between me and Ruby's back. I smiled and nodded.

"Ruby-June! You're all grown up!"

"It's true!" Ruby turned on a haughty tone. "And I even finally got my period."

She let her eyebrows go way high to look extra impressive.

Mom chuckled and reached up to hold Ruby's face in her hands, tucking the loose hairs back behind her ears. "Amazing. And how's Granny?"

Ruby's face fell a little. "She passed a couple of years ago. But she died happy. And I guess we should all be so lucky."

"Can't argue with that," Mom said, giving Ruby an extra squeeze. "Do you know where you're going in the fall?"

"Well, I got accepted to Tech, A&M, and UT, but right now I'm just trying to convince myself that I have any chance in hell of getting my diploma in time to go anywhere."

"What?" I asked. "Why wouldn't you get a diploma?"

Ruby grabbed herself around the middle. "Apparently, you can poop yourself right out of graduating if you try hard enough."

"Are you kidding?" Regan asked slack-jawed.

"I am not. I am allowed ten absences this semester, just like every other kid in Texas—no matter what reason I'm missing a class."

"That doesn't make any sense. What about exceptions?" Regan was already protectively pissed at the idea.

"It's complicated. You can sometimes get a medical exception, but only if you're at school for part of the day, and it adds up class by class. So you could miss one class too many times and lose credit for it, even if other classes are fully attended. But it all boils down to this: Ten days is it. And I'm on absence number ten, so if I miss one more day . . . well, eleven strikes, you're out."

"I know I've missed more than that," I said, confused.

Ruby shrugged, confused, but then Mom spoke. "Yeah, about that," she said. "I had a call from the attendance office after we registered. They have to go through your records to decide how many absences they're going to officially decide you have on the record. It will take them a little time. But whatever they decide, you're gonna be right on the edge, I can tell you that right now. Your Stockwood records show thirteen absences, as far as I can tell." She made an awkward sort of grimace.

My eyes got wide. "What happens if I have more than ten?"

Ruby held up her hands, clueless. "I don't know what you're doing, but I'm going down swinging. I'm giving the principal, Mr. Davis, a piece of my mind every chance I get. And I'm writing letters to the State Board of Education and going to open forums of the school district's board meetings. The state allows schools to give us credit for missed classes via alternate hours—you know, like summer classes, extra work, after-school sessions, Saturday school. But some schools just don't. Blythe offers summer school, which is fine enough before senior year, but once you're in twelfth grade, summer school just means you didn't graduate with your friends. And in the end, it's basically the principal's choice."

"You're telling me that guy gets to decide what methods to accept?" Mom asked.

"True blue. Which is totally unfair if your body is a weirdo like mine, and I guess yours, too." Ruby gestured to me. "And so unfair. Students who have periods are way, way more likely to miss school for all kinds of reasons. My whole IBS situation didn't even start until I got my period."

Regan's mouth fell open. "No shit?"

"Yes, shit," Ruby said, "My period finally came, and brought with it a mighty vengeance. Serves me right for being so rotten to you about yours." Ruby looked at me sadly.

"I wouldn't wish this on anyone," I said.

"I know—me either," she said. "But it's what I've been dealt, and it means that a couple days out of each month, I may be too busy trying to keep my drawers clean to be in class. That's just how it is. But no matter how good my grades are or how willing I am to make up the work, ten days is ten days."

"There are just a few weeks left. Surely you and I can team up to drag each other to school no matter what, right? We have to get across that stage."

Ruby nodded in agreement and held out her hand to shake. "Deal."

"So, I'm starving," Mom said. "We've got to go get pancakes."

"No pancakes." I said. "Ruby and I are meeting Keisha and Priya tonight."

"You are?" Mom asked.

"We are?" Ruby echoed.

"Yeah, we are. I need my old best friend to meet my new best friends."

Regan pretended to gag herself with her pointer finger.

"I would, of course, Deels, but I can't tonight. A friend's

having a party. I said I'd go." Ruby grimaced as if this were somehow bad news.

"A party . . . with a friend? That friend wouldn't happen to be the Iggy formerly known as Nate, would it?"

She laughed, "No, it's not Iggy's party. But I know it'd be cool for you to come. Actually, yes! And you should invite Priya and Keisha, too. Why not? Nobody will care. It will be fun. I don't want to go to any more parties without you. There have been too many already."

She reached over and took my hand, and I gave hers a squeeze.

Aside from the dull ache running up and down my legs, the desperate need to change my tampon, and the sounds of my sister restarting her full-volume rendition of our nation's anthem, which had so recently been soloed into my vagina like a weird, highly ineffective megaphone, everything felt perfect.

CHAPTER FIFTEEN

PARTY WITH PINOCCHIO

My belly was so swollen I couldn't wear the outfit I really wanted. My ever-infuriating period bloat is like a cherry on the sundae of misery. Some days, for no known reason, my belly just randomly swells up so big that I literally look six months pregnant. There's no baby in there, but there is enough gas to set off a car's security system if I let loose too close to where it's parked.

Eventually, I found something to wear that I liked well enough, and right on time, Keisha and Priya plus Ruby and I convened in my front yard to walk to the party.

The meeting of Pri, Key, and Ruby was tense for barely a moment or two. As Pri and Key had only just heard the full friendship horror story for the first time, they were still a bit leery of Ruby, and they wanted to be very sure that I *wanted* them to like her before they let their guard down. But after an extra nod behind Ruby and a couple of targeted facial expressions, the girls believed it, and the four of us were friends, just like that.

"This is going to be the first house party of my public high school career," I said playfully.

Keisha laughed.

"Better get your britches on, 'cause it's gonna be a rager," Ruby said.

We walked a few streets over to where the houses were about twenty years newer than the ones on my block.

I was first up the walkway, so I knocked. Nobody came, but we heard the sounds of laughter inside, so Ruby just opened the door. We stepped inside.

"Oh yes," Keisha said, taking in the whole scene and giggling in my ear. "This is the wild public-school house party you were expecting."

The room was warm and bright, lamps in each corner, but the middle of the living room was crowded by two card tables end to end. There was a couch along the wall, under a big art print—something modern and very thrown-paint-looking. The kids at the card tables were leaning over a large game board and shielding cards from their competitors. There were a few kids not playing, sitting on the couch talking, and I could hear music in the background, but it was soft enough to talk over.

All at once, someone in the game made a play that caused everyone at the table to let out either an "Awwww!" of disappointment or a "Whoooop!" of victory.

"Hey, oh my gosh!" Caleb, the boy who'd held my hair back while I vomited—one of my finest moments—stood up from his spot on the sofa. His head appeared behind the people at the tables and he inched his way over to greet us.

"Oh hey," I said raising my hand to sweep my hair out from behind my ear. On its way up, I smacked it *hard* on the wall beside me. "Ow! Dangit!"

"Oh, shit," he said, reaching for my hand—but I pulled mine away before he could touch it. "Is this one of your classically poised moments, Trip?" His expression was soft and sweet.

My mouth opened with a huge, playfully defensive smile.

Ruby looked back and forth between us. "Trip? Who's that? Do you two know each other?" she asked. As she spoke, she stepped close to him, and they gave each other a big hug.

I said, "No," and he said, "Yes," simultaneously.

"He doesn't even know my name," I said, instantly resisting the urge to burst into flame at the sight of his smile. "We don't know each other."

Caleb shook his head slowly back and forth and then let it shift into a nod. "You're Trip. And yes, we do."

"I like Trip, but just for future reference, I'm Delia," I said, smiling. "Hey."

Caleb's hair was styled in tiny, shiny ringlets in an unfussy pile on his head, and he wore light gray jeans with a deep blue denim shirt, short-sleeved, buttoned all the way up to the top.

Beside me, Keisha pinched my arm. I winced so I wouldn't jerk my whole arm away.

"I'm glad you came," he said, stepping to me and bringing

his face close, close, close so fast I didn't have time to breathe or move or think. One hand held his drink, a ghastly reddish purple mixture of whatever. He wrapped his other arm around and hugged me, giving a little squeeze when our chests touched.

"Yeah," I said. The only word that came to mind. *Nailed it.* "Oh, I washed your shirt."

"Already?" he asked with a disappointed look on his face.

"I threw it in the wash as soon as I got home, obviously. I mean, it was disgusting." I gave a weak chuckle as I realized we were again discussing my vomiting in the street. "Well, anyway, I folded it up and put it in my purse so I'd have it the next time I ran into you, which happens to be right now." *Awwwkward.* I rummaged around in my bag for a moment and pulled out the shirt with its plaid lines of red, black, green, and blue. "Here." I held it out, and just as he reached for it, Priya bounded forward from a few steps behind to enthusiastically put her arm around my shoulder. I bumped forward, knocking Caleb's drink into my hand, which still held his shirt. It sloshed all over, soaking the fabric and turning most of it a dark purple color. "Oh no!" Instinctively, I leaned over and used the dry parts of his shirt to wipe up the drops that had landed on the hardwood floors.

"Crap! I'm so sorry!" Priya looked mortified.

"It's okay," Caleb said, after giving his sneakers a quick check. "Really. It's all okay."

"So much for your clean shirt," I said, folding it over so that the wet part was tucked well inside the outer dry layer.

"I'll wash it and get it back to you . . . again." Maybe my grace and poise was just deactivated by his perfectly gorgeous face. This was getting ridiculous.

He smiled. "Take your time." His eyes sparkled. "So, who else has joined you tonight?" he asked, making eyes at Key and Pri.

"Well, you've just collided with one of my best friends, Priya, and this is my other bestie, Keisha."

"Nice to meet you both. I'm Caleb."

"I heard. So y'all get really wild out here in the suburbs, I see," Keisha added playfully as she glanced over at the full-on board-game night unfolding behind us.

"Oh, we're very intense," Caleb confirmed.

Then he turned to walk us over to the rest of the group. Priya flipped her face to me fast and whispered, "He's seriously cute."

I shrugged, smiling. When Ruby appeared at my elbow, I spoke to her quickly in a whisper: "Tell me fast. Are you guys together? Anything I need to know? You're friends?"

"No. No. And Yes. He's great. He's Iggy's best friend."

Just then Ruby and Iggy saw each other. She rolled her eyes and turned away from him. I couldn't help but grin. I could imagine the whole range of their on-and-off love affair.

Caleb brought our little cluster of people to the center of the room. "Hey guys, this is Priya, and Keisha, and have any of you met Delia?"

At the end of the table, Iggy jumped up out of his seat with a huge smile on his face.

"Oh, of course! *You're* the girl he met this morning? Damn, now I owe him five bucks!" Iggy gestured to Caleb.

"What was the bet?" I asked Caleb, who was standing just a little bit in front of me while making introductions.

Iggy answered for him. "Caleb was late to our study session and he blamed it on a cool, pretty, funny girl he met before school, and I bet him five bucks that he was lying and made her up."

I knew I'd started blushing, but I didn't care. "You put money on the line for me?"

"Easy money. Just as I described," Caleb said, and he gave me the quickest wink.

Iggy ran over to continue a whispered fight with Ruby that only lasted a few minutes before their faces were smashed together like two sucker fish on opposite sides of the same glass.

"Did you decide to leave out the part where I was vomiting into a drainage ditch?"

He gave a sly sort of reluctant nod and said, "Yeah, I kinda did. No offense."

"Oh! Truly!" I laughed. "None taken."

"So are you going to tell me why you were sick this morning? I think we both know you weren't hungover." He grinned, but I pretended to be offended.

"I could be hungover. You don't know me."

"I'd like to." His broad smile lit up his face. It was just like that. I felt a simmer of heat under my skin as soon as I saw that grin. "Can I text you?"

Without saying a word, I pulled out my phone and we swapped numbers. I was fairly sure my cheeks looked cherry-stained, but I didn't mind. The flip in my stomach was a welcome change from the discomfort it was used to.

Beside him, a girl I almost recognized stepped closer and said, "Wait? *Eighth-grade* Delia? I remember you! I remember that thing when you got so sick. God, I felt so awful for you. I hope you're doing better now."

She obviously didn't really care too much about my answer: She was nearly instantly pulled back into some other conversation by another friend. Caleb watched her go, gave a confused look, and then turned back to me with an expectant look on his face. "Eighth grade, huh?"

Part of me wanted to tell Caleb the truth . . . tell him that something was wrong with me and my body and it made me sick. I wanted deep in my soul for him to know that it was true, that I was right, and that no matter what he'd heard, I hadn't made up anything.

But other parts of me just kept remembering kids like Sarah, who had the impression that I was the girl who cried wolf about her misery just to garner sympathy and attention.

What was I supposed to do? Tell this boy my truth? Trust he'd stick around when I was bleeding all over the place and passing out on our dates? Without an answer, I couldn't be a girlfriend. I couldn't be that carefree girl who had the luxury of even thinking about falling in love with someone. The back of my mind would always be consumed with the endless barrage of tears, the searing, ripping pain . . . that would always be first priority.

Right on cue, my legs almost gave out under me as lightning strikes of pain shot from my knees, up my thighs, to my back, and down again.

Caleb must have noticed the expression on my face change. He leaned over and put a hand on my back.

"Whoa, you okay, Trip?"

"I'm fine," I said reflexively. "And you're right about this morning . . . probably just ate a bad yogurt."

"Who'd even be able to tell, anyway?" he asked with a chuckle at his own joke.

"Right." I gave a half-hearted grin. "It's basically bad when you buy it."

"Right," he said, looking down at his shoes and then back up at me. "So, you're okay?"

"Definitely. Don't worry about me. It really was just food poisoning. No big deal." I left him then, stepped back over to the group. He didn't seem upset, but he took a few seconds before following me over.

"And remind me, who are these beautiful specimens?" asked Iggy (who had apparently just decided he was angry at Ruby again) as he crossed over to Priya and Keisha with total *I'm the guy* attitude, which was perfectly matched by Keisha's *you're so not the guy* attitude.

"Priya, Keisha, this is Iggy. Iggy, Priya, Keisha." I gestured between them. Priya, sweet as a dove, held out her hand to shake his, and Iggy actually, and unironically, took it, turned it over, and kissed it on the back. Keisha's left eyebrow shot up as her chin tucked down. Then she caught eyes with Ruby, who said loudly to the room, "Any of you backwater ding-a-lings want to make out?"

Iggy's head shot up and he followed Ruby into the kitchen, where the two started full-volume fighting for about five and a half seconds until suddenly she grabbed his hand and dragged him right into the walk-in pantry.

CHAPTER SIXTEEN

THE PROS AND CONS OF COBBLER

The cafeteria of Blythe High is tired. During most of my first full week, it was an entirely uninteresting place. It has three lunch lines that most kids don't use unless they really have to. On Thursdays, however, one line backs all the way up around the outside of the cafeteria.

Cobbler Day.

Kid after kid, most old enough to be mere days from culturally agreed-upon adulthood, in a line, bouncing on their toes, waiting to buy a Blythe High School delicacy. Students are willing to drop a whole week's allowance on buying enough for lunch, dessert, and an after-school snack. It is *good*.

I licked my lips and put my plastic spoon back into my mouth for the billionth time, even though my cobbler was totally gone. It had been, without a doubt, the best apple cobbler I had ever had in my life. I could have eaten it every day from that moment to the end of my days. The first bite, absolutely warm and perfect, with a spoonful of vanilla Blue Bell ice cream out of a tiny paper cup? Absolute perfection. I'd started BHS on a Friday, so this was my first Cobbler Day. It was memorable for three key reasons. That absolutely delicious first bite was memorable moment number one.

"I told you to buy more than one bowl, but you're stubborn as a mule in the mud," Ruby said, pushing her empty dish aside and pulling another one in front of her for a second helping.

"Oh please. You've never been to a farm, and you've never seen a mule," I said, laughing.

"That's not true," Ruby said, defending her honor. "I did go to a farm on a school trip freshman year."

Iggy chimed in. "Oh yeah, I remember that trip! The creamery . . . there was an ice cream shop next to about a million acres of stinky cows. It was both the worst smell and the best snack ever. Well, second-best snack." He leaned over and playfully pretended to gnaw at Ruby's neck. Her big honking laugh filled the whole room.

On the other side of Iggy, Caleb sat, stacking his second empty bowl into the first. Then he stretched up, pretended to yawn, and put his head on the table. Caleb and I had been walking to school together, meeting each morning at the corner of his street and the main one I reached after I turned off my own. We'd talked about little things, medium things, and even a few big things. Music and friendship, pizza and college.

"So, is today the day?" he asked.

"What day is that?" I asked.

"The day you tell me what mysterious little chaos actually brought you here?"

I grinned. His response to that grin was to blast me with his own wide smile. I know my face lit up at the sight of it, because he sat up a little straighter, obviously proud of himself, before leaning over the table, closer to my face, and saying in a conspiratorial whisper, "What in the world happened over at that fancy prep school you speak so highly of?"

I was in a playful mood. "I'm a criminal. I was kicked out because it was that or I was gonna be handed over to the authorities."

He rolled his eyes at me. "Really? You know, I'm not entirely sure I believe you."

"That's your business," I said, picking at the side of my bowl and raising one eyebrow in what I hope looked like a very cool expression. We could play little games or whatever, but I wasn't actually gonna budge, no matter how sneakily he tried to edge his way around that wall.

Behind us, I heard the lunch ladies shouting, "Sold out!" The collective whine of disappointed people in line implied they were out of something far more important than mere dessert.

By the time my attention had returned to Ruby, I noticed she was shifting her weight in her seat. She seemed suddenly extremely uncomfortable.

"You okay, Ruby?" I asked.

"Oh, sure, sure. You can have the rest of this, though." Ruby said, pushing the bowl in front of me.

Sweet. Bonus cobbler. From across the table, Caleb flashed me his blindingest smile. He winked at me and said, "I'll pay you"—he dug into his back pocket and retrieved a few crumpled bills—"thirteen American dollars for the rest of that pie." (Memorable moment number two.)

He knew he was cute. So I decided to be cuter.

I picked up a spoonful and, for half of a moment, pretended like I might be about to put it into his mouth. Then I zoomed it around to my own face and chomped it right in front of him.

"I may be new here, but I'm not an amateur. This is one of the last Cobbler Days of your high school career. I won't settle for less than twenty."

He laughed to himself before Iggy tapped him on the shoulder. "Caleb, let's go," Iggy said, standing up and kissing Ruby on the top of her head. "We've gotta get to the library—this one here is gonna help me figure out the calc notes. Bye, y'all."

My phone pinged with an email from the BHS attendance lady, and just as I was about to open it, Ruby moaned, just a quiet little squeak beside me.

"Hey?" I said, putting my hand on her back and making a reassuring circle. "What's up?"

Ruby rubbed her stomach and laid her head down on the edge of the table for a moment.

"Was it the cobbler?" I asked.

Ruby looked up at me with sad eyes. "I freaking love that stuff. And I never eat it. I haven't had any in so, so long, but I just really wanted to share that moment with you—and school is almost out and then it will be gone from my life forever."

"Well, maybe you'll be absent again and get held back a grade. Then you get more, right?" I hoped that my joke landed right.

Ruby laughed, but only a little.

"I'm sorry you feel sick," I said. "And I know how horrible it feels to want to do what everyone wants to do, but your body won't cooperate."

"It's such good cobbler," Ruby whined. "I just really wanted it."

"I know."

Ruby's eyes glistened a little, and I was flooded with a rush of sadness for her. It wasn't exactly the same, but it wasn't that different. And either way, it was awful.

Then Ruby reached up slowly and took my hand. I sat there beside her, and Ruby just rested her head on my shoulder. The room was full of people, but it felt silent for a moment.

"Ohhhhh," Ruby said again, whimpering into my shoulder and tightening her grip on her stomach.

"What do you need? What can I do?" I asked. Watching her doubled over, tears welling up and slipping down her face, I felt helpless. "Ruby." She just continued to stare at the floor. "Ruby, what can I do? What can I do?"

"Delia! Stop!" She looked up at me. "Nothing, okay? There is nothing *anyone* can do."

My own eyes went blurry as tears obscured my vision. This feeling was strange and surreal and horrible. And I realized that my friends and family felt it, all the time, over and over, for years. Embarrassed by my getting choked up, I hastily rubbed my eyes. Ruby needed me. It was a rare chance for me to be there for someone in the same way everyone was always there for me.

"I'm sure I'll feel bet—" Ruby's eyes got big, and then she scrunched them closed. She stood and reached for her backpack, which was slumped beside her on the bench. I stood too and grabbed it for her, gesturing for her to go. I would be right behind her.

Ruby started walking quickly, and I followed. We cut through the cafeteria as fast as our legs could carry us without running, until we got to the main hallway. There aren't any bathrooms in the direction she headed. She'd been going on autopilot to her usual single-stall restroom in the front office that Ruby had special permission to use.

"Are you okay?" I shouted forward to her. She was doing a hunched sort of jog that lost its steam every few steps and turned back into a walk.

"Oh my good gravy, past me must have really loved that cobbler!" Ruby yelled over her shoulder.

"Yeah, I think next week I'll pass on the cobbler . . ."

We got through the halls and into the front office in only a few minutes. I trailed Ruby back toward the nurse's office and she reached for the handle, but it wouldn't move. Locked. We listened together and heard the sound of some other poor kid retching inside. The nurse tottered over, clearly in the middle of this whole situation, and told the kid through the door that their mom was on the way.

Ruby looked over at me, her eyes growing big again, before she doubled over and then stood and then doubled over and then stood.

"There's another bathroom just in the hall. Let's go." I took Ruby's hand and tugged her back out the front office doors, and when I looked back at her, there were tears in her eyes.

We rounded the corner and Ruby yanked on my hand, stopping on a dime. I spun and faced her there along the side of the A Hallway. Ruby looked right at me, still gripping my fingers tightly, a whimper on her lips as she breathed heavily.

And then, memorable moment number three: Ruby looked at me, shook her head, and said, "Delia. I just shit my pants."

CHAPTER SEVENTEEN

SHOPPING CART FOR TWO

Gunderson's isn't a big store. There are only twelve aisles, which shouldn't be enough, but usually is. Mom has worked there since she was a kid, and she just never managed to leave. On the one hand, it makes me happy that Mom hasn't ever been tied to some corporate job she hates, but on the other hand I suppose it was strange growing up in a shopping cart rather than a stroller.

"Ray," I hollered, the bell above the door jingling my arrival.

"Eleven!" she called.

I crossed to the right, second aisle from the end.

Regan was pushing an empty cart past the candy. She had the sticks of two suckers hanging out of her mouth.

"Hi," I said, draping my arms over her shoulders, walking

behind her with my feet on the outsides of hers. We took a few steps before I forcibly turned her around by the shoulders to face me.

"What is it? Did you have a bad day?" Regan asked.

"You have no idea." I hung my head and exhaled loudly before looking her dead in her eyes and sorrowfully saying, "Ruby pooped her pants today."

"Hard-core. Get in," she said, mouth clacking as the candy struck her teeth.

I stepped over and climbed into the basket as I'd done probably thousands of times.

I put my back against the front of the cart, my knees pulled up, so I sat facing my sister. Regan pulled one of the suckers from her mouth and handed it to me.

I was too tired and cranky to be grossed out. Plus, it was watermelon.

"So, is she okay?"

"Can you *be* okay if you poop your pants at school?" I asked.

"Fair enough. Man, that's rough. Did she burst into flames?"

"I would have, but no, she mostly laughed it off somehow. Very Ruby. After a quick shower in the locker room she was already making jokes about needing a new set of emergency pants in her bag."

"See? Like I said: hard-core." Regan cracked the rest of her candy off its stick and said, "So, in non-poop-related news, Mom said it's GSD because she has a chamber of commerce meeting until eight," Regan said, reaching for a bag of chocolate-covered peanuts and turning the corner to head down aisle twelve.

"Okay. Everything I want is on two and four," I told her.

"I'll go back over there," Regan said. "I just need this." Aisle twelve houses all the drinks. She grabbed a soda and unscrewed the top.

GSD—grocery store dinner—has been a staple meal at our house since we got old enough to take care of ourselves after school. After eating, we'd take all our empty packaging and wrappers to the front and scan them so Mom could account for what we took. It worked because Mom felt like she was feeding us, but she didn't have to leave work to do it.

Regan handed me her bottle of orange soda. "Hey, James."

We waved at James, Mom's longest-standing employee. He is probably a hundred and fifteen years old and has blond hair that hasn't even considered going gray. He's Swedish, and Mom feels like there is value in having someone on the staff who appreciates Gunderson's Scandinavian roots.

"So, there's one other big thing about today that has me absolutely freaking out."

"What life-altering crisis has come for you this time?" she asked.

I kicked the inside front wall of the cart, which made a large clang just in front of Regan's stomach. "Well, I got an email from the registrar today about my attendance. Do you remember the thing about required attendance minimums and absences and stuff for graduation?"

"Yeah," she said.

"And how Stockwood didn't give a crap if I was absent, as long as I made up the grades? They can pay the teachers to work Saturday school, zero hour, late-night Thursdays."

"Right," Regan said. "So, how bad is it?"

"Medium bad." I said. "I need applesauce."

"Which kind?" she asked.

"Cinnamon," I answered.

"Jar or cups?"

"Jar."

"This must be serious," she said, taking one from the shelf and handing it over.

I unscrewed the lid and upended the whole thing, gulping it down from the oversized jar.

"You're disgusting," Regan said, grabbing a handful of peanuts.

I glowered at her with an applesauce mustache on my lip.

"Says the girl who eats cold SpaghettiOs out of the can." I stuck my tongue out. "So, anyway, the registrar emailed to say that the attendance records from Stockwood show that I've already missed thirteen days of school this semester, but they did give me credit for a few of them that I made up, so it's as if those didn't happen. But the rest of them are immovable, and the number they've landed on is ten. If I miss one more day, I'm pretty much screwed."

I reached up and took her pinkie finger in mine. She gave it a squeeze before letting go and tossing another peanut in her mouth.

"Medical excuses aren't a thing?"

"Well, that's an interesting question." I said. "It's all just gray enough to be annoying, but basically, if I had a concrete diagnosis, they might be able to excuse more of my non-doctor-authorized absences. But without one, they can't."

"So go get a diagnosis! What, like it's hard?"

I pursed my lips and cocked my head to one side. "It didn't happen this time. Scans were normal."

"Wait, seriously? When did he call you?"

I waved her away, "A nurse left me a voicemail earlier this week. It doesn't matter. Same old result, same old answer. But hey! I could get lucky and Dr. Doodle Dandy could call back to say he was wrong about all my scans being clear. And surprise! My scans show a very clear warning label etched into my organs that clearly defines my condition," I said.

"Yeah. Because you're famous for having such great luck."

"True." I said. "Aisle four please. I'm about to up my odds and eat a whole box of Lucky Charms."

"There is one way your luck seems to be changing. You've been grinning and texting a *lot,* and I think we both know that the gorgeous boy you met has you setting up residence in Swoon Town."

"I do not swoon," I said, grinning. "I'm not a swooner. I'm too distracted by my bodily chaos to swoon."

"BS. You're completely obsessed."

"*I'm* obsessed? Okay, then: How's Graaaaaaaaace?" I asked, stretching out her name in a singsong voice. My sister couldn't help but grin. Her smile made her eyes go squinty. "You're not going to do a full-on promposal are you?"

Regan smiled. I loved how her face was always sweeter when she was talking about her girlfriend, Grace. My sister sometimes projects a steely harshness, but Grace softened her like melted butter.

She tried to play coy. "I'm not a promposal person, and Grace and I have been together for a few weeks, of course she asked me to go with her." She looked right over my head, avoiding my line of sight for about three seconds before bending over and getting all bouncy and loud in my face.

"Okay, but if the damn sign seller could have shipped it in time, I was going to buy a custom neon light that says maybe just *prom*? I was gonna put it in my room, on the wall with the others. And put it right above my head, so when I stand there and flip the switch, she'd see the question light up."

"But instead, your senior girlfriend invited you to senior prom, so between you and me *you're* the one who gets to attend," I said, pouting big-time and leaning to reach a bag of pretzels. She steered the cart close to the shelf so I could grab one.

"You're sure the dean wouldn't let you attend? People bring guests to prom. I don't get the big deal."

"People bring guests . . . not recently expelled students. Whatever. It's fine. I didn't have a date anyway. And I'll still go get ready with the girls. It will be fun."

"What about Blythe? What about Caaaaaaaaleb." She mimicked my same drawn-out voice.

"They already had their prom. So, no go."

"Do something else? Go out with him or something."

"No way," I said. "This is fun, but it's not like a *thing*. We graduate in just a couple weeks. We're not defining our situationship this close to the buzzer. He's just . . . sweet. He's sweet and kind and funny. God, his smile. I swear." I pantomimed a knife to my heart.

We were another aisle over when my phone rang.

"Hello?"

"Hi, this is Shannon at the Center for Pelvic Pain Care. Dr. Dubois is on hold and would like to talk with you if you're available?"

I stood up in the shopping cart with huge eyeballs and a box of the clearly magical leprechaun cereal. I'd never really expected a reply from Dr. Steele anyway; in fact, I'd been trying to put him as far out of my mind as I could. Dr. Dubois was not someone I'd have expected to hear from at all.

"Dr. Dubois? Sure, I'll hold."

Regan did a little jump before helping me get down and out of the cart. We sat down cross-legged in the middle of the aisle and leaned back against the lowest shelf of cereal. I held my phone out and turned on speakerphone.

"Delia? This is Dr. Dubois. I hope I haven't called too late?"

"Not at all." I chuckled for absolutely no reason. "And you?"

Regan looked up at me like I was growing a cactus out of my forehead, gesticulating wildly with her hands.

"And I what?" Dr. Dubois asked.

"Oh, uh, I—sorry. Nothing."

Regan hid her face in her hands to cover her embarrassment by proxy.

The doctor started again. "Well, anyway, I don't need to take up too much of your time. I'll get right to it: I was *mortified* for you when you fell on matching day."

My face was turning red and hot. Regan reached up and covered her now-open mouth.

Dr. Dubois continued. "Listen, I don't know any person with a period who hasn't had it absolutely ruin their day before. And *your* period . . . well, it really, really ruined your day. Maybe I'm a pushover, but I believe that you had to have been acting out of desperation. People with academic records as impressive as yours don't typically make such unfathomably bad decisions unless they are."

"You're right. I was desperate for help, so I was desperate to meet Dr. Steele," I said. "My periods are horrible, and I've reached the point where I would do pretty much anything to get to a diagnosis. Including go to school completely out of my mind to have an audience with an expert."

"Maybe I shouldn't . . . use my own experiences to relate, but . . ." She paused. "I relate to you, and to your story. I do. I am deeply familiar with the medical system being inattentive, ineffective, and ignorant. Our stories are different, but my mission isn't so far away from yours. I knew I had to be a doctor because I wasn't going to let patients, especially patients of color, feel like an accurate diagnosis was unattainable. Which is why I founded my nonprofit, aptly named HEARD: Healing Through Education, Advocacy, Research, and Data." She paused again. "And, more personally, my period ruined my wedding day, so I've been there."

"Your wedding day?" Heartbreak surged in my chest.

"Well, *ruin* is a harsh word. We're married, so all's well that ends well, I guess, but yes. My menstrual cup leaked while we were seated for dinner during the reception, and when I got up for our first dance, thankfully my maid of honor noticed it. I completely bled through my wedding gown."

"Oh my god, I would have just imploded right there."

"I almost did." She laughed and added, "We ran back to the dressing area, and I ended up putting on my matching set from before the wedding. White sweats with the word *BRIDE* across the butt in cheap rhinestones. I pulled it off, and I don't think most people even cared once everyone was dancing. And hey, at least I was comfortable."

"Everybody wants to be in sweats when they start their period. I get it. But, wow, I'm sorry that happened to you."

"Believe it or not, that's the least upsetting part of my story. The real kicker is that shortly after, I was misdiagnosed with fibroids that turned out to be cancer. Aggressive cancer. I am lucky that I had people in my corner who kept my voice loud. Who kept my spirit up when I wanted to quit. Periods aren't for the faint of heart, am I right?"

"You're right. I . . . cancer? Wow. I wonder if I could have . . . Oh man." Early in my attempts to self-diagnose, I was sure I had cancer. Every single online symptom quiz seemed to say it was the inevitable conclusion. Dr. Dimitri told me with certainty that it wasn't the cause, so I put it out of my mind. But that's the thing about cancer: it grows.

As if she was reading my mind, she said, "I didn't mention

my story to freak you out and make you think you have cancer. I told you so you'd know that sometimes there's an answer just around the bend, which is why you can't stop moving forward. So, I read the email you wrote Dr. Steele, and it sounds like you're familiar with the work we do here at CPPC. There are so many different things that cause pelvic pain, and it's hard to get a diagnosis. To get the correct one, anyway. Have you heard of endometriosis?"

I nodded, mostly to Regan and the Quaker oatmeal logo man. "Sure, it's one of about a dozen conditions that come up in my searches the most often. It's where cells like the ones in your uterus are . . . well, not in your uterus, right?"

"Pretty much. Endo has been found all over: bowels, bladders, lungs, brains . . . So—and you understand I am not your doctor, and I am not giving specific medical advice here, just general information—you should speak to your doctor about your symptoms and ask them if they've ruled out that condition specifically. Or ask if you have any symptoms that have removed it from their list of considerations. It is a common but complicated disease. It's very difficult to diagnose because it so often looks like so many other things, but knowing is half the battle and all that."

"Okay, wow. Yes, I'll do that." I said. "Thank you. I really, really appreciate it."

"I'm interested, and I hope you'll keep me updated, if you'd like. I know your mentorship kinda crashed and burned, but maybe I can be a sort of unofficial sounding board for you. HEARD would be a good resource for you, too. There's a bunch of information on our website, and maybe it will help."

"That's amazing, yes, thank you."

"Good luck," she said before disconnecting the call.

I extended my arm behind me and reached for two more boxes of Lucky Charms before telling my sister, "I need milk. It's gonna be a long night."

CHAPTER EIGHTEEN

HALF DRESSED UP AND NOWHERE TO GO

"Hold still!" Priya laughed while she held a tiny pencil against my eyebrow. "You're gonna look really surprised all night if you keep wiggling!"

"Not like it matters—I'm not going anyway. I can just stay here, looking weirdly excited!"

Pri, Key, Ruby, and I were living it up in Keisha's massive bedroom late in the afternoon a week or so later on the day of the Stockwood prom. It had been calm for a while as day by day the worst of my period died down. My special-occasion pain had settled into my regular, everyday pain. When I wasn't actually on my period, there were a few good days, but soon after, the headaches would come back, the swelly belly would hit, and it was always a crapshoot if I'd have pain up and down my legs and across my back that was a dull, persistent reminder that I'm not normal. I'd accepted that prom wasn't happening for me, and I was mostly past feeling sad about it, but through the afternoon there had been a few special moments that really stung: when the girls showed me their flowers, when they pulled up their inspiration photos for their makeup goals, and when Keisha gave us our getting-ready shirts.

Keisha's house is in Uptown, just north of Dallas. Her room is at least three times bigger than mine, so there was plenty of room for all of us to spread out. Ruby was feeling pretty rotten and was resting on Keisha's bed. Pri and Key were deep in the process of pre-prom preparations, and they were having the time of their lives. Their own makeup already looked perfect, so they'd moved on to me. The three of us (not Ruby) wore matching button-up shirts that said PROM SQUAD on the back and had our first names embroidered on the front pockets. They were gifts from Keisha's mom, obviously bought before my grand disgrace. I was getting dolled up for absolutely nothing, but it didn't feel like nothing to me.

Priya was trying to glam up my face while Keisha was carefully laying her edges into gentle curls around her face.

"I'm trying to be still. I swear," I said. "How are you feeling, Ruby-June?"

"Much better, actually," she whimpered from her place on Keisha's bed. She was curled in a ball holding her stomach and trying to stay still.

My phone dinged and I instantly looked down. Priya just about lost it. "Dang it, Delia!"

Caleb and I had been going back and forth for days about everything. I'd been talking about my doctor dreams (without mentioning the specific type of doctor I planned to become), and he'd been telling me all about how he'd been accepted to the state colleges he'd applied to, but Iggy had convinced him to send in a few late-submission art-school applications. He worked with large-scale paintings and murals, mostly, but he also loved comics. The thrill of getting to know him was intoxicating. Every time my phone pinged, my heart leaped into my chest.

"Sorry, sorry." Of course Priya was right. I put my phone on silent and tried to turn my attention back to my girls.

Everything in Keisha's bedroom was almost entirely white—everything from floor to ceiling was soft, creamy, dreamy shades of white. I sat on the stool on the far side of her bedroom, in front of her big window. "Oh, good green grasshoppers," Ruby exclaimed out of nowhere, sitting up straight as a board. "I think I'm gonna be sick."

"FYI, I don't know you well enough to forgive you for barfing on my pillow," Keisha shouted, picking up the trash can by her vanity and hustling over to her king-sized bed.

Ruby's posture relaxed. "No, wait. I'm okay. I'm okay." She exhaled and lay back down, rolling sideways to watch us. Her voice groggy and pained, she said, "You're all looking gorgeous. I'm dying to see those dresses!" I watched her pull herself off the bed and cross over to us.

I got sad again. I hadn't cared *that* much about prom, but I'd cared some. At least a little. The corners of my smile relaxed to drooping.

Keisha stepped closer to me, still sitting on her stool. "I'm so sorry. It's not fair."

The other two joined her, pulled me to standing, and put their arms around me. They held me so tight, and for some reason, in that moment, in that room, I just broke all the way down and let myself cry.

"You're going to ruin my beautiful makeup," Priya said, wiping away a few tears with gentle hands.

"It's not like I'm going to the prom anyway," I said, sniffling as we separated. "Anyway, I need to get this girl home. She's not looking so good."

"Keep up the jokes and I'll toss you in the well," Ruby croaked.

"You've never even seen a well. Get outta here." I reached over and booped her nose. "Okay, almost ready," I said, pulling the Stockwood girls toward their dresses, hung high on a door. "I need to send my girls off to the prom."

A few minutes later, Ruby and I sat in the foyer, waiting for Keisha and Priya to make their grand entrances. Best of all, Regan and Grace were going to swing by while I was here so that I could take their photo on Keisha's pretty stairs. Mom made me swear to get about eleventy-billion pictures, and I was in no position to argue.

There was a knock at the door, and I jumped up. I was absolutely dying to see my sister and Grace.

I opened the door and almost instantly burst into tears. Again.

Regan wore a micro-miniskirt of black sequins and a vintage black Dashboard Confessional T-shirt with a heart

163

in the center that said THROUGH THE HEART OF THE SOUTH. Her blue-streaked hair was pinned back on the sides with tiny sprigs of baby's breath above her ears. Grace wore black trousers and a white shirt with a lace Peter Pan collar. Pinned just beside her thin tie was a small boutonniere of the same baby's breath.

I just about crushed my sister in a hug, wrapping my arms all the way around her neck. I whispered into her hair, "You look so beautiful."

"Jeez, calm down, will you?" she said, smiling but pretending to be annoyed. "You're going to squash my flowers!" She was hugging me back.

I took so many photos of (and with) my friends, all looking absolutely gorgeous. I think I mostly kept my jealousy off my face. They left in Keisha's car, which had been totally covered in prom magnets and chalk paint on the windows. I could barely make out Regan waving through the back window as they left.

CHAPTER NINETEEN

PROMISH

Ruby rolled down the windows of the Woolly Mammoth to keep from being carsick on the last half hour of our ride back to Blythe. While I drove, my phone pinged with notifications from Caleb, which got Ruby all riled up about him and us and our whole thing.

"Nothing is better for an upset stomach than distraction. Tell me. Is he a good kisser?"

I let out a loud guffaw and answered far too quickly, "No. I mean, probably. But I don't know."

"You haven't kissed yet?"

I smirked as I checked the headlights in the rearview mirror.

Ruby waved my grin away and kept rambling. "Kissing: Ten out of ten. Highly recommend. Five stars."

I rolled my eyes and said, "I've kissed *people.* I just haven't kissed Caleb."

"Yet," Ruby interjected. "I bet he's a freaking great kisser. Those lips. That smile . . ."

"I know, right?" I took a big deep breath and tried to focus on the road in front of me.

"Iggy is a real good kisser. But of course I trained him myself, so I take every last drop of that credit."

"When did you and Iggy actually get *together* together?" I asked.

"Which time?" Ruby answered, laughing to herself. "Kidding, of course. We're not actually together together."

I shook my head. "Oh please. You obviously are. I mean, you've been *something* since—what? At least freshman year. Right?" Her silence was her confirmation. "I just don't understand how you ever went from awkward ninth-grade kisses to Iggy being the sort of senior-year boyfriend who can be there for you through all your medical stuff."

She held her hand out the window and let it ride along with the wind. "I don't know, it just happened. I knew him so well—our friendship really blossomed freshman year, and one day I was just like, 'I need kissing practice, and I'm ready to graduate from using my own arm. Wanna help?'"

"You're kidding," I said.

"Dead serious as can be. I mean, we talk a lot of nonsense, and I hate him sometimes, and he's *not* my capital-*B* boyfriend, but I love him." She turned sharply to face me, her red hair swinging around her face. "And you *know* he's not enough of a fool to miss out on the chance to love me."

Caleb's face swam in front of my eyes, and I imagined that the gleam of every car's lights was the shine of his perfect smile. Then the thought of Caleb finding me barfing on the side of the road flashed through my mind, and I shuddered. Just the idea of being sick in front of him now made me want to crawl into a hole. "But how did you actually handle it the first time you had a bathroom emergency and Iggy was the only one around? What the hell did you actually *do*?"

Ruby took a moment to think and chew imaginary gum. "IBS is the most humbling thing I've ever gone through. There's nothing I can do to make that part of me invisible. And I had to make peace with that. I'm *gonna* be in the bathroom for an hour. I'm *gonna* let it loose in there, and sometimes he's *gonna* notice it afterward. Maybe it's a good thing that I'm nuttier than a pecan sandy, because other than a few unbelievably bad days, I've mostly accepted that this is my life. I've tried to save my shame for the stuff that's shameful. And this just ain't it. Most of the time I actually believe that. So if Iggy can't handle something that I can't change or control, he's free to let the door knock his ass over on the way out."

Ruby's tone was earnest, not at all like she was puffing up her chest. But I still felt the space where the comparison between her and me would have fit right into the conversation. I was jealous. I wanted to have just a slice of that part of Ruby's personality. Regan's, too. Mom's. Hell, even Priya's and Keisha's. Everyone I loved seemed so much more capable than

I was of setting aside what other people thought. I've never been good at that. I've never been able to just let people think or say or do whatever without getting totally tangled up in it.

"Okay, so, if he's so great, why do you break up all the time?" I pulled off of the highway and onto the exit toward town. In Ruby's lap, my phone gave another ping.

"We break up because sometimes we want to kiss other people. Or we realize we haven't wanted to kiss anybody else for too long. Or sometimes talking to each other makes us want to rip our ears off the sides of our heads."

"What does that even mean?" I laughed again at Ruby's absolutely bananas relationship guidelines.

"Iggy's pretty much been my best friend since you . . . well, since you left. And sometimes kissing your best friend is literal perfection, and I want to just smother him with kisses and let his hands run all over me until I can't breathe. But sometimes kissing your best friend is the worst decision ever, and so we decide to stop doing it."

"Doing *it*?" My cheeks warmed as I asked, "Like . . ."

Ruby shook her head and said, "No, not yet. But after we graduate. I have it all planned out. We're going to be sure we go off to college with a notch in our belts, but we didn't want to do it while we were still together. It would have just made everything more complicated."

"Sure, who wants complicated?" We laughed, which made Ruby grab her stomach again. "I just can't even imagine being ready. I couldn't be less ready. I promised myself I wouldn't have sex until I could do it and not be scared. But nothing could sound more horrifying. My body hurts when I'm totally still, never mind if it were all tangled up with someone else's. My body and I are not on the same page about anything. And I don't feel sexy or desirable. A drawer full of period panties? Not sexy. Pelvic pain as bad as childbirth? Not sexy. Blacking out in the middle of making out? Not sexy. I mean, when does sexiness kick in? How do you get some? Where do you buy it? No, seriously. I'm asking. Like, what do *you* do if you're really getting going and you, I don't know, get the bubble guts?"

"If it's Iggy? I tell him. And I go to the damn bathroom. And I trust him to be there for me if I need him."

The dark of the car was painted with red as we sat at a stoplight. The sound of my turn signal blinking was louder with every click.

"That's a whole lot of faith for a high school boy," I said.

Ruby held up my phone and wagged it in front of my face. Then she read off of the screen. "Caleb texted twice. Once to see how prom send-off was, and once to see if you wanted to get together to see something really cool tonight. What's it going to take for you to trust this guy, huh?"

"Caleb isn't Iggy. And I'm not you. I've only known him for a couple of weeks."

I didn't say anything else, and eventually Ruby just squawked like a chicken.

After I dropped her off, all the way back in Blythe, I gave in to my urge to text Caleb. I told him I was feeling down about missing both proms, and he told me he had a way to fix that. He sent me a geolocation pin, and a few minutes later I drove off into the night.

Mackenzie Street is way on the north side, out past the reach of the suburban sprawl. There's a little town center—it used to be the middle of everything like a hundred years ago. Now it's just empty. Old buildings and small, crumbling houses. Most of the people who still live there are either the original owners or younger people who've moved into cheap housing so they can be starving artists in peace. The Mackenzie Street Bridge is small, two lanes stretched over a creek that dried up long ago. There isn't much on the other side of the bridge either, just a few old farmhouses no one lives in anymore, so it's hardly in use.

I pulled up and parked next to the only other car I'd seen for miles. It was Caleb's black truck, and its headlights were on.

"Aren't you worried you'll get in trouble out here?" I called as I walked toward the bridge.

"Nah, there's never anybody this far out."

I crunched over the gravel and Caleb walked toward the road to meet me. We met right in the middle of the bridge and stopped face to face.

"You look nice, Trip," he said.

"Oh right." I reached up and put my hand on my cheek. "My friends did my prom makeup."

"I like it." He was wearing a denim jacket with a sweatshirt underneath. The hood was down, bunched up against the back of his neck. "I like you." We both took tiny steps forward.

I nodded and tried not to let my face explode. "I like you, too."

"Can I tell you why I like you?" he asked.

I nodded again.

"You're smart and funny and beautiful, but those are not the most special things."

I felt my smile tick up on one side. He was smitten, but it would fade.

"You're strong, but you're soft, too. You're kind of a mess, but you pretend not to be."

I giggled. "I am not. There's plenty you don't know. Like, you don't know that I have a 4.3 GPA and my study method involves a minimum of five color-coded highlighters present at all times. You don't know that I'd eat pizza at every meal, or that my family legacy is the old grocery store on the west side."

He grinned. "No way? The little weird one? Gustav's or something?"

"Gunderson's, yeah."

"Well, I know I've just seen little pieces, but I don't think I'm wrong about you. Everybody I know tries so hard to be one thing, but not you. You seem confident, but you also don't take yourself too seriously. You're nice, but tough. And you want to help people. You're brave."

He knew I hoped to be a doctor, even if he didn't totally know the truth of why.

He stepped a little closer and then brought a hand up to point at my eyes. "You've been crying?"

I shrugged. "Do you feel really silly now for saying I was brave right before you noticed I'd been crying?"

"Whatever." He grinned at me and then cast his gaze to the ground. Half a beat, and then he looked up again, right into my eyes, and said, "You know you can be brave and still cry. Your feelings are fine. Are you still feeling sad you missed your prom night?"

"Maybe a little." I smiled.

"Did you have a big date lined up?" He wasn't asking in a sharp way, but it was pretty cute that he wanted to know if someone at Stockwood had my heart.

"I would have if someone had asked me, but I pretty much only focused on school at Stockwood. I can't say I ever really caught anybody's eye, at least not that I noticed with my head jammed into a book. What about you, though? Did you have a good prom night?"

"I went with a group. Not a date. I don't mind being on my own. We had fun, though."

"You know, if I hadn't gotten kicked out, I probably wouldn't have even appreciated prom. Maybe I would have gotten a little clump of flowers from a boy who asked me to go with him at the last minute, and he would have spun me around, and there would have been some cheesy theme like 'a night under the stars,' and we would have danced and kissed, and I would have treated it like just another expected thing."

He nodded. I felt my face get warm at even the mention of a kiss in front of him. I liked that warmth. I wanted more of it.

"What are we doing here?" I asked.

"I'll show you. Follow me," he said. We walked over to the side of the road and walked down the gently sloping sides and along a little path through a small crop of trees. Once we crossed behind the biggest tree, I could tell we were on an overlook.

I smiled and made a small gasping sound. "What is this? I didn't know this was here. This is what? A big hill?"

Our area isn't known for elevation changes, so it was truly unexpected to look out into the still-deepening darkness and see distant lights from town and beyond for miles and miles.

"It's one of my favorite places, and I thought you'd like it. I've probably painted it about a hundred times. All different ways. All different styles. I love this view no matter how I paint it. Right here." He held up his hands to make a frame. "It's cool, huh?"

"It really, really is."

"Are you . . . okay?" he asked, gesturing to my stomach.

I hadn't even noticed I'd been holding my abdomen, cradling it gingerly as I so often did during times of dull, subtle pain.

"You know, we're all friends with Ruby, and she's got her poop thing. It's really fine if you've got a puking thing or something," he said.

I laughed, wondering if Ruby would have thought it was funny. I decided that I was almost certain she would have.

I looked up at him, thinking about what it would be like to

have a real boyfriend. I'd gone on dates, but I never ended up with anything that stuck.

He knew then, I think, that I wasn't prepared to tell him anything, and he was gracious enough not to call me on it. I shivered, and Caleb said, "Let's get back down there. It's a little warmer by the truck." He guided me back through the trees, keeping a hand on my back, and when we got to the bottom and the bridge, he said, "Prom Squad, huh?"

I laughed and tried to turn my head, as if I'd be able to look at my own back. "Yeah. Keisha's mom got them for us. We were going to wear them while we got ready, until we put on our fancy dresses. Oh well." He pulled off his jacket and held it open for me. I slipped my arms in and soaked up the warmth still inside it from his body.

Caleb smiled and said, "Hold on."

He stepped away to the side of the road, where the grass was hitting its springtime growth spurt, and where he'd parked. He started his car and turned the headlights off so only the running lights were on. They gave a warm glow. He bent over behind the truck then, disappearing from my view, and when he returned, he had his hand behind his back.

I smiled. He stepped up close, half of his face lit by his truck, and he said, "Delia, would you go to prom with me?"

I laughed out loud, and my grin was so big I thought my cheeks might pop. Then he pulled from behind his back a little clump of the best of the Texas wildflowers. Three or four tall, sapphire-colored bluebonnets and a couple of pale pink buttercups from the side of the road.

"You know picking bluebonnets is a criminal offense, right?" I asked.

"You should know. Being that you've been living a life of crime."

Then he held out his hand and said, "And for the theme: a night under the stars." He winked and took my hand. "Will you dance with me?" He guided me as I spun under his arm. Then he pulled me close and draped my hands up behind his neck, and his hands found my waist.

We made little shuffling movements, side to side, spinning in slow circles on the blacktop, glowing gold in his truck's lights, under a sky full of incredible stars. I looked up at them, shining so bright, and he whispered in my ear, "Flowers, boy, spin, stars, dance . . ."

I looked at him, but I couldn't see many details of his face until our rotation let the bright light hit his face again. When it did, his eyes were dancing too, and his lips were so close . . . right there.

"Kiss," I whispered, already bringing my face up to meet his.

He leaned forward and his mouth found mine.

His lips were so soft, and his kiss was so strong.

A sliver of space separated us again, for just a moment, and I tried not to smile too big. Then he was smiling too. We both laughed a few breathy gusts before the smiling slipped back into something quieter. I inhaled deeply and my heart was like thunder in my ears. And then it was quiet. No loud heartbeat, no heavy breathing. There was just Caleb, with his arms around me, and his lips on my lips. His tongue skipped over mine and we breathed in each other. He tasted like cinnamon, or maybe licorice. I closed my arms tighter around him.

He peppered my lips with small kisses, on my top lip, then my bottom lip, then my jaw, and up to my cheek. He kept one hand on my back and the other found its way to the side of my face. When we looked at each other again, still swaying back and forth, he said, "How was prom?"

"Better than expected," I answered.

"Well, that's not all. We voted, and it turns out, you're the prom queen," he said.

"Wow! And the competition was so tough this year! Did you bet on me?"

He nodded. "Easy money."

The drive home wasn't nearly long enough. I felt electrified, warm, and happy. Ruby had been right about Caleb. He was wonderful. I could trust that. Right? I rolled down my windows, letting the wind wildly rip through my hair. I turned up the volume of the Woolly Mammoth's radio until I could barely hear the wind at all.

At the first light past the exit, I felt eyes on me while I was singing at the top of my lungs. I resisted for a second, but when I turned and checked, the car beside me was Caleb's. He was smiling and laughing at my musical serenade, so I only sang louder. My phone rang. He was calling me from his car, and I answered just as the light turned green and I turned the opposite direction from home.

"Where are you off to?" he asked. "Anywhere fun?"

"I need to get gas," I said, "and I've already had fun. What about you?"

"Home for sure. I've got a busy weekend of finishing a report and studying for my last exam."

Deep in the base of my stomach, way down in my intestines, I felt like a knot was cinching my guts closer together. Silently, I opened my mouth to the pain.

"Trip?" he asked, once I'd been quiet for long enough that he noticed. "You there?"

I kept one hand on the wheel while the other came into my lap. "I'm here. Yeah, I'm just gonna grab gas."

My brain was spinning out; my stomach squeezed brutally. I had to find a bathroom and fast.

"You already said that." Caleb's tone changed suddenly. "Hey, are you okay?"

"Of course," I said, trying to focus on the street with the closest gas station.

"You're sure?"

Just before I could let out a sharp hiss of breath, I reached up and muted my phone so Caleb wouldn't hear me breathing through the pain. This wasn't trust. I didn't have any of that. This wasn't a relationship.

Suddenly it all felt so *obvious.* Who was I kidding? Maybe Ruby was brave and proud and able to own her body, but I didn't know how to own something I couldn't understand. I didn't feel capable of boldly claiming something that only ever made me feel misunderstood, weak, and broken. I craved her strength. I wanted it. I saw glimpses of it sometimes, but mostly it felt perpetually out of reach. The urge to pull away, to be alone, smashed into me over and over like bugs on my windshield. When the cramp released for a second, I unmuted and said, "Yeah, for sure. I just need to pull in and get gas. Gonna let you go so I can pay attention and be safe. I'll talk to you later, okay? Monday, maybe."

"Sure, okay. I really did have a great time—"

I hung up. If he mentioned it, I would say I hadn't heard him talking. I didn't have a choice. If I moved wrong or relaxed, I would literally not make it to the toilet. I made the last turn and got caught at another light. My hands clenched the steering wheel tighter. The sign for the gas station flickered—teasing me, it was so close. I whimpered against the pain.

I tried to distract myself by thinking of the good moments I'd had, but they were so gone. By the time I pulled into the parking spot, everything in my heart felt different. I tried so hard to pull back to the feeling I'd had by the side of the road at the only prom I'd ever have. I wanted to return to the feeling of his incredible kisses, the feeling of his hands, but I couldn't. I burst through the automatic doors of the gas station, found my way to the last stall in the bathroom, and almost cried with relief.

While washing my hands, I stared at my reflection in the mirror, letting the water run and run once the soap was long gone. What business did I have leading him on, making him believe he knew me, when I wasn't even brave enough to show him the one part of me that most shaped my life? How could I pretend we could start something real if I didn't trust him with any piece of my truth?

We had hardly even started, but the whole thing was over. It had to be. I just had to get up the nerve to tell him.

CHAPTER TWENTY

THE EYE OF THE STORM

Every little thing that could have been out of whack by Monday was *entirely* messed up. After avoiding Caleb all day Sunday, I hadn't escaped anything—I'd just delayed the inevitably bad day. I'd been researching new doctors who might see me in the coming week and left several messages about scheduling an appointment, but I didn't have high hopes. I was left with only cereal dust and the final drops of milk for breakfast, and we were also out of coffee creamer *and* sugar, so I ended up pouring the last of my cereal milk into my mug. (It was not the unexpected success I was hoping for. My coffee tasted like raisins.) I hadn't managed to get my phone on the charger before bed, so I woke up to an impossible 8-percent battery. The laundry hadn't quite dried my clothes (including Caleb's shirt, which I'd planned to give back to him today), so I was stuck squeezing into almost-damp jeans, which were too uncomfortable to wear. I peeled them off my body and tossed them back into the dryer, even though I could tell it might make me late to school.

I hadn't asked him to, but Caleb was waiting for me at the corner.

"You didn't have to wait for me," I said. "You shouldn't have let me make you late."

"It's not a big deal," he said.

I reached into my tote and pulled out his still barely damp shirt, folded in a clean little square. "Here. I need to give this back to you." We were walking quickly as the sky darkened and thunder rumbled in the distance.

"You *need* to?" he asked, refusing to take it from my hand.

"Just take it," I said, holding it out again as we tried to shuffle quickly over the puddles and flooded corners. I thought he'd reached and had a hold of it, but when I let it go, his clean shirt fell straight into a brown swirl of muck in the road.

He picked it up, and said, "Oh damn. It's okay. Thanks anyway."

"No, no. My fault. I'll clean it. Again," I said, taking it and folding it inside out and onto itself to get the muddy part contained inside a sleeve.

He smiled, reaching for my empty hand then and clasping his fingers together with mine. "Is this all a conspiracy because you want to keep wearing my shirt?" He gave my fingers a double squeeze. I didn't look over. Somehow, in that moment, I felt entirely certain that I would seriously and often disappoint him.

The spring rains were dragging heavy, brutal clouds across

the sky, and so even though speed walking might have barely gotten us there on time, we got caught by a flash of shredding rain, which meant my jeans were soaking wet again by the time I rolled into class ten minutes late. At least I had an excuse to run off without saying much of anything to Caleb.

In class, it didn't seem like the other kids were faring much better on this gross day. Our little group was laid out in the hallway again, but this time Iggy was lying on his back, tossing a giant pack of gum up into the air and catching it at his chest while the others took up the academic slack.

"You're cranky too?" I asked.

He tossed his gum a couple more times before answering. "Ruby got sick again. She couldn't come to school. Had to stay home on the throne, you know?" He was entirely unsqueamish about discussing the bathroom habits of his girlfriend. This was highlighted when another kid in the group made a sort of "ewwww" type of sound and Iggy sat up, instantly, and chucked the pack of gum at his head.

"That sucks," I said. "I'll text her to see if she's okay."

"Do what you want, but don't expect her to be okay. She's not. She isn't okay in any way."

"That bad, huh?"

"It's her eleventh."

My brain took an extra second or two to sort out what he meant, and then I made a sort of involuntary gasping sound. "Oh, of course it is! What is she gonna do? Can we go get her? She's not going to graduate, for real? I can't believe this is happening. Oh man. But there's only two weeks left! Two weeks."

"She'll be able to get her diploma at the end of summer, sure, but she won't walk with us. She doesn't get to do any of the traditional stuff like throwing the ugly hat or walking across the stage."

From across the circle, Sarah said (mostly to the girl who was working beside her), "I just don't get it. I would literally drag myself on my hands and knees before I missed too many classes to graduate."

"Shut up, Sarah," Iggy said. "You know she's got her thing. It's not a secret or whatever. She has big problems with her guts, and she can't just roll up here."

"Come on, man," Sarah said to Iggy and the rest of us, with a look around the circle. "We've all had tummy trouble, and we've all had the shits, but none of us would let *poop* keep us from graduating."

My head yanked back involuntarily.

"'Tummy trouble'?" I snapped. "You have no idea what you're talking about."

Sarah shrugged. "I'm literally not even trying to be mean or whatever. Iggy, you know I like Ruby. Tell her." She gestured between Iggy and me. Iggy said nothing. "I'm just saying that it's a little silly to say you can't come to school when the worst-case scenario is being stuck in the bathroom here but getting credit for attending. Like, show up, sneak into the teachers' single-seater and lock the door for an hour, whatever you have to do. But to not show up and then act like you're being mistreated by having the same attendance requirements as the rest of us?"

I stared at her in disbelief. This was the exact conversation that I believed was happening about me any time I went down for my period, and it was happening right now, in real time, in real life. It wasn't made up. It wasn't a fabrication of my anxiety. This was a real student in my class saying the actual things about Ruby that I always feared people might be saying about me.

"I don't really know you," I said, "but I do know Ruby. If she's out, if she's home, it means there's no other choice. Nobody picks this. Nobody just opts out of a huge life milestone for nothing. You're wrong. She's not being dramatic, but you are being rude."

"Just stop, Sarah, seriously," Iggy said. "This isn't the time for some mean-girl bullshit. Ruby is dealing with real pain, and it's scary, so just lay off. We're trying to figure it out, and eventually we'll know what the specific triggers are and it won't be like this, okay?"

"Honestly, I swear, I'm not an asshole," Sarah said to me on the side before taking back up with Iggy. "It's a little wild to me that there is *so* much drama in this situation. Her health and her attendance and her diploma and her high school boyfriend and—"

"I'm not her boyfriend, Sarah. Drop it." Iggy got up, took his gum back from the other side of the circle, and slipped off down the hallway. The sound of Iggy kicking the bottom of the lockers blended in with the next roaring clap of thunder, and then the halls were quiet again.

* * *

After class, I was fired up, but I had nowhere to go that would make anything better. Sarah's little rant had served to get me entirely in my head. Everything about it had been tailor-made to make me self-conscious and stressed. Iggy had gone from "concerned boyfriend" to "who needs a label?" in the course of two minutes. But Sarah was right, wasn't she? Iggy was eighteen years old. He had absolutely no reason to be eternally yoked to his high school sweetheart when everything about it was so hard. Their relationship had been tumultuous before her stomach problems kicked in, but her issues couldn't have made things any better.

I zoned out through the rest of my morning classes, and then I skipped lunch and wandered the halls for a while. I didn't want to be forced to sit next to Iggy or Caleb or any of Ruby's friends, who would certainly be talking about her no longer graduating. I'd texted her three or four times, but she hadn't replied other than to make some joke about "that's the way the single-ply school-issued toilet paper crumbles" and telling me we could talk later.

Like a dagger in my side, a huge cramp reached up from deep in my bones, and I folded over to hold myself tight.

"Trip?" Caleb's voice appeared like magic out of the previously empty hallway, and then he was just there beside me.

He was all rosy-lipped and sparkly-eyed, and I could tell he was *not* in the same bad mood I was.

"Hey, sorry, I'm not really like . . . in a great mood today." I tried to hold up my hands in a way that wouldn't be off-putting, but I just needed space. For my body. For my brain.

"That's okay," he said, reaching for my waist. "You're allowed to have a bad day. You don't have to have it alone, though."

I twisted away from him just as another cramp cracked like lightning through my body.

"I'm sorry, I'm really not . . . I do, actually, though, want to have it alone. I think." I reached a hand over and gave his arm a pat that was entirely meaningless. I felt it in my fingers, and he looked down to where I was touching him, and I could tell he knew it was hollow too.

"Delia, I'm trying to give you time here, but it's just that, like, I'm not . . . there is obviously something . . . wrong. Like, with your . . . body or whatever. You can talk to me about it, you know? If you need to. Do you . . . have the same problem as Ruby?"

I was already trying to shake my head no as he was making reassuring hand gestures and setting off talking again. "I just mean, I know that people have body stuff, and I just . . . I think you know I like you, obviously. I just want you to know I'm—"

"Caleb, I really don't want to do this now, okay?"

I don't want to talk about my period. I don't want to talk about my bowels. I don't want to talk about blood and guts and poop and puke with the boy that I want so badly to kiss.

Of course I couldn't say any of that.

"This whole thing . . . I just . . . Just give me some space, okay? Leave me alone."

"What are you even talking about?"

Frustration and anger took over my brain and I snapped. "Caleb. You're a great guy, honestly. I'm just not the boyfriend-having type, okay? We can just be friends." His face was painted with confusion, and every cell in my body wanted to say more to explain better or to make him not feel like he'd just been discarded. But I couldn't take another second of any of it. I took a few steps backward and turned. The next corner was D Hallway, and right there, right on the corner, was the single-seater teachers' bathroom that Sarah had been talking about this morning. With nobody around, I went inside and locked the door.

The bathroom had been converted from one that used to have three stalls inside. There were still empty holes from old bolts in the tile floor where the walls used to be. The other two toilets had long been removed, but steel-capped circles still showed where they'd been in a row along the back wall. The room was big. Obviously bigger than a single-seat bathroom needed to be. I hung my bag on the hook on the back of the door before crossing to the far corner and the one remaining toilet.

I sat, checked my undies, and even though they were clean, I could tell something was wrong. I looked at the date on my watch. I was still a couple of days from starting, unless my period was going to be arriving earlier than expected again. I tried to make myself breathe.

I felt my muscles squeeze and I gasped, grabbing onto the side rail for support. I let out a cry of pain, sitting there on the toilet, hand still gripping the rail as if my whole life depended on keeping it clenched in my fist. This time the pain wouldn't let go. It didn't waver or release. It just kept squeezing, sharp, sharper, pain that brought dark spots across my vision, hot shears snipping inside my body but never cutting all the way through. I opened my eyes and bright spots appeared, dancing in front of me. I tried to breathe, in and out, but I could only hold it in. I tried to exhale, but my lungs wouldn't release. The blood drained from my face, and I felt my lips and my nose getting cold. Little beads of sweat popped up under my nostrils and across my brow. I pulled myself up and buttoned my pants, but before I could hobble over to the sink, I started swirling. I was seconds from passing out, and I was locked in a bathroom with a hard tile floor. I sank to my knees. I couldn't have possibly cared less about what germs crawled around me. If I didn't get on the floor, I could hit my head. My bag still hung on the other side of the room, ten steps away. I couldn't get over there, so I just rolled over and scooted my butt up against the wall.

I set my back against the icy tiles just in time for the panic attack.

CHAPTER TWENTY-ONE

RIDE OF SHAME

It was coming. It was coming. The pain was coming. It would hurt. It would take my breath. It would take my words. It would take *me* . . . and it was coming.

I gasped, hot air rushing in and then out again. Light burst in front of my eyes. My chest sucked into itself like I was absorbing my body into my own black hole. The darkness at the edge of my vision crept closer to the center of my view, slowly at first, and then, as my breathing picked up speed and I failed miserably at keeping it slow, it raced toward the focal point, blacking out everything. My hands trembled and patted the bathroom floor, grasping for help that couldn't possibly come. I couldn't release the muscles in my neck and throat enough to make sound. I couldn't cry. I couldn't scream. I was just frozen, sure that I would die. I brought a hand to my chest, my throat, my head. I felt like I was suffocating. It was coming, and I couldn't stop it. I couldn't stop it. There was nothing I could do. Then, just as suddenly, the cramp released, leaving behind an aching, and the sound of my shouted cries shot like a siren from my throat, filling the bathroom with my plea for help. My uterus throbbed like a bruise, like it'd been punched hard, echoing cascading soreness I felt over and over. I sat and blinked and cried as the world slowed and came back into focus.

Knocking. Furious knocking at the door. The handle shook wildly and then I heard him.

"Trip, are you okay! Delia? Delia! Answer me!"

I felt blood fill my cheeks again, and I slowly pushed myself to standing.

"I'm okay." I was entirely too quiet. "I'm okay!" My voice sounded tearful. I didn't realize I was still crying. I brushed off my pants, washed my trembling hands three times, and then grabbed my bag and unlocked the door.

I was a wreck. My tear-soaked cheeks were peppered with flaking mascara, and I wanted to tell him that I was fine. I was even irritated that he'd been there, clearly keeping a vigil outside the bathroom door. I wanted to tell him thank you and also tell him to go away. I wanted to tell him so many things, and I probably would have.

But as I took a step, pushing past him into the hallway, everything went black again in an instant, and I collapsed into his arms.

*   *   *

When I next realized what was happening, Caleb was helping the nurse get me into the campus wheelchair, and the once-empty hallway was now full of students on their way to the next class. The wheelchair was hard to navigate because it looked to be from 1972. Caleb pushed me between dozens and dozens of high schoolers, all looking down at me in my ride of shame, wondering and asking each other what was wrong.

Once we arrived in the infirmary, Nurse Batten told me to lie down on the little cot with the vinyl cover.

I sat there, swirling, and she came over to take a look at me. She was an older, fit woman with pale skin and a severe jawline. She took my temperature and then put on the blood-pressure cuff. She got my name and checked the computer to read my student profile notes and medical information.

"Miss Bridges," she said. "Cordelia. You need to answer me. What's happening? Are you on drugs?"

I realized that Caleb was standing there, expectantly, desperately hoping I'd say the words to her that I wouldn't say to him. Oh god. Perfect.

"M . . . m . . . m." I was frustrated beyond my ability to speak. I looked over at Caleb and scowled. "Make him g . . . go."

His expression fell, he sighed, and then he shook his head and turned, leaving me alone with the nurse.

"Cordelia, what is wrong? Have you taken drugs?" the nurse asked again.

"No," I said, wishing I could scream my frustration in her face. "It's just my period. This is normal."

She looked at me like I'd missed every memo about what is and isn't normal.

"Thissisnormuull," I said again, feeling my eyes flutter.

"Your blood pressure is too low, Cordelia. I'm calling an ambulance."

"No," I tried to tell her. I wanted to tell the nurse I just needed to lie down, I just didn't want to hit my head, but instead I just stared at her. No hospital. No ambulance. No way.

I heard her pick up her phone and type in a number, but then she turned around and said, "Your mom has one chance to answer this call, or I'm calling 911."

On her desk, the speakerphone rang.

The nurse looked at me.

It rang.

A tear slipped from the corner of my eye down the side of my face.

It rang.

The nurse brought her hand nearer to the phone and pursed her lips together.

It rang.

I closed my eyes. Please Mom, please.

"Hello, this is Miranda."

"Ms. Bridges? This is Nurse Batten at BHS. Delia needs you. Now."

CHAPTER TWENTY-TWO

MEETING THE SHERIFF

There may not be anything quite as awful as the self-doubt that comes after a bad flare-up. Sometimes the pain vanishes almost as quickly as it appeared, and for a few brief moments, in those first minutes after, sometimes I wonder, *Did I imagine that? Was it really that bad? Was it?*

It is so hard to hold on to what I know is true. That all of this is real, and it's awful.

By the time Mom arrived, I was fine. By any possible medical assessment.

The nurse had totally changed her demeanor toward me over the past ten minutes. Suddenly I was well enough to go back to class? Suddenly I wasn't in need of a wheelchair? She was skeptical about the whole thing, and she wasn't hiding it well.

The nurse and Mom spent some time talking to each other on the side of the room, as if I couldn't hear what they were discussing. Mom was trying to explain what this was, and the nurse kept asking her if I was on drugs.

Once they were done, and I'd convinced both of them I could stay for the rest of the school day, Mom asked, "Are you sure you don't want to go home?" We turned the corner back to the front of the office and almost ran right into the principal.

"I wouldn't recommend it" came his voice, slow and deep and country-fried.

Principal Davis had introduced himself to me on the first day, but he'd been dressed for some sort of district meeting, and he'd been wearing a suit. Today he was clearly dressed for casual Friday. On a Monday.

"You must be Delia's adult. I'm Mr. Davis." He held out his hand for Mom to shake. "I wouldn't normally just sneak-attack y'all in the office, but as we're in the home stretch, all of the admin meet every morning to touch base about the bubble kids, and so Delia's been on my mind."

"What's a bubble kid?" I asked.

Mom tried to keep things casual. "Don't get excited, kiddo. I have a feeling it's not as fun as it sounds."

He gave a half smile and said, "Well, she has had ten absences this term—which apparently was actually more than ten, but she made up those credits at her last school, which is none of my business. But anyway there are ten absences on record, and that means that she really can't miss any more days here at Blythe High. Okay?"

Neither of us said anything to that.

He looked me square in the face, and his voice got even more intense. "I need to be sure you understand that if you miss one more day—if you have eleven or more absences on your record—you will not receive credit for the classes with eleven absences this semester, and you will therefore be a few credits short, and you will not graduate with your class. Your credit recovery plan will be summer school. Just wanted to make sure we're all on the same page about that. You can't just write another essay or take an extra exam or stay after school. On my campus, we put our butts in the chairs when school is in session."

Mom started getting riled up, making me want to shrivel inside myself and disappear. "That is really unfair. What can we do to appeal that decision?"

"Nothing," he answered. His tone was meant to shut her down. "That's just how we do it. I don't have the funding to pay teachers to work on the weekends or at night, so it's just not something we do. Do you understand?"

"Yes, we do. But," I said, feeling brave, "if the absence is really for a medical emergency, why can't you excuse it? I know that my friend Ruby Walker was absent today, and we all know that's her absence eleven, and I just can't imagine that you really mean that someone as great and smart as Ruby can't graduate. All I'm asking is that you consider, since she's so close to the end, and there are only two weeks to go . . . Couldn't you let her just make up that one day's worth of work? What if all her teachers signed off on it? I bet she could convince them to do that."

He huffed like a bull stamping at the ground and said, "Now, what I can't do here is discuss another student. I can't. And I'm certainly not going to have a disagreement about it standing in the hall."

Mom was basically expressionless. Her eyes didn't blink. Her mouth didn't smile. I couldn't even see her breathing. She looked over at me and I dropped my head. I didn't want to piss him off. I didn't want to start a huge war with the one person standing between me and my diploma.

"I guess we understand. Don't we, Delia?"

I looked down in defeat, and Mom instinctively put her hand on my back.

"It's really straightforward. I call it 'cheeks in the seats,' and the point is, you have to be here a certain number of days. That's it. Medical or not." His voice softened a little. "I know it probably feels personal. But I promise you it isn't personal. None of this is about you."

"Yeah," I said, with just a little scoff. "But maybe it should be."

CHAPTER TWENTY-THREE

EMOTIONAL WHIPLASH

I went to Ruby's house on my way home from school to make sure she was okay.

I knocked on the front door several times but heard nothing inside, so I started talking to her video doorbell. When I still didn't hear her coming to the door, I had to pull out the big guns.

"I'm going around to your window, Ruby! You leave me no choice!"

As I entered the side yard, I froze. Her pool, topped with dirt and leaves, hadn't had its post-winter cleanup. But it was there. That pool. That hot tub. The feeling of everyone's eyes on me. I turned around and forced myself to focus on now instead of then. Ruby's house is two stories, but there is a very climbable tree that goes to a very climbable cedar patio cover.

Ruby's window has three panels, and each of those three panels has blinds, but about a thousand years ago, Ruby's cat gnawed her way through part of the blinds, leaving an open square right in front of her bookcase. I climbed up, finding it much harder at seventeen than it had been at twelve. Scarier, too, transferring my body from the largest tree branch to the pergola and pulling myself to standing against the back of her house.

"Ruby-June, you open this window!" I shouted, looking inside and trying to pick her out in the pile of pillows on her bed.

"Would you get down, you weirdo? You're gonna kill yourself." Ruby had appeared in her backyard, behind me, under the trellis. She looked, honestly, awful. I clambered down and was glad to be back on the planet's surface when I came face to face with her in her big pink bathrobe and fuzzy slippers.

"Explain to me how your parents didn't literally carry you into class rather than letting you stay home today."

"They're out of town. They're supposed to be back tonight, though." Then Ruby sniffled, turned, and walked through the sliding glass door, and I followed. I closed the door behind me, but she didn't turn. I was still staring at her back. My spicy tone wasn't right, so I softened.

"Hey," I said. "I know you've got to be so upset about graduation. I know how crushed you must be. Are you okay?"

She turned. "I know the graduating thing is horrible, and I know that I should be crying about that, but . . ." She took a huge inhale before letting out a loud sob. "Iggy and I broke up for good this time. He dumped me early!"

"What?" I asked, shaking my head. "Early?"

Her shoulders shook, and I wrapped my arm around her. Every cell of my brain wanted to come up with a funny "dumping" joke to cheer her up, but something told me this was one occasion that Ruby wouldn't want humor infused into.

"He called me, like, two hours ago and told me he loved me, but it was time to call it off for real this time. For good. We were gonna break up at the end of senior summer anyway. But now I won't really have a senior summer because I'll be in classes, so what's a few months early? Since we wouldn't be able to spend as much time together, why bother?"

"Oh, Ruby." I felt my jaw go slack. No matter how banana-pants their relationship seemed from the outside, she didn't want it to vanish like this. This one was gonna hurt.

Suddenly, she jerked. She didn't say anything but just doubled over in pain, a gesture that was so familiar it made my heart beat fast. She almost stumbled as she took a few steps from the back door through the breakfast nook into the den. Ruby had that space all set up. The giant sectional had been rearranged to make a huge bed, with about a thousand blankets in the middle, and she had small tables at both sides. There was a cup of water, a package of crackers, a small bowl of rice, two bunches of bananas, and a bowl of mashed potatoes that couldn't possibly be warm.

"I don't understand. He and I talked this morning. He was fine. We were fine. He was worried about me. But in the few hours since we talked, he realized that my senior summer and his senior summer were going to be very different. He was going to be moving on from here and I was going to be stuck." The TV was on—playing real TV, which seemed strange, but I knew it was actual TV because it was playing a commercial.

"Why are you watching commercials? Why aren't you streaming something?"

Ruby lay down on the couch, gently, and groaned her reply. "I don't know? I just like it. It makes me feel like I'm making fewer choices. Picking a show just feels like too much pressure sometimes."

Ruby abruptly buried her head in the blankets and started to sob again.

I said, "If Iggy was willing to break up with you like that, that just means he's an absolute asshat and he doesn't get to have three more months of your heart or your time, Ruby. You deserve better."

"I'm not crying over Iggy now," she said. "This time I'm crying 'cause it hurts."

My heart ached. It was like looking in a mirror, almost. It was wild how familiar it all seemed, and how strange it was to watch it happening to someone else. She was tucked up so tiny, and she was rocking her body back and forth a little. There is an unfortunate side effect of hurting that badly: It's hard to keep anything in your brain. You feel so overwhelmed by the pain, it short-circuits your mind until it's difficult to process anything at all. And if you're in so much discomfort that you can't reason properly, you can lose track of what you might have been thinking or feeling or doing. Everything gets sort of lost to the pain.

"I can't. I can't," she cried. "Owwwww, owwwww." A few rhythmic sobs came from her mouth.

"Oh, Ruby." I didn't really want to say anything else because I know how hard it is to listen to platitudes when everything you want and need and feel is paper thin.

I lay down with her, beside and over her, petting her hair and rubbing her back. "I know it hurts. I'm so, so sorry it hurts."

"I'm not crying about the pain anymore. I . . . I can't believe I'm not graduating," she cried. "I can't believe it." She coughed, choking on her tears. "And just a couple of days after I made the decision to pick UT."

"Ruby! You did? Congratulations!"

"It doesn't matter now—I'm not gonna be there this fall anyway. Did you know some of the kids in my drama class had an idea about having all the seniors—the ones with absences to spare—stage a walkout in protest for their senior prank? Isn't that so sweet? I feel like everyone was rooting for me. And now that I missed today, all these people at school know that I'm not graduating. It's embarrassing. I can't actually let them try to make a big demonstration for me, right? Just because I can't go to graduation?" Her voice was quiet, and then: "I need to go."

"I'm sure there has to be something we can do to get you to graduation. I'm sure there has to be some way we can pull this off, right? I had the idea that we could petition all your teachers to sign off on you doing some sort of makeup work?"

She made herself laugh, but only for a second before she said, "I've tried. The teachers aren't stepping up to their boss. But, I'm not even talking about graduation now . . . try to keep up, will you?" She redoubled her grip on her waist. "I need to *go* so bad."

"I can help you to the bathroom?" I offered.

"No, I mean, I need to go, but I can't. I can't go. I just keep trying and trying, and I just can't." The TV was playing a commercial for some sort of medicine then, and as we got quiet, it got to the part where they listed off the potential side effects. "Oh please. Old people would not be skipping down the beach at sunset if they had this side effect. They really should be more hesitant about signing up for anything that causes *this*." She gestured to her stomach and then her butt.

I smirked at her. "Oh yeah?"

"Yeah. A drug that gives you diarrhea and constipation? That would be a fate worse than death. I mean, just take me out to the back roads and drop me off to die. I'm tired."

"I know," I said.

She looked at me sadly for a few seconds, and then tossed out like it was just casual conversation, "Distract me. What's new with you?"

"I'm up to two acceptances . . . a school in Chicago, and Texas Tech. I don't really care at all about attending either, but I guess it's called a backup school for a reason, right? And, ummm, a doctor had a cancellation and is going to be able to give me an appointment. I'm going to see a Dr. Evans after school this week."

"Boring. Don't care. Tell me about kissing and quivering nether-regions and things that actually matter."

I laughed. "Oh, well. Let's see. Saturday night, after I dropped you home, Caleb and I met up at this gorgeous overlook on the other side of the Mackenzie Street Bridge. Did you know that was there? Anyway, I was still all made up, and he did this adorable fake prom thing. He picked wildflowers for me; we danced. And we totally kissed. A lot."

Ruby screamed with delight.

"Oh my gahhhhhd! I just knew y'all were gonna be sweeter than Granny's tea for each other. I love it. How was all that smoochin'?" She waggled her eyebrows at me. I grinned sadly at what would come next.

"But on the way home, I almost crapped my pants, which got me all in my head about things, and then this morning, everything seemed even more impossible. And I realized that I couldn't do this to him. So I broke up with him—officially—or whatever. I ended this thing between us—"

"Delia, you tell me you're lying right now."

"It gets worse. And *then* I locked myself in the faculty bathroom way back in D Hall, and proceeded to lose consciousness, complete with lying on the bathroom floor."

"You did not."

"I absolutely did."

"Caleb has been so heart-eyed for you. Why on all of God's green earth did you dump him? I'm so confused."

"There's nothing to be confused about. I just can't take the pressure of trying to deal with managing a guy's feelings on top of everything else I'm dealing with."

She repeated my words in a slow, exaggerated way. "*Managing* his *feelings*? What did he do to make you think his feelings need managing?"

"Well, nothing. I mean, not yet anyway. But come on. Dating a girl with problems like mine is not something that any reasonable guy our age wants to deal with. Clearly Iggy is proving that rule."

She gave a little sigh.

I added, "Caleb is great, he's super nice and cool, but I don't need him to resent me before it's even started. Being with me is exhausting. Being my person just costs too much."

"And you're just going to decide that's true for him without giving him a chance to say it isn't. I think you've gotten the memo about how messed up it is to try and make somebody else's decision for them?"

I rolled my eyes and said, "I expected you to understand. I'm cutting him loose. Giving him an out."

"You're trying to be sure you break up with him before he has the chance to break up with you . . . maybe . . . eventually . . . in a theoretical future that probably follows weeks or months of happiness and making out and fun? Isn't that a *little* dramatic?"

I gasped as if she'd just slapped me across my face. "Ruby-June! You did *not* just pull out the word *dramatic* with me right now? That's an unspeakable word!"

"Well, I'm real sorry, but if the dramatic-ass shoe fits, then put it on," she said playfully.

"How is this dramatic?"

"You have a beautiful boy who likes you, wants to be with you all the time, made a personalized prom just for you, and is gentle and smart and fun! And you're just chucking it out in the garbage with the gnawed-off corn cobs? That's what I would call dra-mat-ique!"

"Look, maybe if I had a diagnosis? Maybe if I had a plan? Maybe if I wasn't still floundering in this, drowning in it, after six years?" My voice got shaky, and my eyes started to sting. I blinked a dozen more times. "Maybe if I wasn't still being just beaten down by this over and over? I mean"—my vision blurred with tears, and I angrily wiped them away—"I don't feel like I know anything. I don't feel like I'm any better at any of this, and that's the most hope-wrecking feeling, I . . ."

Ruby grabbed my hand. She held it and gave it a big squeeze, and then she reached up and brushed my stray hairs back behind my ears.

Then she used the palm of her hand to smack me right in the middle of the forehead.

CHAPTER TWENTY-FOUR

GTFOBGYN

A few days later, I found myself once again draped in paper and hoping that the doctor I was about to meet would be the one who had all the answers. I was sitting there, trying to focus on how very fortunate, how very privileged it is to have medical care at all when, at 3:49 p.m. Dr. Evans entered the room, accompanied by his nurse.

My eighth gynecologist was not what I expected.

In the photograph on his website, he looked like any regular middle-aged dude with a receding hairline, heavy features, and coffee-stained teeth. In person, it looked like somebody had had a bit of a makeover.

Dr. Evans, it would seem, had decided to get some new hair, start working out, get a tan and some veneers. He was just handsome enough that I felt my chest go red.

"Hi," I said, more quietly than I had intended.

"I'm Dr. Evans. It says here that you've been making the rounds?"

I gave an awkward sort of head shake, unsure of what he was trying to say.

He noticed my reaction and added, "The notes from the intake nurse say that you've been to quite a few OBGYNs. Is that true?"

"Yeah. It is. It's been hard to find the right fit."

He sat on his little wheeled stool and pushed back to where my folder lay on the counter. "That's not very common for someone your age. And since you are young, you might just not entirely know how all of this usually works. Can you tell me why your mom hasn't come with you today?"

Ooof. He'd landed right on a sore spot. The truth? We'd had a little argument this morning when I told her I'd have this appointment after school and it was the first time she was hearing about it. She was pissed that I hadn't mentioned it, and she was irritated that she'd had to nudge me to tell her about what Dr. Leavy had found too. I'd been pushing her farther and farther from my doctors' appointments, and maybe I didn't even completely know why. Embarrassed maybe? I was sick and tired of feeling so ineffective. I don't see myself that way, or I don't want to anyway. I don't want my mommy to have to handle my problems, no matter how willing she may be. Even when your mom is one of your best friends, you still want to find ways to be independent. "Well, I'll be going off to college soon, and I . . ." I forced myself to take a deep breath. "I need to be able to talk to my own doctors, right? If I have a medical condition, I'm going to have to be able to manage that for myself really soon. I'm almost eighteen."

"That's fine. I just think it's important for me to ask, right from the start, why you think you're going to hear something different from me than what you've heard from a half a dozen other doctors. I don't mind seeing you, but I want to manage your expectations here. If you're walking into an appointment with a self-identified 'medical condition,' as you say, but the science doesn't indicate that, you still may not get what you're gunning for here. Does that make sense?"

The nurse checked her phone, leaned over, whispered in the doctor's ear, and left the room.

Dr. Evans got up from his stool and said, "Will you excuse me for just a moment? I need to take care of one thing and then I'll be back and we can talk some more."

Was that supposed to be something to look forward to?

I couldn't believe how rude his reply had been. Nobody would believe it when I told them about it later.

A thought shot across my mind. They'd believe it if they could hear it. Maybe Regan was onto something.

I hopped off the table as fast as I could, my bare butt exposed to the door. I pulled my phone from my pants pocket, opened my voice-recording app, pressed the red button, and set it partially under the edge of my folded-up T-shirt before retaking my seat.

When Dr. Evans came back in at 3:55, he took the seat on the little rolling stool and got right back to the business of making me feel like some kind of manipulative con-artist. "It looks like you don't need a pap smear today. You had one not too long ago with your previous doctor, right?" He glanced up from the chart in his hand. "So we're just going to take a quick peek."

"Right," I answered. I hated how difficult it was for me to force out words. Every time, I'd rehearse the things I wanted to say or the questions I wanted to ask, but then the doctor would come in and everything would get stuck in my throat.

"Okay, just lie back," he said. I put my head on the table and locked my eyes on the ceiling.

There he was again. The cartoon cat of my nightmares. What was it that compelled every one of my gynecologists to put cheesy posters above the exam table? Dr. Evans's poster had Garfield the cat standing at a chalkboard. Whatever had originally been on the poster had been replaced by a hand-drawn card that covered the blackboard words and changed his equation. Now the cat was teaching that PMS is a simple math formula: PMS = pain + moody + snacks.

He asked me to scoot even farther down. (I'd been *sure* this time that I wouldn't need to be adjusted. I am determined to get there someday without being asked.)

"Just try and relax for me," he said.

I let my knees fall open, and I locked eyes with that cat on the ceiling, and I forced my breath in and out. He inserted and opened the speculum, took a little look around, removed it, and told me to sit up. The whole thing couldn't have lasted more than sixty seconds.

"So, let's talk. You're worried that your period is abnormal?"

"Well, I *know* it's abnormal," I said, instantly defensive. I didn't scowl or make a face or anything, but I absolutely wanted to. "I've got really horrible pain, and it usually starts a couple of days before my actual period, then it's at its worst on the first few days of my period, but my period lasts a long time anyway, and sometimes it still hurts even when my period is over."

"When you have your period, your body is shedding and releasing this uterine lining you no longer . . ."

I felt my face getting warm again. I knew what my freaking period was. I waited for him to finish.

"This pain is so bad that I sometimes p-pass out, and I can't go to school."

Why was I stammering? Why did I feel weird and nervous? How many times had I explained this to someone?

He looked at me, and a sly grin crept up the side of his face. "Well, let's just say that I can't give a school excuse to every girl who says her period hurts," he said, chuckling. "You're young. You're still getting used to it. You'll be better able to handle it over time. That's just how it is, unfortunately."

I wanted to correct him, and tell him he was missing the point, completely, but he was already writing on my chart. I remembered then that Dr. Dubois had pointed me to all that information on endo, and that I'd told myself to be brave and ask about it. But as soon as I was about to start asking, he spoke again.

"Are you having sex?"

Even if it was a reasonable question, the way he asked it threw me off.

"No, I'm not."

He made a little note. "Well, there are some indicators that maybe you have a slightly tilted uterus. That can cause painful periods, but there's nothing you can reasonably do about the tilt. You're probably going to have painful sex, too. I just wanted you to know because it's along these same lines. Periods can hurt. Sex can hurt. It's usually normal, and if your uterus is tilted, that's something you'll have to learn to deal with when you become sexually active."

My jaw was barely open with shock. His delivery was shocking.

"So, I'm going to put you on a low-dose birth control pill. That should make your periods a little more predictable, so you'll be able to keep track of when you're going to start. That way you can start taking some over-the-counter pain medicine early enough to head off some of the discomfort you have from your cramps."

I wanted to scream when he started in on predictability. Why do they all assume predictability is the magical cure for everything? "Oh, uh. No, I'm sorry. You're not understanding me. I track my periods religiously. And I've—I've been on birth control before."

"Well, I under—"

"No!" I snapped. I took the deepest breath I could, fueled by frustration, worry, fear, anxiety, and every other horrible feeling that had been flooding my head lately. *This* should at least be easier than all of *that.* "Sorry. I just—" I added under my breath, "I feel like I'm losing my mind." I looked down at my hands. "I can't take it. I'm anxious all the time; I'm feeling depressed. I've done birth control, more than once. It was awful for me. Every time. I had horrible mood swings, and I know it helps some people, but for me it seemed to make the pain worse."

"Delia, you've had scans, bloodwork, ultrasounds, and exams that came back normal."

"Some of those were years ago. Why can't we do new scans? Isn't it your job to figure out what this actually is? What about endometriosis?"

"It's possible, sure. But it's just as possible that it's two dozen other things. And it's also possible that it is nothing at all. I have treated hundreds of patients during my career. Almost every one of them responds as expected to treatment. This is exactly why it's so important for patients to listen to the experts."

"You said *almost* all," I pointed out. "What am I supposed to do if I'm the exception? Somebody is the exception. And what if it's me?"

He scoffed. "It's probably not. Everybody thinks they're an exception, and they're almost always wrong. It would be irresponsible of me to recommend exploratory surgery without being sure that everything else has been tried, and that's why I'm recommending this course of treatment as an option. Maybe you expect that surgery isn't a big deal because of medical shows that pull it off successfully every week, but there are risks. Big risks. Surgery is scary and complicated. People have complications all the time. Why would you want to take that on before we've even figured out if there's anything out of the ordinary?"

His *if* set my brain on fire. "Then I want to talk other procedures that would stop my period. Maybe I'm done. Maybe I can't do this anymore. I read about an in-office procedure where they kind of burn the middle of your uterus and you never have a period anymore. Maybe I need to think about that."

He laughed. It wasn't a chuckle. He actually put his head down and let out a few beats of heavy laughter. "Delia, no doctor in their right mind is going to give you an ablation, or remove your uterus. You're asking to be sterilized. You can't make that sort of decision without thinking about your future life—your future husband and kids."

I shook my head with disbelief.

"You're still young. You wouldn't be able to have kids. Don't you want to be able to have kids someday?"

"I . . . well . . . I don't know."

"See," he said, throwing his hands up in slight exasperation. "You don't even know if you want them and you're going to make a decision as a teenager that will change the course of your life forever? You're *probably* going to want kids, and you're going to look back on these moments and be so glad that nobody let you casually toss away your ability to have a healthy pregnancy. Not to mention, there are many people who had painful periods who say their pain stopped once they had kids. You could find yourself pregnant anytime and then, who knows? You may find you're only nine months away from never having pain again."

I felt my mouth drop open just a crack. He said this as if it were a selling point for teen pregnancy—that maybe it wouldn't be so bad if I got knocked up before too much longer.

He paused to collect his thoughts and then said, "Delia, I'm going to make a referral for you, and I want you to seriously consider what I'm saying, okay?"

"Okay?"

"You're telling me you're experiencing depression, anxiety. You're expressing a willingness to take extreme measures for a medical condition that according to *many* doctors does not exist. It sounds to me like you need some better tools."

Relief surged. "Yes. Exactly. Something has to change. I have to get a diagnosis. Maybe a specialist would be able to—"

"I have a friend who is an absolutely incredible psychiatrist. She could work with you on breathing techniques. Relaxing through the pain. And she could prescribe you something to help with your anxious or paranoid thinking. If you want a diagnosis, you have to consider that's the place you should start. She's brilliant, so smart, and she knows what cramps feel like."

The relief vanished instantly, replaced with rage that made my nerves melt like an ice cube on a hot Texas sidewalk.

He wasn't referring me to someone who could help my body.

He was telling me I was delusional. He thought I was making it up and needed a mental-health intervention.

I imagined my eyes turning to black steel, and I started counting off my fingers.

"She knows what *cramps* feel like? Cramps that make it so that I can't walk or speak. Cramps that make me lose consciousness. Vomiting. Diarrhea. Constipation. Bloating that makes me fluctuate three pant sizes only one day apart. Tremors. And the almost-debilitating anxiety and depression."

He held his hand up, just barely out of his lap but enough to silence me. "I am sorry. I know this is difficult for you to hear." He said this calmly, and it was clear that even though the words were horrible, he hadn't meant them to be mean. "But you have to understand that the overwhelming majority of patients grow out of their fear of their period. It's normal to be scared of this change. But what you're feeling isn't a mysterious medical anomaly. It's common," he said. "And a good doctor is not just going to give you some pain pill and send you on your way."

"I never, ever asked for a 'pain pill'!"

"I hope you'll consider seeing her," he said, tearing the slip of paper off, tapping the notepad, and standing. "Let me guess. You also need an excuse for school?" He made another scribble and tore that off for me too. "I'll make you a deal. If you will commit to three months of this birth control, we can talk about it after, and then, if things are still the same, we'll run more tests. You have my word." Then he held out his hand, I shook it, like an absolute chump, and then he walked out of the room.

I looked at the clock on the wall.

It was 4:01.

Dr. Evans gave me less than a mere twelve minutes of his time . . . and I had the audacity to be excited by his reluctant and conditional promise to return my call if I did what he asked.

In the pile of clothes, my phone was still recording. I could just barely see the little line sliding across the screen as the scribbles of sound passed and flattened in my silence.

CHAPTER TWENTY-FIVE

THE BOTANIST

It wasn't even nine when I flopped down across the foot of my bed that night. I buried my face in my covers for a minute, then rolled over and stared up at the ceiling.

There was no chance of sleep at this point.

I always knock on Regan's door, even though she never knocks on mine. I don't know, maybe I hope the courtesy will subconsciously rub off on her. Anyway, I knocked on her door, and while I stood there, listening, I heard distinct sounds of *oh crap, I'm doing something and I don't want to open the door until I hide the evidence.*

"Hey," she breathed, her face practically pinched by the three inches of door space she allowed. She literally couldn't have looked more suspicious if she'd tried.

"Um. Hi." I shoved the door open and pushed past her.

"What the hell?" she complained.

At first glance, everything looked normal. Her collection of small neon signs—saying things like FML and SAPPHIC AF—all glowed mostly pink and blue on the wall above her bed. She's been known to say that regular bulbs are hideous and have no place in society. She even took the regular bulbs out of the fixture above her bed, which I saw as ridiculous, but then again, I don't have such a particular aesthetic to maintain. So it was very surprising when I scanned the room and saw a light. Bright white light in her closet. The thin strip of open door was like a line of highlighter across the floor.

"You're being weird," I said by way of excuse and explanation.

Regan noticed me noticing the closet light, and for a second we stood still.

At the same time, we both lunged for the closet door. We smashed each other against it, fighting over the door handle and knocking each other back and forth. She's taller than me, and stronger, but I'd had a rough couple of days, and I guess I wanted it just a little more.

I knocked her in the boob, and when she recoiled, I gripped the knob and pulled.

"You hit me in the *boob*? *Seriously?*" she barked.

I didn't answer. I was silent.

At the bottom of her closet, in the spot behind her shoe rack, a desk lamp shone brightly upon the saddest little pot plant the world had ever seen.

I just shook my head a little, then plopped down on the

floor right inside her closet and crossed my legs. It was only a second or two before she sat down in the doorway just behind me.

"I know you told me you grew it, but honestly, I . . ."

Regan set her chin on my shoulder.

We looked at the little plant growing out of a big yellow smiley-face mug. The plant was essentially two bare pale green stalks. There was not a single leaf to be seen, just a few tiny nubs on the sides of the naked stems.

I reached over and picked up the cup, pulling it out of the stream of light.

The yellow mug smiled at me. The plant definitely did not. I stared and stared and then set it back down.

"What are you doing with this decrepit specimen?" I asked.

She hesitated for a second, and when she talked, her chin bobbed up and down on my shoulder.

"I just didn't know if it would keep growing. I wanted to see if it would come back and make leaves again."

"Why? Do you need more leaves? Is this your life now? Are you a bedazzled weed-juice artisan? I don't think there is a track for that at Stockwood."

"Bite me. And, no. I was curious. Do you have any idea how hard it is to make a pot plant grow? This tiny twig-ass plant produced exactly four scrawny leaves after six *months*."

"You had this in the works for six months?" Somehow this was an absolutely jaw-dropping detail. "That's . . . a really long time." Gratitude for my sister swelled, and my nose started to sting. "I don't know what I ever did to deserve you as my sister."

"Don't be—"

"Hey." I interrupted sternly. "No quips. No jokes. Just for a second."

She let her lips draw closed.

"Thank you," I said. She gave a small nod and an even smaller smile. "Okay, that's enough. We can go back to our regularly scheduled reality check. You cannot let this thing keep growing in your closet. You just can't."

"I know."

"But for real . . . if it weren't illegal, you'd be rich making more of that stuff. Those first few drops gave me more relief than I've felt in years. They made me hopeful for the first time in a really long time."

"It was nothing," Regan said, bobbing her chin by my head.

"It wasn't nothing. I mean, it's great that nobody found out you made the dang tincture, but it was a risk that you took for me."

"Anytime," she said.

I reached over and turned off the little desk lamp. The smiley mug looked way less happy without the bright light shining on it.

Regan picked her head up, and the brightness came back to her tone. "It was pretty cool of you not to make a big deal out of that detail. I mean, can you even imagine Mom's face if she knew I grew the pot plant that got you kicked out of Stockwood?"

"Oh, there's no need to imagine it." We froze. It was Mom's voice, and her face, right behind us.

The argument started in Regan's room, where Mom blasted Regan for growing the plant; then it moved to my room for a while, where I got some more heat for taking the tincture; and now we were in the midst of round three in Mom's bedroom, where she was taking more of a combo approach. Mom was pissed all over again about how her two brilliant girls could have made such a wildly horrible string of choices. This time, however, she was absolutely railing on my sister. Regan was a minor who'd bought marijuana seeds off the internet—a practice that was ambiguously, theoretically, and occasionally legal for adults, but certainly not for her.

"It *was* a bad choice"—I started up again—"but it was a choice. She wasn't just being reckless. Regan made that stuff because she'd been researching, and she thought it might help me. She's peeled me up from the bathroom floor so many times, Mom. And even though it ruined everything, you have to know that in the moment, I would have tried anything. I mean, I really can't even imagine what I might have put in my body." The tears stung my eyes even as my lips curled and I tried to fight a deep frown. "The pain is so complete. So . . . impossible. And ignoring the fact that I later took, like, ten times more than I should have, those first couple of drops Regan put under my tongue in the middle of the night were miraculous."

Regan squeezed my hand. I knew right away that her squeeze meant she would do it all over again, just for me.

"The question is, do you trust me? I feel like I've earned your trust, Mom."

She pursed her lips sideways and said, "You know I trust you."

Regan chimed in, "And do you trust me?"

"Hell no. Absolutely not. And to prove it, you're grounded for a month."

Regan pulled a facial expression that said *fair enough,* and we all grinned at each other.

"Well, since you do trust *me,*" I said, giving Regan a wink, "you are just going to have to believe that at the time, in that moment, I really believed it was my only option, okay?"

She was quiet. She started to say something, and then she pulled back.

I pushed her to just say it. "Come on. What?"

"I . . . It's only that you've had it bad before. For a long while. Really bad. But you've always been able to . . . I don't know . . . push through it? It just seems like such an incredible jump from something that you're suffering through but surviving, to something that you're just letting completely steamroll you."

My eyes closed against the hurtful words, and my heart lurched in my chest. *"Letting?"*

"I didn't mean . . . you know what I mean," she said, trying to backpedal. "How has it become suddenly insurmountable? I know you're tired . . . none of this is coming out right."

I was exhausted. "Mom, I've already lost so much. I had a chance to have this wildly successful life. It was right there. A first-rate university, a relationship with an expert. I was gonna be a doctor. I've lost almost everything. I really, really can't deal with thinking your faith in me is gone too."

Regan gave me an impressed thumbs-up, which I waved away with a roll of my eyes.

Mom nodded slowly. "What do you mean you *were* going to be a doctor? Just because you can't take this one route does not mean you can't get there." She shook her head.

"I'm tired, Mom. I've had a lot of time to think about it since everything went down, and honestly, I just don't know anymore. I wanted this thing, but I think I wanted it for all the wrong reasons. Is it reasonable to decide to *be* a doctor because I *need* a good doctor? I can admit it—I really screwed this up. I think we both know none of this should have happened."

"Speak for yourself. I'd do it again in a second." Regan grinned.

"Come here, girls. I love you both so much. You know that right?" She waved us over, and we made our little triangle hug.

"Well, speaking of good doctors that I definitely haven't had yet . . . the new doctor today was completely unhinged."

"What happened?" Mom asked. "Damn it, Delia, I told you that I needed to be there. I knew it."

"I'm not having the same fight with you again, Mom."

"Don't tell me what we're not fighting about! I'm the boss of you, and I am very intimidating, and I'm so mad at myself for letting you win this one. I just don't understand why you didn't call me over once you decided he was being an ass? You knew I was just across the street considering which toddler-sized scented candle I had to buy."

"I already told you. I wanted to try to deal with it. You know I'm really trying. But can we pause the repeat of our spat and focus on the point? This guy . . ." I reached into my back pocket, took out my phone, and pulled up the audio recording.

"It can't possibly be worse than the Star-Spangled Pap Smear guy," Regan said.

"Well, the punch line for this one is that he referred me to a shrink, told me it was normal for sex to hurt, and implied that I was trolling for drugs."

Mom's face did the one-two punch of growing wide with shock and then shrinking in anger. "He said *what*? Press play right now."

"I'll get the popcorn," Regan said.

CHAPTER TWENTY-SIX

A REALLY BAD PARTY FAVOR

Keisha's house is the kind of big that makes you feel like you don't understand wealth as much as you thought you did. Like, the kind of big where you know that no matter how much you work, even if you have an incredibly high-paying job in a regular sort of way, there's absolutely no chance you'll ever have a house this big. It's the kind of big where they have a pool inside and also outside, and more bathrooms than bedrooms, and a library with a rolling ladder going up the wall. It's a wonderland.

It felt odd to arrive at a party that might have been partly mine. I'd planned on being part of this big Stockwood graduation celebration's setup and taking my rightful place in the hostessing trio with Pri and Key. But in a moment of depression this week, after Ruby and I'd spent days avoiding both of the boys we couldn't stand to be in the same room with, I'd told my besties that there was no way I could really do much right now. Life was too out of control.

The music was loud when I entered, even though it was playing in a completely different part of the house. Stockwood's best and brightest were living it up, celebrating the near end of the most challenging years of their lives. I wandered into the kitchen and found Priya and Keisha hanging out by an absolute mountain of red plastic cups just waiting for drinks to be poured.

I was grateful for the Stockwood-only party, and I was so glad to ignore BHS for the night. I was desperate to forget about all those people who had noticed my running with Ruby to the nurse, watched me get bathroom passes out of class nearly every day, or seen me being wheeled down the hallway looking green.

"D!" Priya squealed, ran forward, and tackled me with a full-body hug. Keisha joined us, and we huddled together in a ball.

"You're so late! We weren't sure if you were still coming. But we're so glad you're here," Keisha said, giving my arm a squeeze.

Something about the use of the word *we,* meaning them and not me, made my heart ache.

"Yeah, it's been a really bad pain week. But this party is something we've planned for literal years, so I really couldn't miss it."

"No Ruby?" Priya asked.

"She wasn't feeling well enough. It's just me."

"Just nothing. You're everything, my love." Priya gave me a little squeeze.

"Well, it's good that you came because we got you a present," Keisha said. "Stay here, get a drink, and we'll send it in."

They ran out of the kitchen, giggling with each other, and I took the chance to sit on one of the large wooden stools along the island. People came in and out, grabbing snacks and new cans of soda, shouting and dancing, and a few minutes later a familiar voice found its way over my shoulder.

"Hey, Trip."

Caleb gave me a slightly awkward hug that was so far from what a hug from Caleb should be that it was almost unpleasant.

"What . . . what are you doing here?" I asked.

His grin fell. "I . . . well, your friends texted me to come, and you'd had like a week to cool off. I assumed you told them to invite me? They didn't know that we . . . I thought you . . . ah man."

I was embarrassed and sad at the look on his face. His gorgeous face. He reached up and ran a palm over his cheek.

"You . . . didn't ask them to invite me, did you?" he asked.

I looked down, over, up, and down again before shaking my head. "But I can say thank you for the other day. Thanks for helping me get to the nurse. I'm sorry I was a little intense about everything. It was a bad day."

"But . . . you meant what you said, I guess." He shoved his hands into his pockets and straightened his arms out all the way. I took a moment to think, looking at him, remembering the feeling of his lips on mine. My cheeks flushed. Before I could answer, he spoke again. "I just want you to tell me one thing, and then I'll leave you alone, if that's really what you want." He stepped closer, making the space between us unreasonably small. "Why does it seem like you only want me gone when I'm checking on your—*obvious, by the way*—health issue? Why is my asking if you're okay, wanting to help you, to make sure you're all right . . . why does that seem to be the only time you push me away?"

A thud in the middle of my body radiated pain to every inch of my skin. My eyes closed tight, only for a second.

"See? You're obviously going through something awful. In the hall that day, you were so pale you were almost blue. I watched your eyes roll back into your head and caught you before you collapsed on the floor. This isn't a reason not to like somebody. I just don't get it. Have I done something to make you not trust me? Is it so impossible that I might want to be there for you? Help you?"

"It's not impossible, Caleb. It's certain. I have the most wonderful people around me, and they're all constantly doing the *work* of being there for me. I don't want that for you, okay? It doesn't make me feel desirable or cool or sexy to have the guy I'm falling for playing nurse."

I got up, instantly full of regret for having come to the party at all.

I walked toward the front door, and of course he followed me out of the kitchen. I grabbed the doorknob and paused as my body clenched. The pain was so infuriatingly brief.

"So what if we're just friends, then?" he asked, right as I opened the door and stepped into the night. "If we're just friends, then would you let me drive you home? You've got that weird coloring again. You don't look good."

I was embarrassed to hear him say that I looked awful. That was exactly what I didn't need right now.

"I don't need any more friends, Caleb. And I don't need a ride home. I just need to get out of here, out of high school, out of this town. I just need anything other than this life."

I closed the door behind me, leaving him in the foyer at a house party full of people he didn't know.

I climbed in the Woolly Mammoth, turned it on, and pulled away from the dozens of cars on Keisha's gorgeous tree-lined street. I didn't want to be here. But I didn't want to go home. The only thing left to do was drive. I wanted to go—to get on the road and drive until there were thousands of stars.

Highways in Dallas are a new driver's worst nightmare and best teacher. We have to conquer the fear of getting on the highway or else we are stuck with an hour-long journey to get anywhere. But once you're on the highway, the speed limits are fast, the roads are straight, and the rhythm of the concrete under your wheels is a lot like a heartbeat. Leaving Uptown, heading north, I spent the first few minutes thinking just about the road. But once I was situated, I couldn't clear him out of my brain. Caleb's face punctuated my thoughts with every streetlight I passed. For the first minute I was calm, but for the next few minutes I felt my breathing catch with each inhale. And by the time I had the cruise control on, I was crying over everything that I wasn't able to control.

As my hands held the steering wheel, I sensed that my grip had gotten tighter and tighter as the pain in my abdomen grew. I told myself to relax, to breathe, but there was no way to make my body listen to my mind. The next burst of pain drew a low, loud moan from my lips that I couldn't breathe through. Panic threatened to slink from the shadowy corners of my mind, but I made myself focus on the road and the shape of it, stretched out through one of a thousand suburbs on the way home. As the blood drained from my face, my skin got clammy, my nose chilled, and my vision became peppered with black stars.

You have to get home.

You have to pull over.

I tried to convince myself that one of those truths was worthy of winning, but the battle between them had me locked into place. Nothing like this had ever happened before. It wasn't reasonable. None of this was reasonable.

Another sob, a wail of pain, and my stomach lurched. Nausea churned in my belly, and the other cars kept flying past me while I argued with myself about what I should do.

More pain. More self-doubt. More fear.

Pull over. Pull over.

You're fine.

Get home.

Calm down.

You have to get home.

I felt my head wobble on my neck as I got into the right lane. I thought about stopping on the shoulder, but the first reasonable exit for Blythe was only a quarter of a mile away.

Anyone would say it was too dramatic to stop on the side of the highway because of a period cramp. I was being ridiculous. I could make it. I would exit, pull over somewhere. Park, call Mom.

I would.

I could.

But before I did, my eyes fluttered, my hands fell, and the Mammoth veered into the guardrail with a thunderous scrape followed by the furious crunch as it smashed into the base of a light pole.

Everything was loud, and then quiet, and then dark.

CHAPTER TWENTY-SEVEN

THE ABSENCE OF PAIN

My eyes fluttered open once, but closed again right away.

In that moment I saw my hospital room. Mom was sitting in the chair beside my bed. Regan was in the corner, slumped over and sleeping in the other, more comfortable-looking chair. My legs were draped with a light blue blanket, and there was a TV above the bed, but it was off.

The next things my brain processed were the sounds outside my room. Talking, random movements, beeps, and bumps. My own breathing. My own heartbeat, a dull thud in my ears.

And once the sights and sounds had been accounted for, my brain had time to focus on the biggest sensory input of all. Pain.

My heart started to thud more heavily in my chest, and

then I realized that one of the beeps I'd heard was my own monitor with its volume down low.

My mouth pulled into an involuntary deep frown, and my eyes, still closed, flooded with tears, which slipped out and down my cheeks.

"Delia! Delia, baby?" Mom sounded frantic as she shouted out the open door, "Nurse!"

One arrived just as I cracked my eyes open.

"Momma. Momma!" I felt my voice croak first, then get louder and stronger. I sounded desperate and afraid.

Deep, sharp pain filled my abdomen, and it radiated through both thighs and behind my back. It was brutal and unrelenting.

Mom answered, sounding similarly panicked, as the nurse addressed the beeping and checked more little screens all around me. "I'm here, baby. I'm right here. It's okay. You're okay."

"I'm not!" I wailed. "I'm not! Momma, please. I can't!"

"Can you tell me your name?" The nurse tried to draw my focus. "I need you to try and tell me your name."

"I can't," I cried. "I . . . Delia."

"That's good," the nurse said. "You've been in a car accident. You don't have any broken bones or significant injuries we can find. But you may be experiencing shock right now. I need you to breathe."

As she spoke, I was crying uncontrollably, but I wanted her to understand. I knew that here, at the hospital, there would have to be answers. I didn't want to be in the hospital, of course, but if I had to be, maybe they could find something. Anything that would help me make sense. "Please," I said, "it hurts so bad."

"We can definitely give you something for the pain, but I need you to try to tell me what hurts, okay? We need to know if there is anything else wrong. You have some bruising on your forehead and chest from your airbag and seat belt. You have some scrapes on your arms."

I tried to calm myself down so I could speak, so I could be understood. So she wouldn't write me off as a liar. I took my hand, the one that wasn't attached to an IV, and brought it to my abdomen. "It hurts. Please. My uterus. I can't."

Each word was slow and punctuated by ragged breaths.

A second nurse had entered at the sound of my sobs. The nurses spoke to each other while Mom was silent from stress and worry.

"We just got the scans, and there are no signs of internal bleeding. Her appendix is normal. There are no particular areas of bruising developing on her abdomen." They chattered about the bathroom, the buttons beside my bed, and the TV remote. I didn't care.

The first nurse spoke to me again in gentle tones. "Delia, can you tell me where you're feeling pain?" She reached for my abdomen, way up under my ribs. "Here?"

"No. I told you. Please. Down here."

She took a hand and gently pressed over the right side of my pelvis, and I wailed for my mother one more time before I passed out.

* * *

The second time I woke, everything was quiet. The door to my room was completely closed, Regan was gone, but Mom was still sitting in the chair by my bed.

When I called for her, my mom almost jumped up and into the bed with me, she was so close to my face.

"How do you feel? Are you okay?" she asked.

"It's . . . gone," I said. "It's gone."

My body felt heavy, still, and calm. My eyes were full of tears again, but this time I wasn't crying because of pain. This time I was crying because of the absence of it. My heart felt like it would burst with joy, and my smile grew so big, it felt foreign to the muscles of my face. There had been so many uncountable hours, days, and weeks of pain. Small pains, big ones. Sharp and broad. High and low. Acute and spreading. There had been pain, some sort of pain, for most moments of most days for most of my memory. And there in that hospital bed, my body was hollow. Emptied of pain. Not even a ghost of it bouncing around the walls of my wicked body. Euphoric, manic joy rose up and out of my mouth in a laugh. The sound of it faded as a warm stillness came back into the front of my mind.

"What's gone, honey?"

"The pain. I can't feel any pain."

"They gave you something strong for the pain. It should have taken the worst of it so you could sleep."

"No, Mom." Even half-asleep and drugged, I was tired

of feeling impossible to understand. "I can't feel any pain in my uterus. None. Nothing. And it's—" My voice caught in my throat. "Mom, I haven't felt this in years. I don't know what to do. I . . . I don't want it. I know you're going to say I haven't thought this through, but I promise I have. Please. I want you to tell them to take it out. All of it. Momma." I sobbed. "I know you are going to be upset with me if I can't have a baby. I know you want me to have a grandkid for you someday, but I promise I'll use a surrogate or adopt or something. I don't want you to miss out on that, but I can't." I coughed and sputtered. "Please, Momma. I can't do this anymore. I'm so tired of hurting. Of feeling alone. I am so tired of being a chore and a burden. Nobody believes me. Nobody cares, Mom."

"Honey, that's not true. Plenty of people believe you. We'll figure it out. I promise we will."

"I can't wait anymore. You heard Dr. Evans. That's how they all feel. He just had the guts to say it out loud."

A knock at the door, and I heard Regan's voice from the other side of the little curtain that blocked my bed from the hall. "Just a second," she told someone.

"Hey, sis." She came around the curtain, made a beeline for my bed, and with glistening eyes of her own took my hand. "I'm so glad you're okay."

"Me too," I said.

"Well, she's been dying to see you, and the nurse told me you woke up, so I brought her back."

"Who?" I asked.

"Who in the hellfire and tarnation do you think?" Ruby

said, billowing the curtain out beside her as she came to my bedside. "How are you, sugar biscuit?"

I grinned. "I think I'm okay."

"I should have gone with you . . . to the party. I'm sorry I stayed home. I—"

"No way. Absolutely not," I said. My sluggish speech took a moment to formulate in my mind and my mouth. "You didn't feel good. You get to not go when you don't feel good." I sounded so much like my sister.

Ruby reached over and put a hand on the side of my head. "I'm sorry I didn't understand that when we were kids. I really am."

"I know. I'm sorry too."

"I'm going to go out and talk to the nurse about what's next, okay, love?" Mom came over, kissed my head, and left us alone.

Regan said, "I can't believe you tried to kill the Woolly Mammoth. Don't you know those are going extinct?"

"Oh no," I said sadly. "Is it okay?"

"Are you kidding? That thing is a tank. It's never gonna die," she answered. Regan had my phone in her hand and said, "So I did get a message to Priya and Keisha, but they are still at the party and it isn't a good idea for either of them to drive. They're gonna come see you in the afternoon tomorrow . . . er . . . today."

I nodded. "Great."

"But there is one other thing," she said. "Caleb was texting you . . . kind of a lot. He was asking if you got home okay, and then of course at first I didn't answer, but then he got worried and called, and I couldn't just let him freak out. Especially since, well, the thing he was afraid of happening had actually happened. So I told him about the wreck, and, well—"

"Let me guess," I interrupted. "He came up here to see me?"

Regan looked at me for an extra second before she spoke. "Actually, no. He didn't ask to come. He kinda just got quiet and then said that he's glad you're gonna be okay, and that he'd see you around sometime. It was very obviously *not* a plan to see you. What's the deal with that? I thought you guys really liked each other."

Ruby chimed in. "They do. Delia's just got the brains of a scarecrow."

"Listen here, 'Dorothy,' don't start this crap with me again. If anyone should understand this, it should be you. Especially now that Iggy enacted your breakup a few weeks early for exactly this reason. Why should he take on any of this? I mean, I feel like I already have enough people carrying the burden of being my support system. Why would I need *him* to, specifically?"

"Well, *I'm* sure not gonna make out with you," Ruby said.

"You're being ridiculous. You're just going to, what? Be alone forever?" Regan rolled her eyes. It was nice to see that her sympathetic bedside manner had already expired.

I let her words hang in the air, though, the button for my IV pain medication under my thumb. Maybe I would be alone forever. Maybe that was all I could actually have: A great mom and sister. A few good friends. But otherwise on my own. Some people get to have everything, and some people don't. Someone had to draw that card. Maybe it was me.

As Ruby and Regan continued to chatter, my eyelids drooped. I blinked, slowly, watching them come in and out of focus, until my eyes closed and didn't open again until morning.

CHAPTER TWENTY-EIGHT

NERVES OF STEELE

The next day, Sunday, I was released with little more than a few bruises and scrapes and told to go on my way. The doctor on call had taken pity on me after I begged her to cut me open and give me a diagnosis. I'd panicked and started to hyperventilate at the idea of the pain meds wearing off, and she'd given me a small prescription for pain medication that I could use in case of emergency and some prescription-strength patches I could stick on my lower abdomen.

All packed up, we left the room, passed the nurses' station, and made our way through the hospital maze toward the exit we needed. As we rounded a corner, I stopped short, almost plowing right into none other than Dr. Steele himself. He was dressed head to toe in the most impossibly obnoxious scrubs that could have been designed. They were covered entirely with footballs, big ones and small ones—every single inch from head to toe (including his scrub cap) was brown and white.

I spoke automatically, and probably startled him for no good reason. "Dr. Steele! Oh my god, hi! What are you doing here? It's me, Delia Bridges. Stockwood Prep."

He smiled at me, a good-natured, surprisingly un-angry smile that I was sure I didn't deserve. "Delia? Hi. How are you?"

"I just got in a car accident. I'm fine. I ran into a pole. I was slowing when I hit it, so it wasn't as bad as it sounds. I mean, it was still bad, of course—it was a head-on collision, so obviously not good—but you know, it wasn't that bad. All things considered. How about you?"

Speaking to this man obviously turned me into a blithering buffoon.

He smiled at me, gave a little chuckle, and said, "Your thoughts really do just pop right out, don't they?" He gave a little wink before reaching a hand out to my mom. "I'm Dr. Steele. To answer your question, I just finished up a surgery. I'm on my way to check on my patient."

"It's great to meet you," Mom said. "I've heard so much about you. You're something of a symbol of hope. A unicorn among doctors. We wish there were more like you." She gave a nod and told me she'd be across the waiting room if I needed her.

"Since you're here, Delia," the doctor said, "I hope you'll accept my apology for not following up with you after your message. My schedule is impossible, as I know you've heard.

I've got an email half drafted in response, but I haven't found the time to finish and send it. I wanted you to know that there are absolutely no hard feelings on my end. I really was very excited to work with you on your mentorship, and I'm sorry it didn't work out. Truly."

Even though his words were obviously kind, they landed like a punch in the face. Hearing him say it out loud, admit that it was all over, was painful.

"Dr. Steele, I was wondering if there was anything at all that I could do to prove to you that I would still be the best mentee you could possibly take on. I was thinking that if you would be willing to still be my mentor next year, Gleeson University would probably put me back in the accepted pile, which would be great. I've already applied to several other schools, and I even have a couple of acceptances, but Gleeson is the dream. I'm sure you understand." I was rambling again. I took a deep breath. "Anyway, if you would just consider if there is anything at all I could do to prove myself to you, I know I wouldn't let you down."

"No," he said calmly while he slowly, sadly shook his head back and forth. "I'm sorry, but that's not going to work out."

I felt my hands shaking again, and my neck got hot.

"Doctor, I know that day was embarrassing for you. It was incredibly embarrassing for me, too. I am so sorry for what I said about your name. I accept full responsibility for what happened. But I assure you, that's not who I am, and if you reinstate me as your mentee, I will show you just how incredibly capable I am."

"I have no doubt that you're capable. And I can promise

you that my ego has nothing to do with my decision. As a doctor, thick skin is one thing you can't lose track of. But even so, I won't be serving as your mentor."

He said this last bit with an almost smile on his face. Not like he was trying to be evil or anything—he just had a peaceful finality to his demeanor. My adrenaline kicked in.

"Dr. Steele, you don't understand my situation—"

"Delia, can you promise you'll let me say a few things before you respond? I'm not quite as good at talking as you." He made a big smile and widened his eyes.

I laughed and nodded that I would listen rather than talk. I stood there rubbing my thumb across the back of my hand. There was a sting behind my nose, but it wasn't there for long. I swallowed once, and it was gone.

"There are a lot of really important things doctors have to know. There's all the obvious stuff, the stuff you've already started learning—the body and the blood and the science of it all. But that's not the part that's actually hard to learn. The hard stuff is learning how to tell a mother her baby is gone, or how to know when to push through a certain rule because you know you might just save a life if, and only if, you break it. Learning that you can't count on plan A always working out. But I think one of the biggest lessons a doctor has to learn— one that's possibly the hardest to teach young doctors—is that their choices have consequences. Everybody thinks they know that, but when you're holding somebody's well-being, somebody's life, in your hands, you quickly realize how high the stakes are. Every bad decision has consequences. Every minute you don't sleep that makes you drowsy, every mile you speed over the limit, every second you wait before you act has permanent, irreversible consequences that you can't always predict."

I nodded. Everything he said was like gold in my heart.

"I will not be your mentor, Delia, but it's not because of what happened with your school, or the comments about my name. It's not even because you showed a serious lack of good judgment when you got high or brought that bottle to school. It's because I know that I have a chance right here and now to make a bigger impact on your future by telling you no than I ever could by telling you yes. I have one chance to show you how hard the impacts of your choices can hit. You were going to be my final mentee anyway, but with you out of the program, I'm going to start my retirement a little earlier than I planned."

"You're really retiring early?" I asked. My stomach dropped. Part of me must have still held a flicker of hope that eventually I'd make my way to the top of the new-patient list.

"I am. I don't have all the details worked out yet. I'm not exactly sure when it's going to be officially over, but I'm handing the reins of my practice fully over to Dr. Dubois."

My eyes opened wide. "Oh, wow. That's amazing."

"She's amazing. A fantastic doctor, and a fantastic surgeon. But, Delia, med school is going to be so much harder than you can imagine. You're going to fail more tests. Lots more. It sounds like high school was easy for you, am I right?"

I nodded slowly. "With the exception of the past few weeks, I'd say so."

"Well, then, if you want to be a doctor, you need to look

at those weeks, and the next many months and years of your life, as the new normal. You're going to have setbacks and self-doubt, and you're going to be pushed so far from comfort, you won't even remember what it feels like when it's all over. But it's worth it. And if you choose to stick it out, and push through that, you could be an incredible doctor. These plans changed, but you've got fight in you. You're going to find the route to what's next, whatever you decide that is. And I wish you all the luck in the world."

I sniffed back the sting in my nose. "Thank you."

He reached up, gave my shoulder a gentle squeeze, and walked down the hall deeper into the hospital.

CHAPTER TWENTY-NINE

LESSONS IN FUTILITY

On Monday morning, when I got to the corner where Caleb and I had been meeting to walk together (after days of getting to school an hour early so I wouldn't run into him), I saw him at least three blocks ahead of me. He hadn't waited. I shouldn't have thought he would after a week of walking without me, but still, knowing he knew about the wreck, part of me wondered if he might. He'd been clear in the way he'd talked to Regan that he wasn't going to keep trying to make this happen with me. Which sucked. But I had absolutely no right to expect anything else. I'd absolutely demolished our relationship before it really started.

Ruby had made me swear that I would keep my butt in the chair at school for the last four days no matter what, but the rumors had swirled into action and the seniors were planning to walk out some time this week in honor of Ruby's situation. Some of the cooler teachers had talked to the seniors in their classes about how to "skip responsibly," which basically meant not skip unless they had absences saved up. Sure, for a lot of kids it was mostly an excuse to cut class for a cause, which was nonsense, but it made them feel better about themselves and made their choice more defensible to their parents.

My group project with Iggy was finally over. Last week during class, Iggy and I had tried to behave as if we didn't even recognize each other. Now that we'd turned in the work and gotten our grades (we had presented first), we spent the rest of the class time at our desks, listening to the others make presentations. He and I glanced at each other a few times, but we didn't talk. And at lunchtime, Ruby and I surveyed the cafeteria after a week of eating in the courtyard and found Iggy and Caleb sitting on the other side of the room, far from our old table. With only a few days left, our little circle was dwindling. The friends in outer rings of closeness with Ruby were fine, but it wasn't the same.

"You have to tell somebody about what Dr. Evans said," Ruby continued as she picked at her buttered noodles. "I know you're worried about him getting madder'n a tick or whatever, but he's your doctor. He's supposed to be taking care of you, and instead he was an absolute jerk. I think you should post it all over the internet—make him go viral for being an ass. Don't you think the internet would lose their minds if you posted that? It would serve him right."

"Maybe, but he also said he'd run more tests on me.

Several more. That's closer to what I want than any other doctor so far. That's the best offer I've had, you know what I mean? I have to do three months of this birth control pill he likes, and that's it."

"You're going to take them? I thought you were aggressively against birth control pills."

"Well, yeah, I hate them, but I have no choice if I want his tests. So, I feel like I'm being held hostage by his prescription, but what else can I do?"

"That's it, huh? In three months, you will hopefully be on your way to college, once you stop being stubborn and pick one, that is, and he's going to be here trying to get you to keep doing the treatment plan he thinks is the right answer. I don't understand why you would trust him at all when he's given you zero indication of being trustworthy."

"Well, what exactly would you suggest I do, Ruby?"

"I don't know, man. I'm not saying you haven't been fighting in your own way, but you could fight louder. You say you want to make a difference, and a way to do that is sitting in your hand!" she said with more intensity than I'd have expected. "I'm over here shitting my pants, but I'm also writing letters to the mayor and the school board. I'm trying to drum up interest in a protest. I'm trying to get a reporter to call me back for a news story. I don't know, I'm just trying to figure out why you've been so . . . just a . . . passenger in all this? If it's so bad, I just don't get why you aren't raising all hell."

"*If?*" I said, my defenses standing up at attention. "*If* it were actually bad, I'd be acting like you? And since I'm not, what does that mean? That it isn't so bad?" I pushed myself up and off my chair, frustrated and ready to be somewhere else. Ruby wasn't going to pressure me to stay, and I couldn't tell if that was making me feel better or worse. "I had a *future*, Ruby . . . I had plans to be something great. But now all I have is schools I don't care about and one doctor who may be able to help me prove that all of this is real. Because it *is* real. Tell me the truth. After all we've been through these past few weeks, do you really still just see me as the drama queen who ruined your birthday party?"

"Well, aren't you just sharp as a marble?" Ruby quipped, rolling her eyes. "You know I don't think that."

I grabbed my stuff from the table. "Sure you do. I mean, what's more dramatic than running my car into a pole because of some period cramps, right?"

I stormed out and didn't check over my shoulder.

And for the second time since middle school, Ruby just let me go.

That night, when Priya and Keisha got to my house, they had a bouquet of flowers that was as big around as an extra-large pizza. They'd been too busy recovering from their party and studying for finals on Sunday to make it to the hospital before I was discharged, so they hadn't actually seen me since I'd left the party and literally gotten wrecked. I didn't want to be jealous, but it was crawling all over me. We'd sat on the floor of my room about a million times, but this was the first time in forever that it was mostly quiet. None of us could get a conversation to stick.

After exhausting six or seven talking points within the first half hour, I decided to get what I actually needed from them: some empathy about how bad it all was. Caleb couldn't feel as strongly as he'd said. Ruby didn't actually believe me. I was right to play nice with Dr. Evans and try to get closer to a diagnosis at the end of the summer. Principal Davis was never going to change his mind about school policy, so I definitely couldn't join some protest walkout and get marked absent for the eleventh time.

"We're on your side, like we always are," Priya said, painting the second coat on her next finger before passing the nail polish around. (We'd perfected the at-home polish by slowing it down and rotating after every nail and every coat.) "But . . ."

I swiped the rosy color on my left thumbnail. "I really don't want to hear the second half of that thought."

"Best friends get to say the hard stuff," Keisha said. "That's the deal."

I handed the bottle to her and tried to do anything but huff like a child.

"We've just noticed that you're pushing and pushing, and you deserve friends who will tell you so," Priya added. "Like, you like Caleb, but you're pushing him away. You got hurt by us for hosting the party without you—don't try to deny it— after you told us you didn't want to do it. You're pushing Ruby away. You're pushing med school away. You have backup schools you could say yes to today, but you're dragging your heels 'cause you're what? Holding out hope that if you go slow enough, everything will come back together? You're pushing away the future you can actually have to preserve the memory of a future that's *gone.* That doctor is never going to be the doctor you need. And like Ruby told you, you have the power to tell the world what it's like to come in, ask for help, and be told you're just nuts."

"You're going through a lot right now, and we know how independent you are, but you don't have to deal with all of this all alone." Keisha passed the bottle back to Priya.

"There are a lot of people who have done nothing wrong in this situation—including you, by the way," Priya said. "So why can't you point your fire at all the people who deserve it instead of picking fights with the people on your side?"

I sat on the edge of my bed and flopped backward so I could look up at the ceiling.

Priya finished her manicure and handed the bottle to Keisha, who ever so carefully painted my last nail.

"Have you decided if you're gonna to come to graduation?" Priya asked gently, after a few more seconds of silence.

I wiped the tear that was streaking down the side of my face. "Why? None of it matters anymore."

"Just because they have loud voices doesn't mean you have to let them have the last word," Keisha said, kissing the back of my hand. "You know we love you, but we do have to head out. Finals, blah-blah."

"Love you," Priya said, standing and grabbing her bag.

"I love you, too," I told them as they backed out of my

room and closed the door. I let my neck release and my chin turn to face the pinboard opposite my bed. Who was that girl? She was a stranger.

When the moon came up, I was still wide awake. I wanted to sleep, but only kinda. I had been lying there, thinking and trying to figure out what the hell I was going to do with my future, fall semester, graduation, or even just the next twenty-four hours.

I was flailing. I'd been in free fall for weeks, and I was tired and sore. Literally sore.

From running my car into a pole.

I got up, dug in the clean laundry pile, pulled out Caleb's shirt, and held it against me. What was I doing? I put it on and slipped out the front door. It wasn't that late, but Mom and Regan had already retired to their rooms.

I walked down the sidewalk, stepping over the cracks and around pools of light to keep my brain busy. I turned and found myself at the corner where Caleb and I had been meeting, and a lump formed in my throat. The air had been warming steadily for the past several days, but it was still breezy. I sat on the curb and wrapped my arms around my knees, staring out into the streets that were sleeping and quiet. The sky was still more blue than black, but the stars had come out. There weren't even half as many visible now as there had been on the Mackenzie Street Bridge, on the only prom night I'd ever have. My history, my story, had already been so changed. Nothing had turned out how I thought it would. I hadn't graduated from Stockwood with my 4.3 GPA; I hadn't landed that mentorship; I wasn't going to Gleeson; I was struggling to decide how I felt about med school. Everything was tangled.

"Hey." Caleb's voice was soft behind me, but I still jerked at being startled. "Sorry, sorry," he said, holding up his hands.

"Hey," I said. "What are you doing out here?"

"Just coming back from Iggy's. How about you?"

I turned away from him, looking past the glow of the streetlamp. "Just thinking. Taking a walk. Do you wanna sit?" I gestured but didn't turn. I didn't want to see his face if his answer was no.

A moment of silence was brushed away when he took the two steps toward the curb and sat down beside me. But once he was seated, everything was still again, and the quiet came back to the street.

"So, I've got really bad periods," I announced.

He didn't reply, but I could see the very slight nod that he rocked back and forth.

"Really bad. Worse than they should be," I added. "But I don't know what's wrong. It's horrible, and it's scary. Most of the time, the only thing I have room for in my life is pain, anxiety, and fear."

I turned to look at him, and he waited a moment before turning his head too.

"I got kicked out of my super-intense college-prep high school a few weeks ago because I tried to self-medicate with marijuana drops my kid sister whipped up for me in the bottom of her closet. I went to campus, got so high I fell down the stairs, got busted with the drug paraphernalia, and torched my fast track to med school by calling my mentor a stripper."

His eyes widened with every word. By the end he looked like a cartoon character whose eyes were popping in and out of his head.

"I'm a mess, Caleb. I don't know what I'm doing. I don't know what's wrong with me. I don't know what any day will be like. I'm really sorry. It's not an excuse, but I hope you know deep down that in my own way I am trying to protect you." I swallowed.

"Protect me? From what? From you?"

"Having feelings for me . . . being in my life . . . it isn't easy. It's frustrating and annoying. There is always something wrong or something unexpected. And I know how much we like each other, but we're young and there's no reason for you to sign up for some highly difficult and taxing relationship that takes and takes and never gives."

"Is that what you think?" he asked.

"I think it's exhausting to love me."

"No, it's exhausting to *try*." Caleb had a frustrated look on his face, and he wrapped his knees with both arms. He turned to look at me with an expression of confusion, hope, and compassion. I couldn't resist the urge, so I brought a finger up and brushed it lightly across the back of his hand. It only lasted a second, but it made my skin buzz. He continued, "You're so worried that you're a burden, you're not considering that some costs are worth paying. I know we're five minutes from the next epic chapter of our lives, and I'm not fooling myself about what this is—I know we don't know what's coming. But you were more willing to drive your car off the road than you were to let me be there for you. You're so busy trying to run away from what's real right now, you don't even care that you're running toward a future that, as of right now, is completely imaginary."

His words echoed my own revelation in a way that made my whole body feel warm. I knew he might not be my forever, but I wanted him to be my now.

I paused, turning over my fears before saying them out loud. "What if it gets too hard? What if it turns out that I'm not actually worth all this?" I gestured vaguely around me. My thoughts jumped to my sister, my mom, my friends, my doctors, my teachers. "What if I'm not worthy of this much effort or time or love or any of it? What if I'm too much?"

"The only person who thinks you're too much is you," he said.

I leaned over, ran a hand across his cheek, and brought my lips to his.

The smell of his skin rushed in with my breath, and his hand made its way behind my head, his fingers gently cupping the back of my neck. "I knew you were conspiring to keep my shirt," he whispered. He ran his hand down my arm, down the sleeve, and took my hand. When we finally pulled apart, his eyes were sparkling and bright. "I have to go back to Iggy's. But I'll see you in the morning, right here?" He stood, reached for me, and helped pull me up.

"Iggy's? But it's so late." My cheeks were still flushed, my lips rosy and warm.

He turned to walk backward, the wrong way from his house.

"Yeah, but he owes me another ten bucks."

I grinned. "Let me guess. You made a bet that I'd come to my senses and realize we're made for each other?"

He continued taking steps backward without turning around.

"Easy money."

CHAPTER THIRTY

OR FOREVER HOLD YOUR PEACE

The next morning, I got up and got dressed—a standard pair of soft joggers and a T-shirt to stay cool. I dabbed a little makeup on the greenish bruises that remained on my cheekbone from the wreck. Caleb and I walked to school, and as soon as I turned the corner, I felt my heart crawl up my throat.

There were dozens and dozens of people, some students but many just involved citizens, standing in front of the school. Most were holding signs and chanting, though I couldn't make out their refrain just yet. As I approached, their words got louder. Their signs got clearer:

CREDIT IS CREDIT
AN HOUR IS AN HOUR
SCHOOLS AREN'T DOCTORS

A few more steps and I could hear the chant, too.

"Two, four, six, eight! They just want to graduate!"

It wasn't exactly surprising to get toward the front of the crowd and find Ruby there with her parents. I was passing too close by to ignore them—not that I wanted to, necessarily.

I told Caleb I needed to talk to Ruby, and he left me and headed into the school after kissing me on my head. He planned to walk out with the rest of the seniors after first hour started.

"Hey, Mr. and Mrs. Walker," I said. I was instantly met with Ruby's mom's open arms.

"It's so good to see you, Delia," her dad said.

I mumbled at Ruby, "I like your poster."

Ruby gave a sort of pout and looked down at the sign she was holding that said EXCEPTIONS EXIST. The letters were huge and beautifully drawn with big contrasting shadow lines drawn in.

"Thanks," she said. "Does your speaking to me mean you know you *were* in fact wrong about how you handled all that?" Ruby gestured up the steps to where Caleb was disappearing inside the building.

At that point I didn't feel like talking anymore. Each of us waited a second for the other to speak again, but neither of us could manage it. We were caught somewhere between knowing the other was right and wanting the other to acknowledge that they'd been wrong too.

"Are you staying out? Here, I mean? Out of school?" Ruby's mom asked.

Ruby answered before I had a chance to, "No, Mom. She really can't. She doesn't have any absences left, and she's gotta get that diploma next week—at least one of us should, right?" She reached up and tried to grin, and I could tell that she was doing everything she possibly could to keep her half-hearted smile in place. I knew the wide range of Ruby smiles, and this one was unquestionably lacking.

I still didn't say anything, but I gave a pitiful sort of wave and started making my way to the front doors. Once I got to the other side of their little cluster, I could see that there were more people outside than I'd expected: There could have been sixty or seventy-five people chanting their frustrations in the crowd. Some of them were seniors, but a lot of them weren't.

I could read some of the signs more clearly, too. They weren't only from Ruby's supporters, either. There was a sign being held by the parent of a kid who had a sensory issue that hadn't been diagnosed or excused. And then I saw her. A girl a few years younger than me, holding a sign that said MY PE-RIODS FEEL LIKE LABOR. WOULD YOU MAKE ME GIVE BIRTH IN MATH CLASS?

I felt the band of guilt running through me, plucked like a guitar string. I dropped my gaze to the concrete and walked up into the school.

The front hallway was mostly empty, but looking out the doors was Principal Davis. He looked furious. When he saw me, his scowl melted, and he made his way to greet me.

"Delia! I'm glad to see you inside the building today. Not that you have much of a choice, of course," he said, flashing me a quick ten with his fingers. "We heard about your car accident this weekend. Glad you're up and about, though. Would have made a whole other can of worms if you'd had to miss. I know you're trying to keep your nose clean here at the end." He gave a thumb jerk toward the street outside. "And I'm glad to see you're not getting tangled up in all that *drama.*"

One eyebrow ticked up as I looked at his smug grin.

That was it. The condescending straw that broke my back. What was it that made all these people so sure they were smarter than the people they were supposed to be serving? It wasn't right.

And if he believed I was staying put because I was avoiding trouble, then he didn't realize how used to trouble I'd gotten over the last month.

It would mean my diploma. It would mean summer school.

It would mean graduating without the rest of my class.

But it would be right.

And everyone who loved me was right. I didn't owe anyone my quiet compliance. I could fight out loud.

"One thing you've got to know about me, Mr. Davis," I said. "I'm a card-carrying overly emotional lifelong drama queen, and I don't think that's changing anytime soon. See you in summer school."

I smirked, turned, and pushed back out through the double doors.

* * *

I burst forth from the front doors of the school and ran down to where the crowd had gathered on the sidewalk.

My running had drawn attention, so I wasn't totally surprised to have several people listening when I got to Ruby and pulled her over to talk to me.

"I'm sorry," I said.

"Me too," Ruby said. "I have to stop telling you what to do and how to live. It's your life. You have to do what's right for you."

"No, but this *is* right for me."

"Delia, no. You need to turn around and go inside. It's bad enough that I'm not graduating, but you? That is basically a fate worse than death. You've gotta go back in there and sit at your desk and get this done. You've got to save yourself here."

"I can't." I was panting, but I spoke between big gulps of air. "Too many people aren't being heard. Doctors, teachers, principals aren't listening . . . Complicated medical issues call for complicated solutions. We have to try. These absence policies are nonsense. These doctors withholding diagnoses? Also nonsense. Now give me that poster."

"You're sure? One hundred percent?" she asked. "I can't have you resenting me, or feeling like I'm the reason this happened when next week rolls around and you're devastated."

"I'm sure," I said. "One thousand percent. We lost four years of friendship. We can make up more than just credits in summer school together."

She smiled. "Yeah. And my birthday at the end of the summer? We'll have the biggest three-months-late graduation party of all time. Deal?"

"Deal." Over my shoulder Ruby waved her hand, beckoning to a cameraman, who turned and signaled the reporter with him.

The final start-of-school bell rang, and the teachers and administrators on duty took positions to monitor the protest and be sure that things stayed calm. Mr. Davis descended the steps quickly, and when he saw me standing with the protesters, he did an honest-to-god double take. I gave him a shrug.

Behind the teachers, more seniors pushed out the double doors, staging their act of rebellion in honor of Ruby's cause. And my cause too, even though they didn't know it.

I guessed it was time to change that. I turned to face the camera when the reporter asked me if I was the spokesperson, and Ruby, ridiculously, said yes. That was good enough for the anchor, who shook her hair back and got into her spotlight. Caleb, Iggy, and my other new friends had circled us. The cameraman gave a nod, and the reporter stuck her microphone in my face. "Tell us your name and why you're out here today?" When I spoke, I felt steady and sure.

"My name is Delia Bridges, and I'm a senior at Blythe High. I have a 4.3 GPA, but I will not be graduating with my peers next week. I'm going to have to retake my last semester of high school because of medical absences beyond my control." I took a deep breath and looked up at the faces in the crowd. "I have debilitating period pain that sometimes keeps me from being able to attend classes. The school isn't giving students with medical complications enough avenues to make up missed time. It's not our fault that we need accommodation. And expecting us to provide concrete diagnoses and specific doctors notes for general complications, when that's not something in our control, is wrong. All eight of the doctors I've brought my concerns to have assumed that I'm too young to know my own body. Between physicians who don't listen and administrators who won't accommodate, many good students are being held captive by medical problems in school systems that don't seem to care. We just want to be heard."

The crowd erupted with cheering and chanting, which the cameraman instantly panned to.

We wanna be . . .

HEARD!

We wanna be . . .

HEARD!

The word echoed in my ears, over and over, and then the idea came smashing through my brain like the Kool-Aid man.

Not only did I need to be heard, but I needed HEARD.

I needed *her.*

CHAPTER THIRTY-ONE

SNITCHES GET WISHES

Shannon, the receptionist at the Center for Pelvic Pain Care, was nicer than I deserved. Showing up unannounced is never a good look with a doctor. Ruby had driven me all the way to Dallas and left, since Mom was on her way. I tried not to make a big deal about it when I asked Mom if she would come with me to meet with Dr. Dubois, but she cried happy tears anyway. I asked Shannon if she'd please tell Dr. Dubois I was here, and that I'd be willing to wait all day to see her for just a few minutes. As I'd already sacrificed my last absence, I didn't have to worry about missing class—it was already done.

Mom arrived in the waiting room about forty minutes after I'd called to fill her in on the whole thing: the protest, and Davis, and being absent, letting go of graduating on time.

She walked in through the automatic doors and I stood to hug her.

"Hi, baby," she said. "You okay?"

"Yeah," I said. "A little shocked, maybe? But I'm okay. I can't believe I did that. You're sure you're not mad at me?"

She grinned and reached up to hold my chin. "At some point you're gonna have to stop worrying about if I'm mad or not."

"Well, today is not that day," I said, scoffing.

"Delia?" Shannon said my name from the side door. "You can come on back."

I took my mom's hand and we followed her through a few turns in the maze until we reached two side-by-side office doors. Dr. Steele's was closed and dark inside. Dr. Dubois's was open and waiting. There was a desk set diagonally in one corner, with a chair tucked right in the far nook, and the rest of the room was fairly simple. Two chairs in front of her desk, a couch along one wall, and a number of framed certificates outlining Dr. Dubois's accomplishments and her career. She had more diplomas than I'd expected.

Mom sat first and then gestured for me to join her, but I couldn't stay sitting for long. I got up again and started looking at the diplomas on the wall. Years and years of studying and learning. So much time and focus, so much ambition. Many schools . . . none of them Gleeson. She'd found her way. Maybe I could still find mine. Her dedication was evident in every frame. Aside from the obvious doctoral degrees, she had an associate's degree diploma from a community college, two bachelor's degrees, one from a school called Ressidio University that I'd never heard of. It was a bachelor's in Health Communication. I didn't have much time to be intrigued before I was interrupted.

"Have you considered Ressidio in Chicago? It's a great, small, really progressive school." Dr. Dubois said behind me.

"I haven't," I answered.

"You should look into it," she said. "There's a whole lot of work on that wall. How are you, Delia? I don't mind telling you that I really barely have time to talk today."

"I know. Shannon told me she'd schedule something if I could do it another day, but I just didn't want to lose my momentum or my resolve. I need your help."

"Well, I'll see what I can do. Let's sit. You must be Delia's mother?"

"Mom, this is Dr. Dubois. Doctor, this is my mom, Miranda Bridges."

"It's so great to meet you." Mom leaned closer to whisper, "I can't believe I've met both of your doctor crushes now." I nudged her with an elbow to make her hush.

"I don't want to waste your time, so I'll get right to it." I cleared my throat and pulled my phone out of my back pocket, leaving it face down in my lap. "You know I've been burdened with horrible periods that seem to get worse every month. It's creating so much discord in my life. I missed out on graduating from this incredible prep school, which ultimately resulted in my being unaccepted from my first-choice university. I'm trying to take responsibility. I know that it was my series of choices that led to that moment, but I also know that I only acted the way I did because I was desperate. I have all the horrible symptoms you would expect: widespread pain, digestive problems, migraines, mood swings. I just had a minor car accident because I lost consciousness from the pain while driving home from a party. I know that part of what made me feel like I had to become a doctor, part of what made me desperate for a connection with Dr. Steele, and you, was that I was tired of meeting doctors who think I'm a liar. I saw my eighth doctor recently, and it didn't go well. I did ask about endo, but the whole thing was pretty horrible. Needless to say, he decided I probably didn't actually have anything wrong other than some big mental-health problems."

"I'm so sorry to hear that, Delia."

"Yeah. It's been really hard to deal with. But this last time, I decided that I would protect myself and record the conversation. This doctor made a lot of mistakes, but he is just one out of so many who are more willing to call a patient a liar than they are to believe a patient's own lived experiences. I was prepared to accept all the inappropriate things this doctor said, because he said that in a few months he would be willing to do more tests."

I picked up my phone and unlocked the recorder app.

"But I know that what he said wasn't okay, and even if it means delaying a diagnosis for me, I need someone to know what happened so that it won't keep happening to other people. I know that your organization, HEARD, provides advocacy services, and I was hoping that you might be able to figure out what to do with this information. I'll set my own diagnosis aside if it means nobody else has their doctor talk to them like this."

I pressed play and set the phone on her desk. The sound of my meeting with Dr. Evans rose up between us, biting and even more condescending each time I heard it through.

"Well, let's just say that I can't give a school excuse to every girl who says her period hurts. You're young. You're still getting used to it. You'll be better able to handle it over time. That's just how it is, unfortunately . . . You can't make that sort of decision without thinking about your future life—your future husband and kids . . ."

There were so many other tiny words and phrases that contributed to the tone of dismissiveness and judgment. These were not the words of a doctor listening to a patient. These were the words of someone trying to gaslight me into believing my medical issues weren't real.

Dr. Dubois graciously listened, keeping her head down. When it was over, she raised her face and looked back and forth between me and my mom. It was a few seconds more before she spoke.

"Speaking strictly as the head of HEARD, and based only on this recording, I can say that his behavior is wildly inappropriate. Reporting it to the medical board isn't our only option, but we should talk about what we can do, because this line of dialogue is problematic, even if it's legal. We can do something, definitely—bring this to light, and hopefully help Dr. Evans make some changes. One of the things we do with our volunteer legal counsel is present calls for change to physicians, offering them free classes and additional tools to improve these behaviors. But we also have people who work in media if we are ready to move on to the public-shaming phase."

Joy sat up in my chest, proud and straight. I wasn't sure what would happen next, but it was going to be *something*, and that was so entirely better than *nothing*.

"I don't know what to say. Thank you. I wasn't sure what could happen, but I knew I could trust you to understand. I know that my experiences are intense and probably a little hard to believe. I know that most people who are in pain aren't, like, crashing their cars and getting high and tumbling down stairs, but I promise it's real. I know it is. It has to be. I know Dr. Evans said I was just mismanaging my period, but it's more than that." My eyes started filling with tears again, so I tried to keep them down.

Dr. Dubois nodded at me, her kind smile growing, making her eyes scrunch almost totally closed.

"Delia, I need to tell you something. And I want to make sure you're really listening. Okay?" Her smile relaxed, and her eyes opened wider as she locked them on mine. "I believe you. I believe you, and I'd like to take you on as a patient."

I froze.

Nothing.

No oxygen, no air, no heartbeat.

"Delia?" Mom said my name again. "Delia?"

All at once, my nostrils flared and my chin trembled. When I blinked, two fat tears rolled down my cheeks. "What?"

Dr. Dubois leaned forward slowly and said it again, not

breaking eye contact, slowly, with a pause after each word. "Delia, I believe you." Her eyes started glistening, just like mine—or maybe it just looked like it because I was watching her through tears. "I believe in your pain. And I want to help you try to figure this out. You deserve to have a full life that's not run by or ruined by your condition . . . whatever it is."

"B-But this practice has years-long waiting lists for new patients." My head kept shaking side to side, even after I stopped talking. I was still straining my face, trying hard not to fully lose it.

"That's true. But HEARD partners with a handful of doctors and surgeons who donate pro bono consults, exams, even surgeries each year. The CPPC can't take you on, but I can. Now, there's a lot to think about. It's my opinion that the benefit of exploratory, laparoscopic surgery would in all likelihood outweigh the risks. But that doesn't mean there aren't some big ones. We need to talk about it, more, later, in a couple of weeks when we get this all official. But I've got an inkling that this is endo, and there is just no other way to be sure."

The tears came, slowly at first, and then in a rush.

The doctor was talking, Mom was asking questions, but I was just sitting, trembling, tears streaming into my open hands.

In that moment, I didn't care about surgery, graduation, or college. I didn't care about high school or med school or independence or jobs.

She believed me.

CHAPTER THIRTY-TWO

DOUBLE THE FAILURE, DOUBLE THE FUN

I expected the Stockwood graduation to be tough. I didn't expect it to make me want to punch myself in the eyeball in order to avoid it.

Mom had saved me the embarrassment and told the extended family weeks ago that my graduation wouldn't be happening the way they'd expected. And even though Key and Pri had told me a thousand times that I didn't have to come for their sake, I knew in my gut I had to be there.

I walked down the center aisle of the beautiful hall with its vaulted ceilings and wooden beams, Regan and Mom on either side of me. I hadn't exactly asked them to come, but I hadn't told them not to come either. As soon as the room quieted down, and the sound of the school song started floating into the air above us, lifting up to those high ceilings under which the girl I'd thought I'd always be had met her untimely demise, I couldn't help it. My breath caught in my throat and my eyes welled right up.

I crossed my arms over my stomach, aching now in a way so unlike my usual pain.

Without a sound, Mom and Regan found my hands, each holding one gently in her own. They held on with a softness that pushed those tears right up and out of the crease where they'd gathered.

I cried through the whole song, the opening remarks, the invocation, the valedictorian giving their beautiful speech, and every name in the As till they started calling the Bs. I wiped my eyes and sat up higher in my chair, watching Priya rise with her row and stand by the stage.

When they called Priya Balakrishnan, I stood up, screeching my applause, as did the entire section of her family. They had four rows full of people clapping and watching just like I was. Priya strode so confidently and so proudly to the center of the stage. She grabbed the little tied scroll, gave a small wave to her family, blew a kiss to me, which I pretended to catch, and then she switched her tassel to the other side.

I sat back down, and the adrenaline slowed.

It came up quicker than I'd expected—the sting in the back of my throat just a few moments later. The space in the line of graduates that should have been mine. Bridges. The brief seconds between Laurel Bell and Joseph Brock felt like they stretched out forever. In that tiny slip of silence, I closed my eyes, imagining the sound of my name being called. I imagined myself walking, looking out at my mom and sister, seeing the pride in their eyes and knowing my smile had never been brighter. I could imagine my face, and the way it looked as I shook hands with the dean and took my diploma and waved it above my head. But the stretch of time snapped back like a rubber band, and it was over. My moment had come and gone without me.

I stared straight ahead through the rest of the Bs and didn't do, say, or feel much of anything until the Ps, when I got excited again. Keisha bounced a little as she waited, but when she got to the top of the tiny little staircase on the stage, she pushed her shoulders back and waited for them to say Keisha Perkins. When they did, she strode across to the other side, waving like a beauty queen at the two rows of her family, about three rows in front of me.

I relaxed once her tassel was turned.

This was the graduation that for me would never be. I'd just watched them walk and take that rolled-up piece of paper, impossibly tiny.

When Keisha had finished crossing, I leaned to Mom and said, "Can we go?"

"Are you sure? You don't want to wait for the final words? The hat throwing? Pictures with the girls?" she whispered.

I shook my head.

I walked slightly in front, Mom and Regan just half a step behind me. The rows and rows and rows and rows of parents and siblings couldn't help but watch our little trio strutting over the dark wood floors. Our steps matched so perfectly that the sounds of the three of us crossing to the massive double doors a thousand miles away in the back of the room became like one person's clop-clop echoing up into the ceiling.

It felt like the whole room was silent, waiting for us to be out the door.

But I swear to god, that aisle grew two feet with each step we took. Every cell in my body wanted to turn around and look back at the hall, at the place that was almost my alma mater but would never actually be. I wanted to see if Priya was raising her fist in my honor, or if Keisha had involuntarily put her hand over her heart at the sight of my only true act of defiance against this school.

Regan hissed at me, barely audible above the sound of our perfect steps: "Don't you dare turn around."

I didn't pause or falter. I pushed my shoulders back farther.

I was almost to the door now, just a few feet left.

They'd all watched me. Every one of them. Or maybe none of them. But it sure felt good.

I got to the huge doors, dark wood with inset sections almost as tall as me, and I pushed against them. It was this epic, damn-the-man moment—or it would have been, if both sides of the double door had been unlocked.

The left side was locked tight, and the right side was the opposite of sticky, and my force was far more than necessary, causing it to open really hard and fast. I smacked my left shoulder against the doorframe and almost grabbed it, ready to wince and screech with pain, but Regan whispered again,

"There's no crying during a dramatic exit, Delia—now get out the damn door!"

I got through the door, followed by my mom and sister, and it closed behind us.

"Oh . . . my . . . god, that felt amazing, right?" Mom said to the pair of us with a giant smile on her face.

I was still rubbing my shoulder, but my smile was wide too.

"I wonder if they really were watching us. Probably not, right? I'm sure it was just one of those moments when it felt like they were, but they really weren't, because that's just not actually likely—"

"It doesn't matter if they were or weren't," Mom said, taking a strand of my hair in her hand and twisting it. "What matters is how you feel right now. I want this feeling for you. So much. And I'm so proud."

I hugged her, and Regan piled on.

The next afternoon was the graduation ceremony for Blythe High.

Mom, Regan, and I entered the stadium seating and climbed way up and toward the back to find Ruby. It felt very much like the place to watch from, unnoticed and out of the way.

The administrators called everyone to sit so they could begin, music started to play, and I plopped down on the metal seat so hard my tailbone sizzled with pain for a few seconds. Regan stifled a laugh, and I bumped her shoulder with my own, knocking into the bruise I'd earned at the first graduation I attended that wasn't my own. She pursed her lips together even tighter against the urge to crack up.

Down in the center, where all the seniors were seated, Caleb finally caught my eye—or, well, the waving white flag I'd told him to look for in the stands. I'd surrendered in so many ways, after all. I blew him a kiss, which instantly felt absurd, but he caught it and pretended to tuck it behind his ear.

Beside me, Ruby said she wasn't looking for Iggy, but when she found him in his row, she grabbed my hand and just pointed him out to me. "I'm gonna miss him," she said.

"I know you will," I said.

She whispered again, "We talked last night. Cleared the air."

"You did?"

"Yeah," she said with a soft, sad smile on her face.

I squeezed her hand tight.

The BHS valedictorian was in the middle of her speech. "We graduates have reached a point in our lives that we have dreamed of for years. The point when what we do stops feeling like it's for everybody else. As we move forward from this place, we'll come to find that our lives are more our own now than they've ever been. And maybe you made it here today because someone else wanted or needed you to, but in the end, you chose to be here. You chose to do the work. You chose to take the steps along your path that led you to this moment. Nobody gave it to you. And nobody can ever take it away."

She was right. My choices had put me here—in the audience rather than on the stage. But I'd grown numb to the feeling of missing something that I'd thought I was going to have. It wasn't useful. I had to move on. My future was coming for me, whether in the way I'd planned it or not.

CHAPTER THIRTY-THREE

THE END(O)

I've become surprisingly chill about waking up in a pool of my own blood.

At least most of the time.

But it turns out the level of chillness I feel is directly related to being in my own bed, ruining my own sheets.

I felt the same damp feeling, but it was entirely the wrong place and time.

Please let me just have peed the bed.

I was in fact praying that I'd wet myself rather than bled all over the impossibly white linens of my hospital bed.

I pulled the covers back, pulled a big fluff of tissues out of the box, and dabbed between my legs under my hospital gown.

"Not now," I whined quietly, realizing I was holding a

bloody tissue I couldn't easily discard. I tried to tip myself over to check and see how big the spot of blood would be, but as I clenched my muscles, pain sparked through my abdomen. Obviously. I wasn't supposed to be wiggling around just a few hours after having surgery. I tried to focus on feeling the size of the wet spot on my butt . . . it wasn't small.

Even among medical professionals, Elvira was determined to embarrass me.

"Whoa, whoa. Where did this blood come from?" asked the night nurse, Donna. Her face stayed perfectly calm, but she was immediately focused and at work.

Out of a dead sleep, Mom's head shot up from where it had been smashed against the window. "Blood? What blood? I didn't see any blood during my last check. Is it an incision?"

"Mom, calm down. It's not an incision."

Donna answered too, pulling on a glove, dropping my tissue in the medical-waste bin, and pulling my hospital gown up to take a closer look. "No, it's not an incision. It looks like it's coming from . . . Oh."

"Donna, meet Elvira, my period." I gestured to my lap.

She gave a very sweet smile and started shifting all my wires and attachments. "Let's get you over to the bathroom so we can clean you up and get these sheets changed."

The anesthesia had left me a little groggy, but as each minute passed, I felt more and more aware of the stiffness throughout my body. I was a little sore, but it wasn't terrible. I didn't feel too hungry, but I was very thirsty. I expect they'd given me a healthy dose of pain medicine, and

I could tell that my mouth and brain were still behind the curve.

"All right, Delia, I'm going to set this down here, and you just take a seat and let me know when you've peed, okay?"

She set a sort of bowl with measuring lines into the actual toilet.

"What's that for?" I asked.

Donna explained that now that my catheter was out, I would need to prove I could pee on my own before I could leave. It sounded silly until I thought I'd peed about seven times only to discover that I hadn't.

Once I was back in my bed and all my connections and wires were back in place, I fell asleep for a while, and when I woke up, I was sure it had only been a few minutes, but it had actually been a couple of hours. Mom looked like she hadn't moved a muscle that whole time. I asked, "Have you seen Dr. Dubois yet? Has she come by? How was the surgery? Did she find anything?"

The weight of my mother on the edge of the bed made my hip dip ever so slightly toward her. She took it as an opportunity to reach an arm over and around me.

"She said it went well." Mom brushed the back of my hand with her thumb.

"And?" I asked. "Aren't you going to tell me what she said?"

"She didn't really tell me much, and she said that we'd have a more detailed report to go over in a few days."

"Come on, Mom. I've gotta know more than that."

Before Mom could answer, Donna came back to have me try to pee again. This time I'd do it. Second time's a charm.

"There," I said.

"Really? Good!" Donna took my hand and helped me stand up from the toilet. "Nope. Dry as a bone."

"You're kidding me! I swear I went."

"It will happen soon," Dr. Dubois said, entering my little room and pulling the curtain around behind her. "It can take some time. How are you feeling?"

At the sight of her, I felt a rush of emotions, and I wished my head were a little more able to focus.

Mom came over to my bed and helped me get my covers situated again while Dr. Dubois checked my chart on her tablet.

"I'm okay. But I'm about to lose my mind. You have to tell me what happened in there. Did you find anything?"

It felt weird to be hoping for her to have found something, but I was. I wanted so much for her to tell me, for sure, that it wasn't all in my head.

Dr. Dubois smiled. The tight knot of braids at the base of her neck caught the light each time she looked down at her notes. "We're going to have a much longer conversation soon, and there are still a number of things that we'll confirm once we hear back from the lab, but there are some main points I can lay out for you now."

Mom took my hand, and we both looked up at her expectantly.

"I was able to see the formation of endometriosis throughout many areas of your abdominal cavity. You have endometriosis on and around your intestines, your stomach, and bladder."

"I have endometriosis?"

"You have endometriosis."

"Officially?"

"I saw it with my own eyes, and I removed it with my own hands. Well, my tiny robot hands. And not all of it, but as much as I could during this first look."

The lump in my throat seemed to grow larger until, finally, I had to swallow it to breathe. My chin trembled for a moment as my eyes filled with tears. I smiled, threw my head back with closed eyes, and let out a joyful "It's real. It's real." Beside me, Mom wiped a tear from her own eye and then let her face fall into her hands.

Dr. Dubois continued. "It's real. We have more exploring to do to get to the bottom of this, but I expect we'll call it stage three."

"What's stage three?" Mom asked, looking up, trying to keep her cool and mostly failing. "What does that mean? What is that?"

"Well, it is directly about how much and how widespread the endo is. But it's worth mentioning that some people with widespread, stage-four endo have little or no pain, and some people with stage one can hardly function. It's more of an indicator of the endo's development than it is of your experience."

My brain had already slipped back into its state of euphoria while Mom asked more questions of the doctor. *It's real. I can't believe it's real.*

* * *

At the end of the summer, just two months later, I woke up to an ovarian vise grip, rolled over, and glanced at the clock. 4:20 a.m.

The universe is irony's best author.

Despite the pain, I grinned for just a second until another surge squeezed my lower half, all the way to my knees.

I looked across the room, still dark, but the moon gave enough light for me to see the pinboard across from my bed. It looked different now—new clippings, new dreams. The cartoon uterus with its middle finger in the air; photos of me, Priya, and Keisha from the weekend that we all spent in Boston, helping them get unpacked; a selfie of Regan and Mom on either side of me, standing in the kitchen, holding my high school diploma. It had arrived soon after I'd earned my credits during summer school. The district had put a new credit-recovery policy in place following our little protest, but it wouldn't take effect until the next school year. So Ruby and I worked that summer, and got it done—there were photos of Ruby and me outside the school from the last day, only a couple of weeks ago. There was a giant sticker for HEARD, and a hook where Caleb's shirt hung next to the letter he'd written me for my eighteenth birthday in July. He was driving up from Austin to visit in just a few days.

I opened my nightstand drawer and took out a bottle of pain medication carefully prescribed and overseen by Dr. Dubois. I broke a pill in half, swallowed it dry, and prayed for relief to come soon. Until it kicked in, which could take twenty minutes or an hour, I wouldn't be able to sleep anyway, so I rolled over and took my phone off the charger. It lit up my dark room and made me squint against the brightness until I could dim the screen. I opened my mail app to do the refresh-a-few-times-even-though-it-automatically-updates-because-just-in-case thing, when I saw there was already a notification. I blinked a few times as my inbox came into clearer focus.

Subject: REGARDING ADMISSION STATUS: C. BRIDGES, RESSIDIO UNIVERSITY

I sat up so fast, my head spun, and the jerking caused my pain to roar up with new urgency. Ressidio had drawn my attention for about a million different reasons, and I wanted to get in *bad*. I'd spoken with Dr. Dubois about it a few times since, and she even personally recommended me to the admissions board. Along with her letter, I thought my admissions essay for them about my newly diagnosed endometriosis was one of the best things I'd ever written. It outlined my recent involvement with HEARD, my budding advocacy with local districts and the State Board of Education. It shared my most embarrassing moments in a way that I hoped would make any reader understand how universal my experiences really were. I thought I'd nailed it, and the email with their decision was now in my inbox.

I wouldn't have thought anything could keep me from opening that email, but I doubled over, eyes closed for several minutes, rocking back and forth, gritting my teeth and trying to remember to breathe through the pain.

When it calmed again for just a moment, I picked up my

phone, screen still showing my inbox's contents, the subject line still bold and unread.

I swallowed hard and then opened the email.

C. Bridges:

The Admissions Committee at Ressidio University is delighted to announce your acceptance, applicable any session start date within the next twelve months.

The scream was involuntary. I started waving my hands around and shaking my head back and forth, and then I threw myself back onto my pillow and hugged my phone to my chest. I started to kick my heels against my bed, but as soon as I engaged my lower ab muscles, I regretted it.

When Regan and Mom burst into my room just a few seconds apart, it looked like the pain was the reason for my scream, and both of them rushed to my bedside with worry all over their sleepy faces.

"Are you okay?"

"What's wrong?"

"No," I said, facing them and trying to put my smile back in place. "I mean, I did just start and I'm in crippling pain, but the scream was good news! I got in! I'm going to Chicago!" I pushed myself up gently so I could see them better and scooted back against my headboard. Then I handed over the phone so they could read the email with their own eyes.

It only took a few seconds before they were both screaming

and jumping. Regan actually crawled up onto the bed and jumped a few times before flopping down to her knees, panting.

"I'm so proud of you," Mom said.

"Me too," Regan huffed.

Mom and Regan nodded, breathing heavily. It felt like pure joy, sitting there, seeing them beaming, and knowing that I'd done it. I'd been accepted into a school I really wanted. College would still happen. Different place. Different time. But I would still make the future ahead of me my own.

The happiness was short-lived, as another swell of ache, simultaneously sharp and dull, derailed our celebrations. Regan and Mom sobered pretty quickly, each of them moving to tend to my typical needs. Regan got the heating pad. Mom got a few crackers from the stash.

As fast as it had come, the lightness I'd been feeling sank deeper and deeper into a heavy weight at the base of my tailbone.

How could I possibly survive life beyond this house? How could I expect to do college when my pain could still knock me completely and literally on my tush? How could I study and take classes if I couldn't get out of bed, and how would I be able to manage all the pieces of it on my own? I'd only been working with Dr. Dubois for a short while, which meant there was still a lot of trial and error happening and things to consider. Pain management was a good place to start, but we'd already been talking about the surgeries that were sure to come next.

Mom and Regan saw the change in my face, and they

didn't even say anything. They just watched me and waited for me to say what was on my mind.

"What if I can't do this alone?"

They both just kinda stared at me with faces that looked like maybe they agreed with my assessment.

"What do I do?" I asked them.

They shook their heads slowly and shrugged. They didn't have the answers, and it would have to be my decision anyway.

"I'm not sure if I'll be ready to start right away. I think we should take some time. Think about it. Together."

"Wow, Mom," Regan said. "I think our baby is growing up."

Mom's eyes were locked onto mine, and her sweet smile parted to say, "You're sure this is okay? It's not what you thought was gonna happen."

"Yeah, well, plans change, don't they?" I said.

Understatement. My life turned in directions I never saw coming. I hated it. I moved forward kicking and screaming for the expectations I'd picked for myself. But if things hadn't gone wrong, so many of the most important parts of my life wouldn't exist.

I wouldn't have Ruby back in my life.

I would have been working with Dr. Steele, who might not have retired early, so I probably wouldn't have been as close with Dr. Dubois, and maybe I wouldn't have gotten connected with HEARD. I certainly wouldn't have had surgery when I did.

I wouldn't have met Caleb. I wouldn't have had my first love.

And worst of all, I still wouldn't have a diagnosis.

But maybe life is just a series of messy moments that laugh in the face of what you plan and expect. It's when you dive out of the way or get shoved off the path that you accidentally find yourself on that less-taken road.

An unexpected consequence doesn't always ruin.

Sometimes, it renews.

So, yeah. My period has ruined my life . . . twice. So far.

But I hope I've learned that sometimes beauty hides in ruins.

I just hope that *when* life is ruined next time, I'll remember that I'm strong enough to pull up my period-stained big-girl panties and put it back together again.

Because if I can survive my period, well, I can survive anything.

A NOTE FROM KELSEY

Believe it or not, many of the most embarrassing, cringe-worthy moments in this book were taken right from my own experiences. I lived with undiagnosed endometriosis and adenomyosis for well over a decade, and I am one of the countless people who has felt misunderstood and alone while trying to navigate it. Endometriosis is a complicated disease that impacts millions of people with uteruses, and as this story centers on Delia's quest for an answer rather than her treatment plan post-diagnosis, there are many important details about this condition that aren't part of her story. Severe period pain is one of the most common symptoms of endometriosis, but there are many others. For endometriosis-specific resources and information, visit endowhat.com and femxx.health. Sexual and reproductive health and education resources for young people can be found at amaze.org.

Take care of yourself, stand up for yourself, educate yourself, and most importantly, *trust yourself.* You deserve to be believed.

With love,
Kelsey

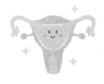

ACKNOWLEDGMENTS

Having the opportunity to share parts of my own experiences with endometriosis is a gift I never could have imagined I'd receive. My period brought pain and sadness countless times in my life, but this time, it's brought me so, so much joy.

To my editor, Kelly Delaney, I extend my most heartfelt gratitude. Your faith in this story and my ability to tell it has transformed who I am as a writer. Each story I create for the rest of my life will be better due to the myriad ways you've helped me grow through this book's development. Our easy collaboration has been such a gift, and I am honored you chose to give my voice a home. All my gratitude to the team at Random House, including Caroline Abbey (thank you for being such a proud champion for this book), managing editor Rebecca Vitkus, production manager CJ Han, copyeditors Clare Perret and Karen Sherman (for literally blowing my mind with your talents), cover designer Angela Carlino (I can't thank you enough for the perfect tone you set for readers before they've even cracked the spine), sensitivity readers Jasmine and Jordan Wilson (for the early encouragement and for helping me focus on what really matters), publicity and marketing pros Lili Feinberg and Rachel Jensen, and interior book designer Cathy Bobak.

To the team at BookEnds Literary, and particularly my agent Moe, thank you for fighting for my book, and for being so confident that we would find a place for it to shine. Moe, your guidance, patience, and encouragement on both my brightest and darkest days has given my career new life, and I am so grateful.

To the doctor who changed my life, Dr. Dulemba, I wish I could tell you how transformed I am by the care you provided and the belief you gave me without my having to earn it. You were the first doctor who felt like my partner, and I can't thank you enough.

I am so thankful to my friends who kept me alive and loved during the wildest time of my life. Annie, you are so much more than my writing partner and my creative backbone; you are the bedrock I bloom from, and there's no me without you. Megan, you make me feel known and safe in every way, and I have never known anyone as effortlessly beautiful and magical as you are. Tameka, thank you for being willing to sit with me during the times when I felt impossibly alone; you help me remember that I am always loved and always worthy of loving myself. Other dear friends who have shaped my heart: Jessica N., Missy, Jess T., Laura, Kaley, Lola, Abdalla, Boone: Thank you for never making me feel like I'm too much. Tons of thanks for the old school, evergreen writing friends and to the newest on discord: Andrea H., Angi, Sarah B., Tess, Dahlia, Jessica S., Diana, Megan E., Jessica L., Alex L., Lisa, and the CGWWDC writing sub girls. My assistant, Madison Houle: thank you for sharing your talents with me and for helping me make it through this launch! My potato-land tech editor friends: you're the best.

To my family, I am so grateful for your support and encouragement. Mom, Dad, and LaDonna, thank you for being such beautiful parents. Mom, you've been my safe harbor so many times, and I can't imagine who I would be without the influence of your humor, strength, and graciousness. Dad, you are the warmth in my soul, and I know that so much of my tender, earnest heart came straight from you. LaDonna, your evergreen presence and generosity inspire me to never underestimate the value of my role in the world. To my creative, brilliant Grey, you'll always be my weasel, and I love you so much and I love being there with you through every twist and turn of this life. Grams and Art, your steadfastness has always anchored me, and I will never be able to express how much of you I continue to find in myself. To my newest family tree branch, Mike, Edie, Dayna, Tom, Grammy, Preston, and Nolan, I am so grateful to be a part of your lives and so grateful for all the ways you make mine brighter.

To my Tater Tot, Eli, I love you bigger than all the planets, and all the sky, and all the universe. You are the most beautiful bonus of my life, little love.

Derek, my lovey, you are my home, my sunrise, and the best leap of faith I've ever taken. I know that even if I wrote for all the rest of my days, I'd never be able to create a love story as wonderful as ours. I love you.

ABOUT THE AUTHOR

KELSEY B. TONEY is an author and speaker who loves sharing stories made of wit and warmth. Her novels usually feature some combination of big choices, big mistakes, and big dreams, as she considers herself an expert on all three. Kelsey taught in public schools for seventeen years, which fed her love of public speaking and her passion for youth mental health support. Of course, it also gave her a near-endless supply of storytelling inspiration. Kelsey believes there is no greater joy than a very early morning and a very strong cup of coffee. Learn more about Kelsey on her website, podcast, or in her newsletter.

kelseybtoney.com

X ⊙ ♪